IMAGE COMICS, INC.
Robert Kirkman – Chief Operating Officer
Erik Larsen – Chief Financial Officer
Todd McFarlane – President
Marc Silvestri – Chief Executive Officer
Jim Valentino – Vice-President

Eric Stephenson – Publisher
Corey Murphy – Director of Sales
Jeff Boison – Director of Publishing Planning & Book Trade Sales
Jeremy Sullivan – Director of Digital Sales
Kat Salazar – Director of PR & Marketing
Emily Miller – Director of Operations
Branwyn Bigglestone – Senior Accounts Manager
Sarah Mello – Accounts Manager
Drew Gill – Art Director
Jonathan Chan – Production Manager
Meredith Wallace – Print Manager
Briah Skelly – Publicity Assistant
Sasha Head – Sales & Marketing Production Designer
Randy Okamura – Digital Production Designer
David Brothers – Branding Manager
Ally Power – Content Manager
Addison Duke – Production Artist
Vincent Kukua – Production Artist
Tricia Ramos – Production Artist
Jeff Stang – Direct Market Sales Representative
Emilio Bautista – Digital Sales Associate
Leanna Caunter – Accounting Assistant
Chloe Ramos-Petersen – Administrative Assistant
IMAGECOMICS.COM

EAST OF WEST

JONATHAN HICKMAN
WRITER

NICK DRAGOTTA
ARTIST

FRANK MARTIN
COLORS

RUS WOOTON
LETTERS

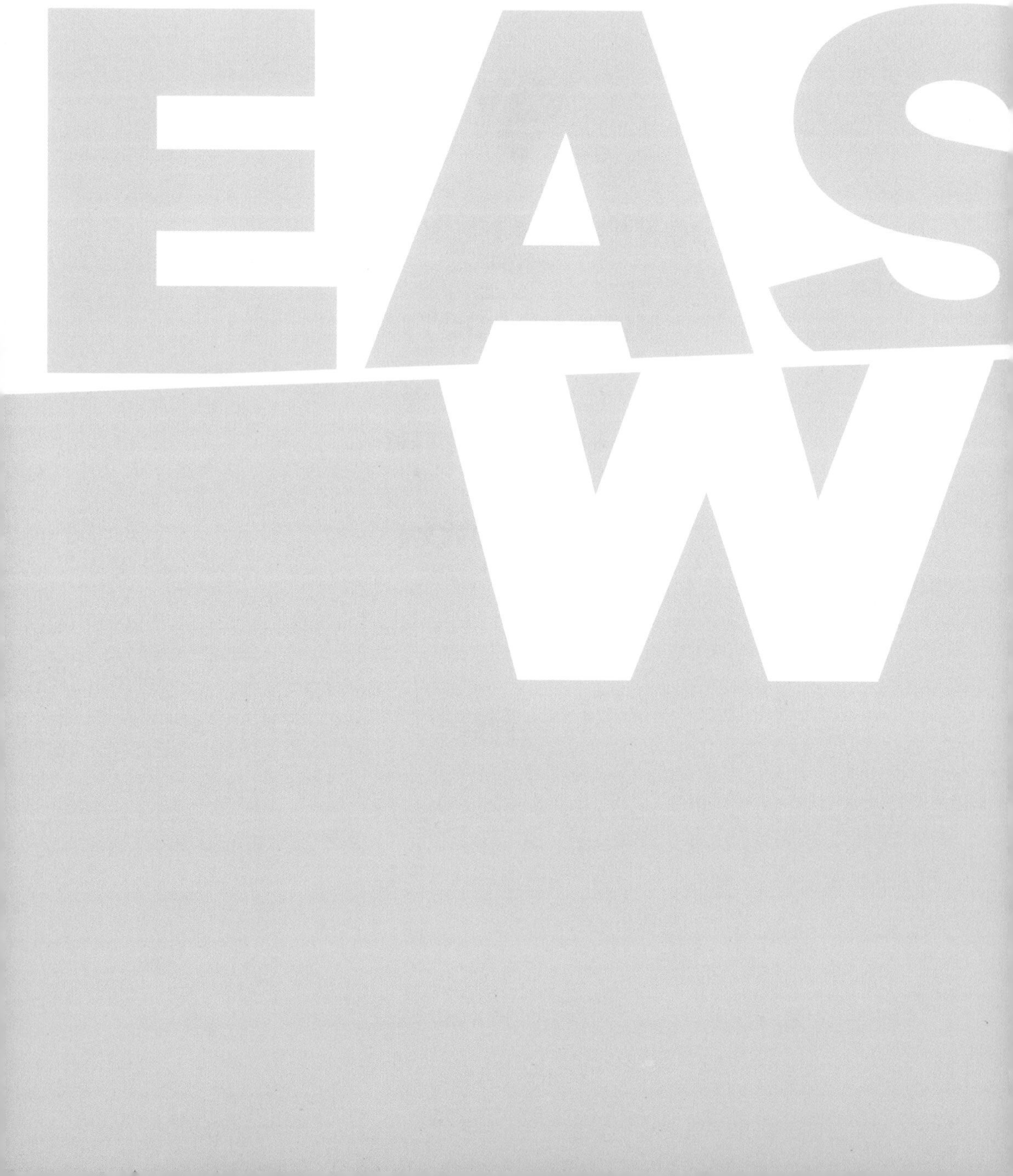
EAS
W

T OF

EST

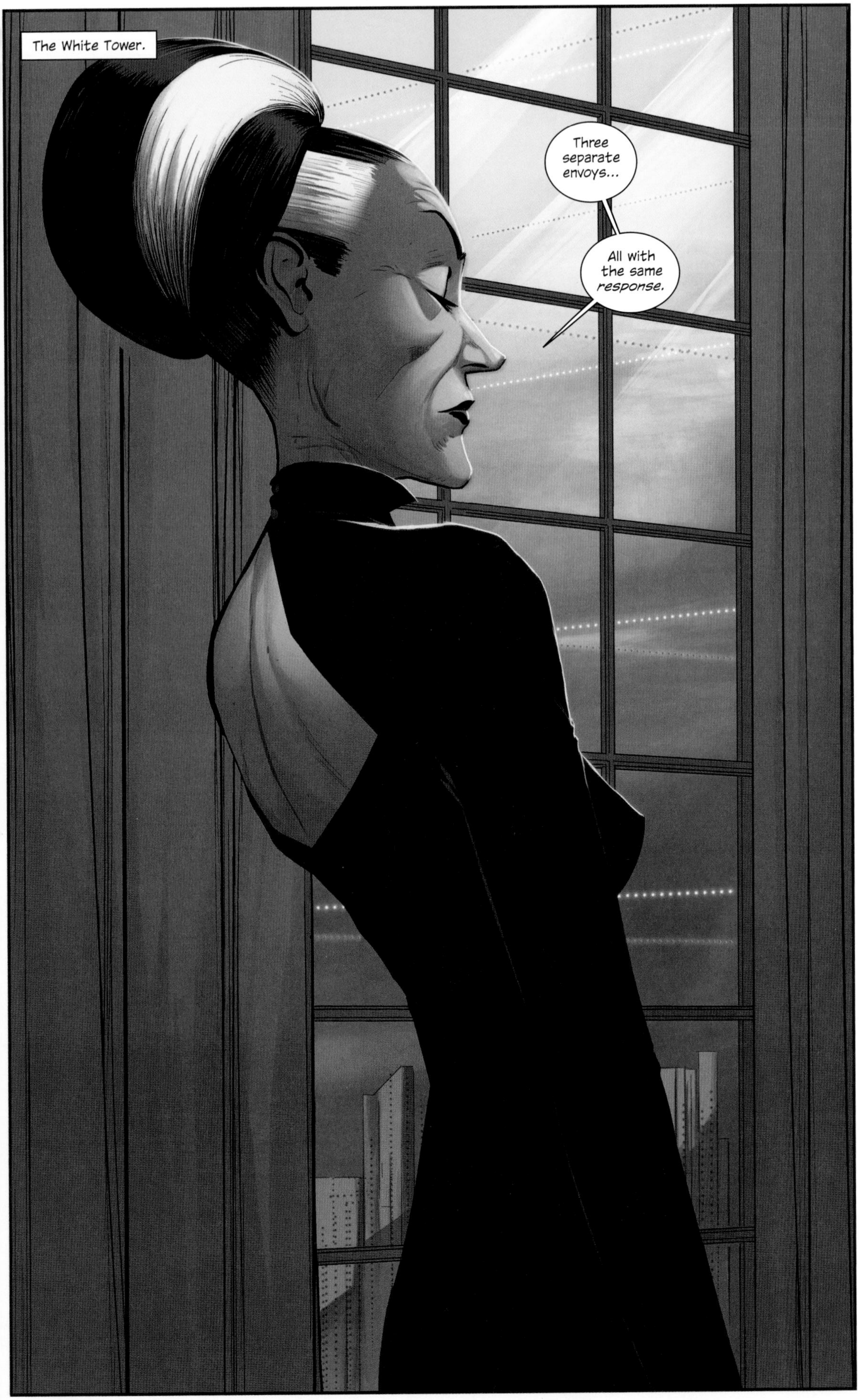
The White Tower.
Three separate envoys...
All with the same *response.*

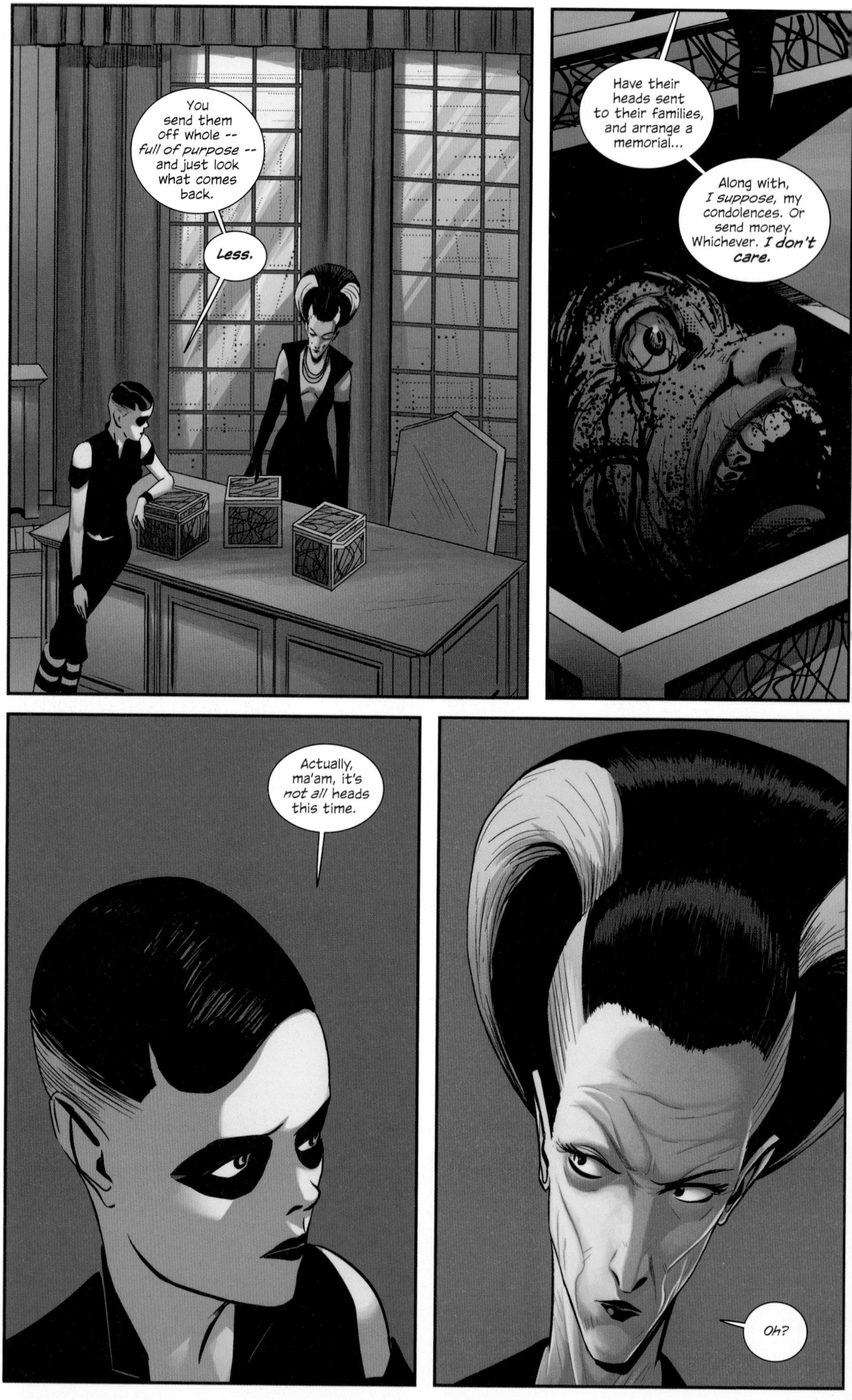
You send them off whole -- *full of purpose* -- and just look what comes back.
Less.
Have their heads sent to their families, and arrange a memorial...
Along with, *I suppose,* my condolences. Or send money. Whichever. ***I don't care.***
Actually, ma'am, it's *not all* heads this time.
Oh?

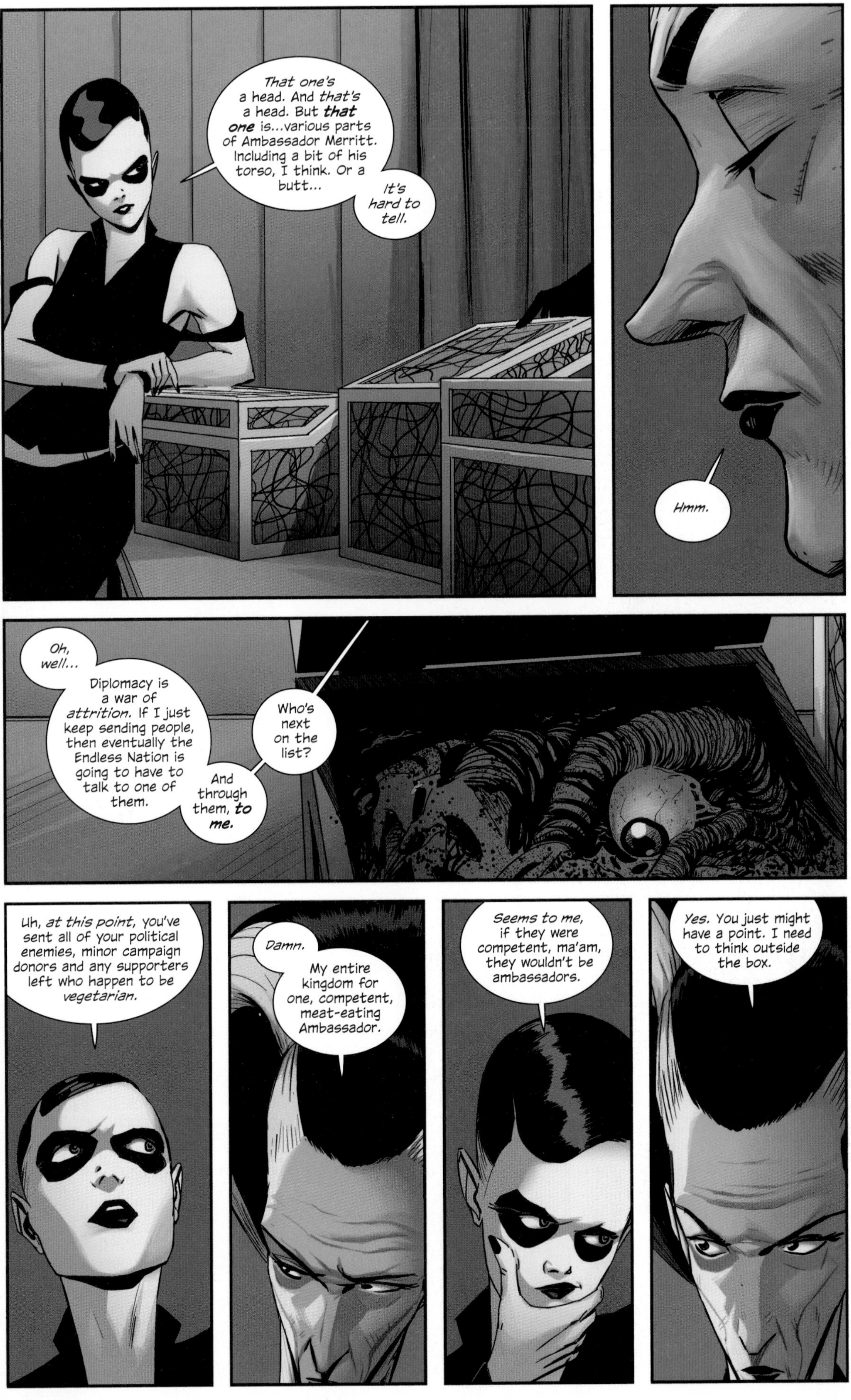
That one's a head. And that's a head. But **that one** is...various parts of Ambassador Merritt. Including a bit of his torso, I think. Or a butt...
It's hard to tell.
Hmm.
Oh, well...
Diplomacy is a war of attrition. If I just keep sending people, then eventually the Endless Nation is going to have to talk to one of them.
And through them, **to me.**
Who's next on the list?
Uh, at this point, you've sent all of your political enemies, minor campaign donors and any supporters left who happen to be vegetarian.
Damn.
My entire kingdom for one, competent, meat-eating Ambassador.
Seems to me, if they were competent, ma'am, they wouldn't be ambassadors.
Yes. You just might have a point. I need to think outside the box.

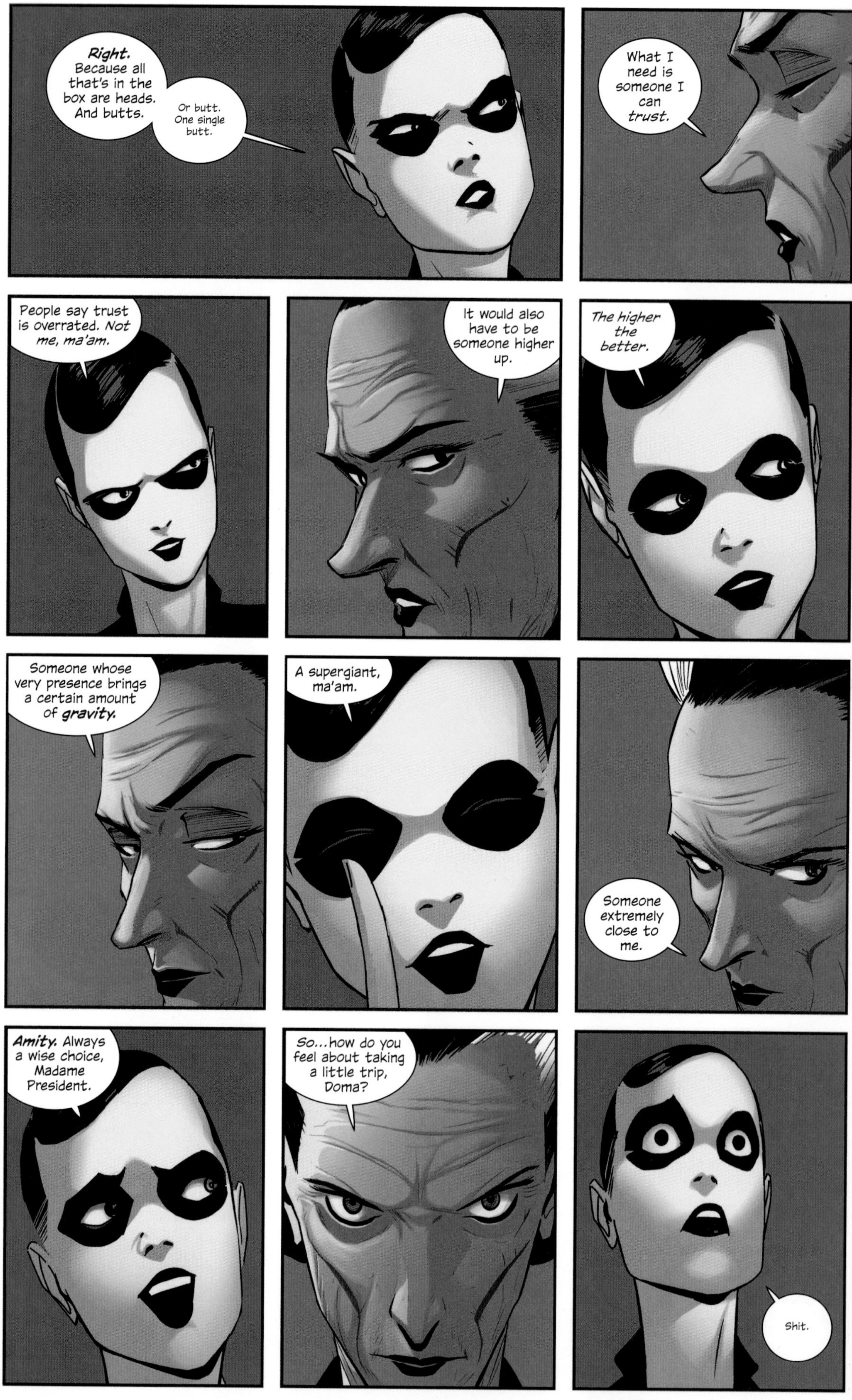

Right. Because all that's in the box are heads. And butts.
Or butt. One single butt.
What I need is someone I can *trust.*
People say trust is overrated. *Not me, ma'am.*
It would also have to be someone higher up.
The higher the better.
Someone whose very presence brings a certain amount of ***gravity.***
A supergiant, ma'am.
Someone extremely close to me.
Amity. Always a wise choice, Madame President.
So...how do you feel about taking a little trip, Doma?
Shit.

PAY CLOSE **ATTENTION.**

YOUR **ENEMIES** ARE
EVERYWHERE.

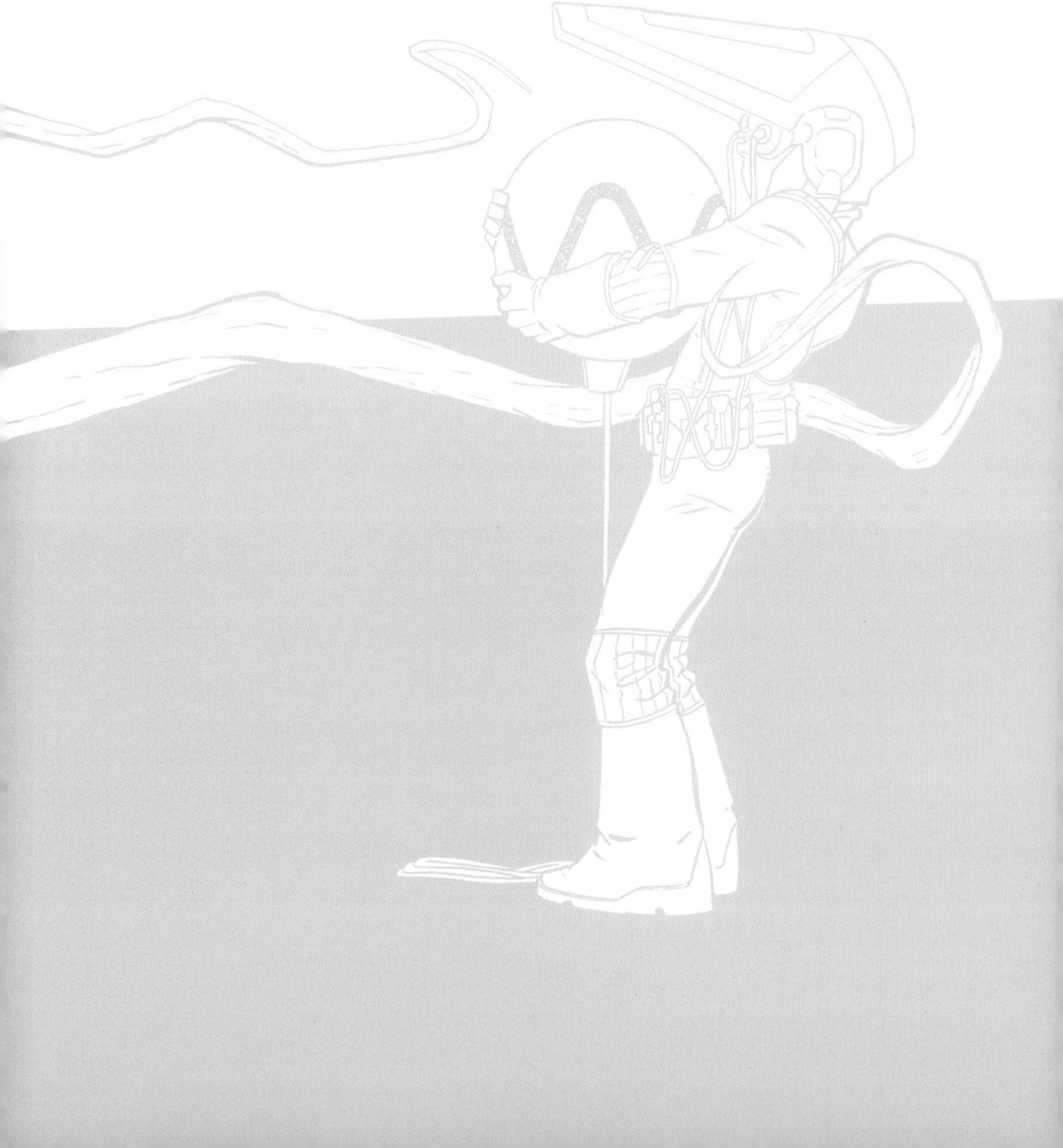

20

TWENTY: THIS TANGLED WEB

WHAT ARE YOU **REALLY,**
CHILD?

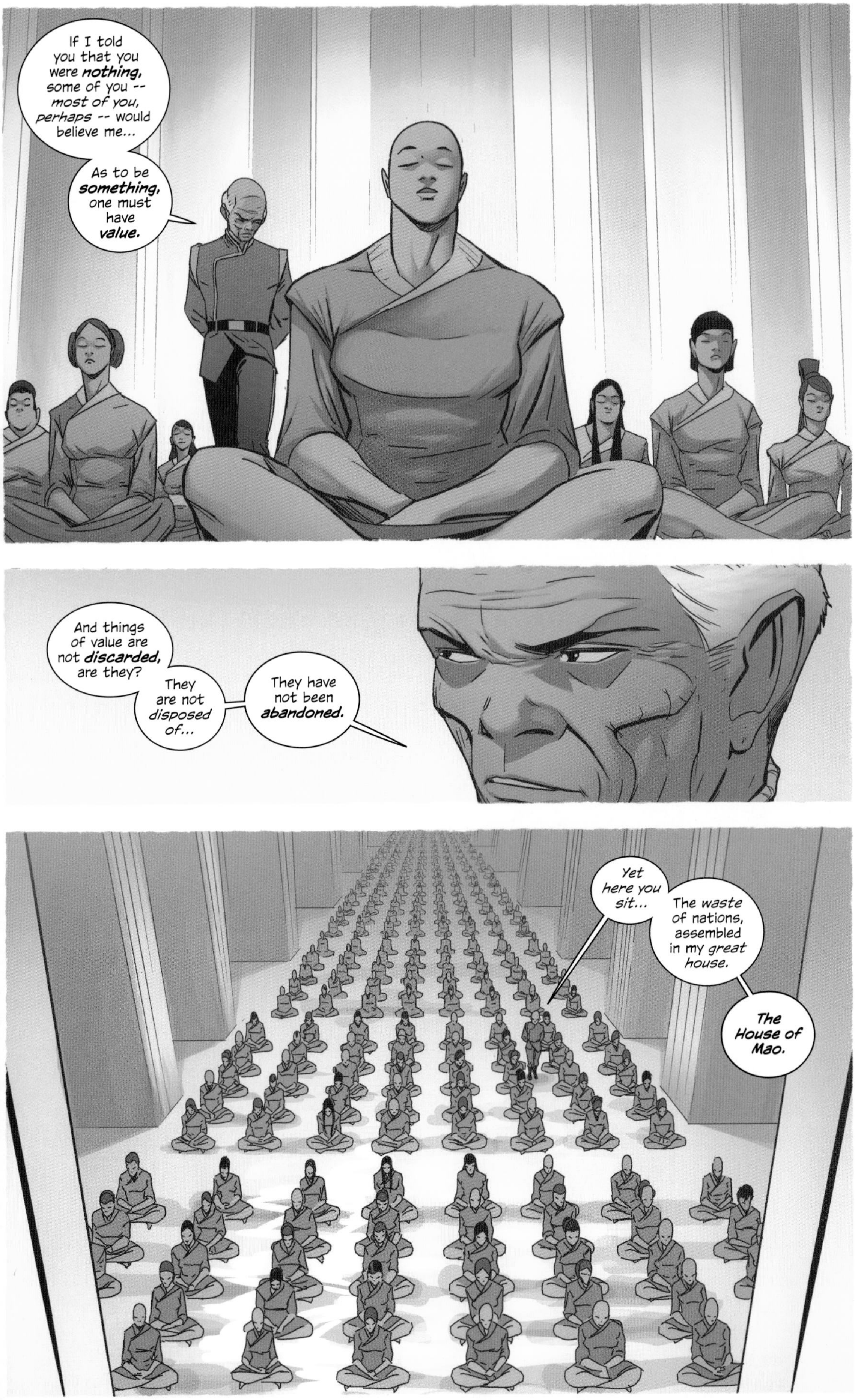
If I told you that you were *nothing*, some of you -- *most of you, perhaps* -- would believe me...
As to be *something*, one must have *value*.
And things of value are not *discarded*, are they?
They are not *disposed of*...
They have not been *abandoned*.
Yet here you sit...
The *waste* of nations, assembled in my *great house*.
The House of Mao.

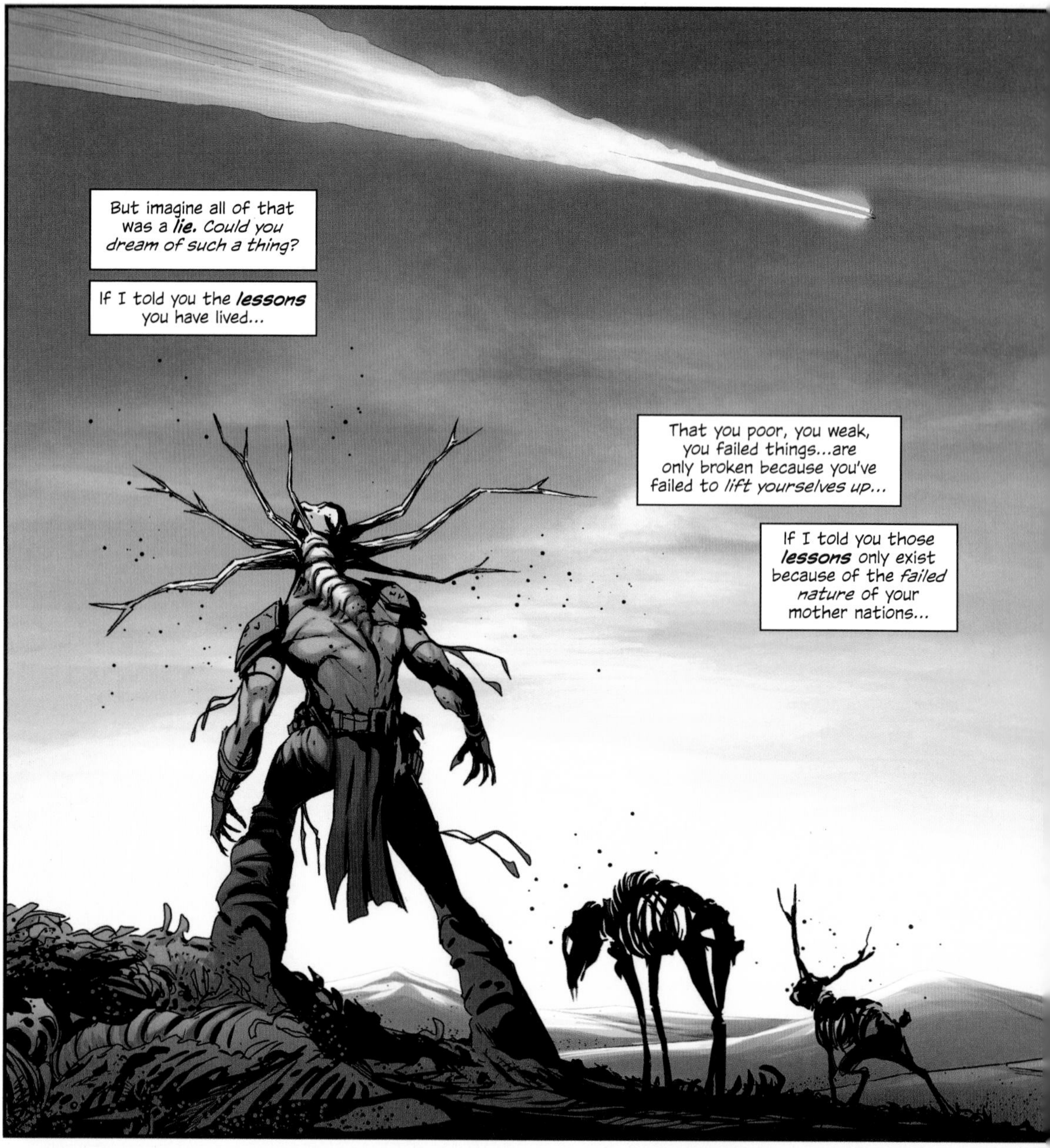
But imagine all of that was a *lie.* Could you dream of such a thing?
If I told you the ***lessons*** you have lived...
That you poor, you weak, you failed things...are only broken because you've failed to *lift yourselves up...*
If I told you those ***lessons*** only exist because of the *failed nature* of your mother nations...

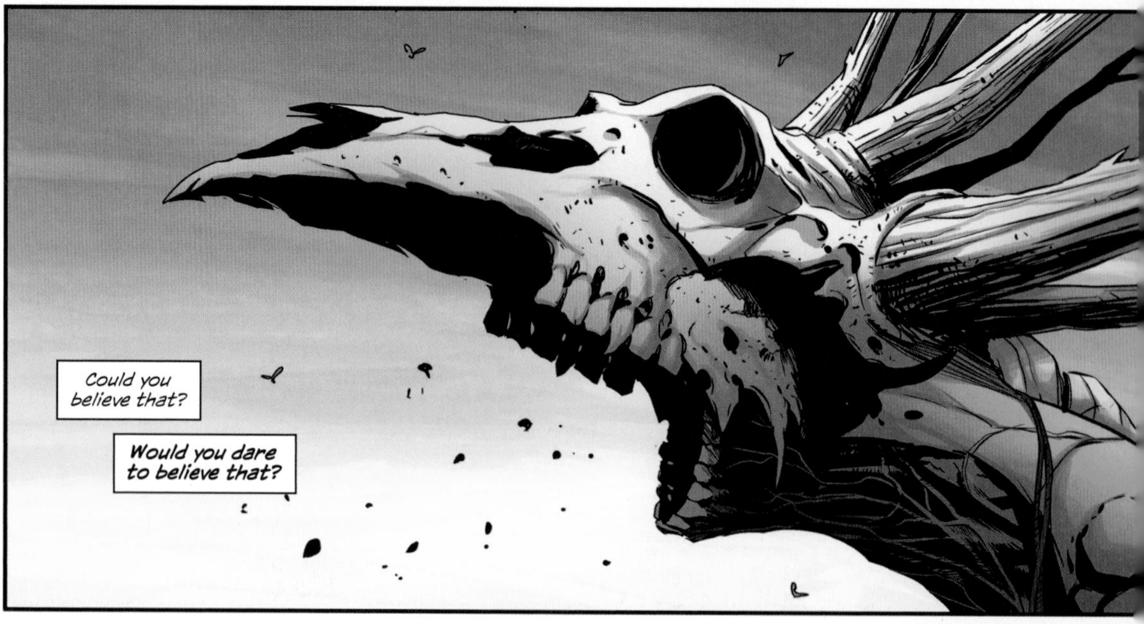
Could you believe that?
Would you dare to believe that?

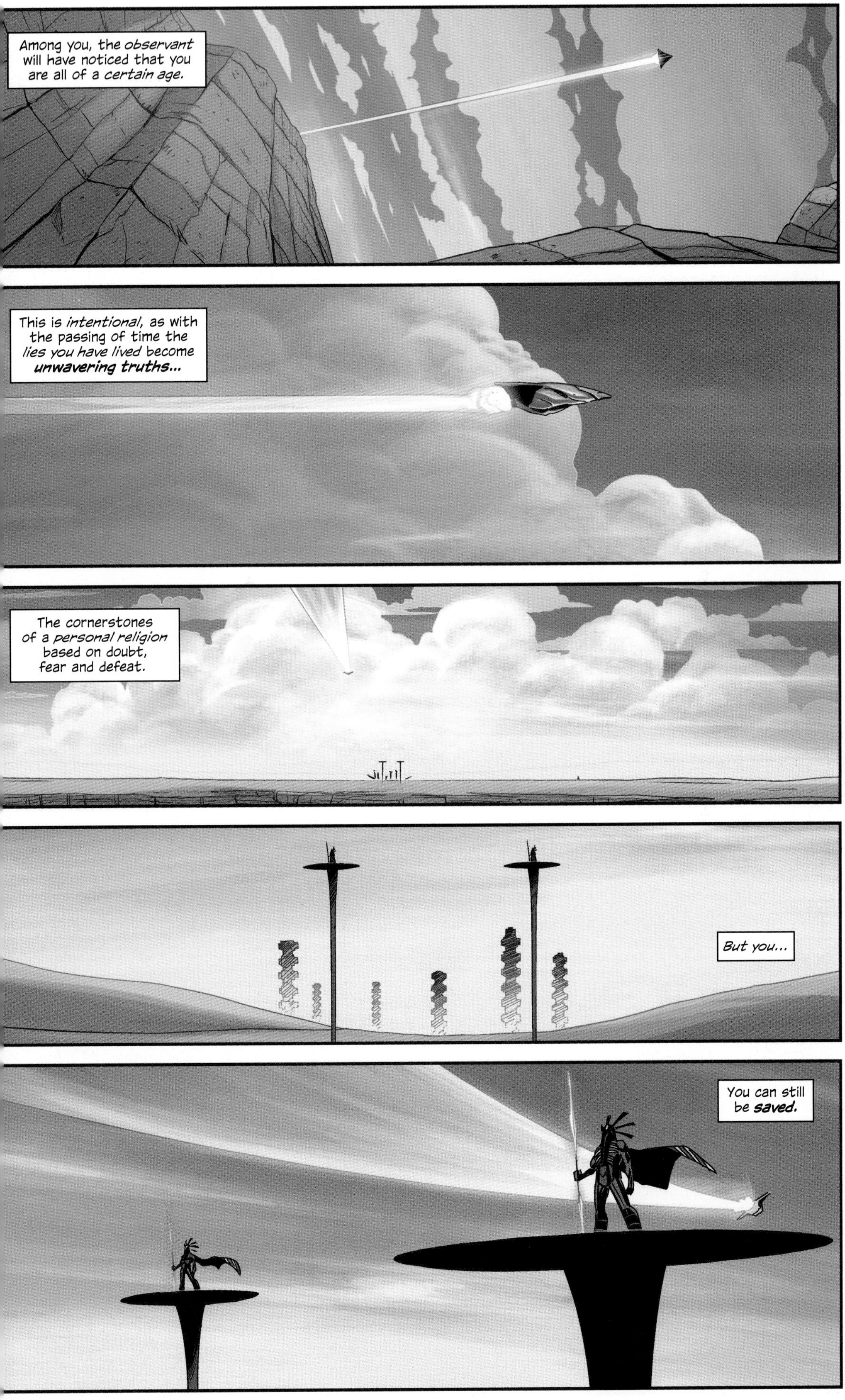
Among you, the *observant* will have noticed that you are all of a *certain age.*
This is *intentional,* as with the passing of time the *lies you have lived* become ***unwavering truths...***
The cornerstones of a *personal religion* based on doubt, fear and defeat.
But you...
You can still be ***saved.***

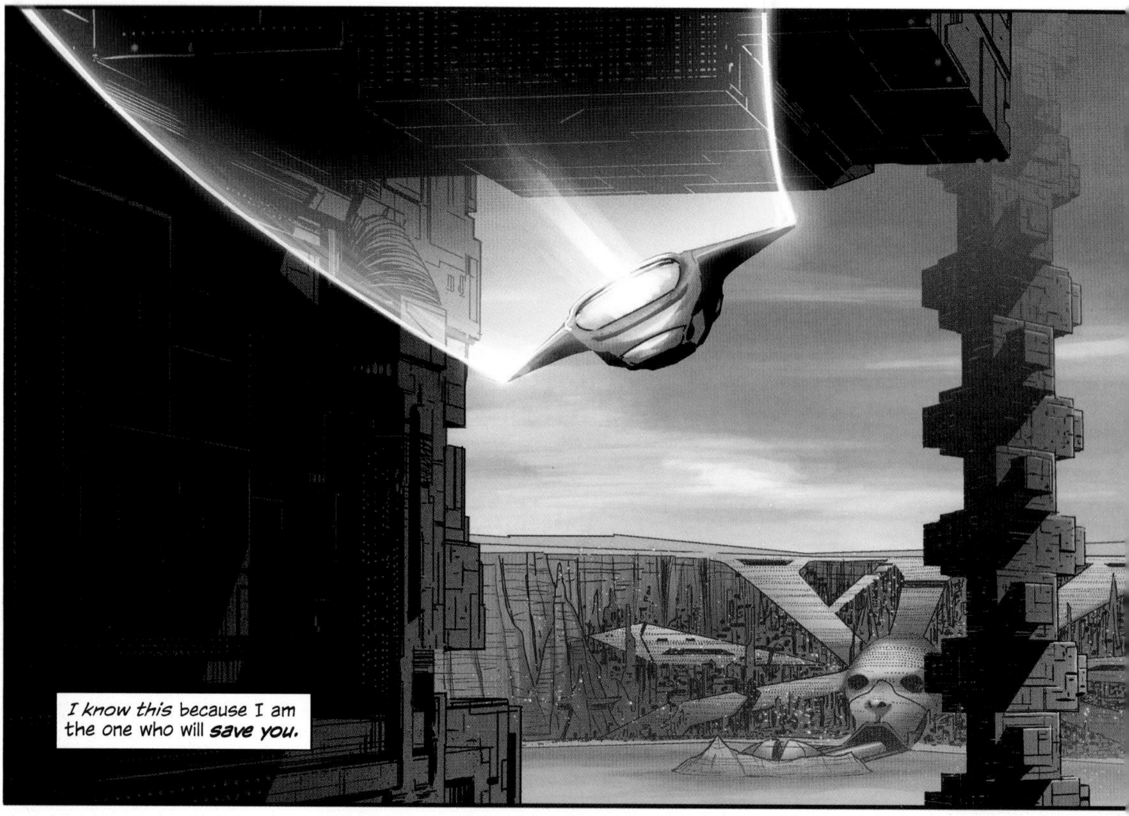
I know this because I am the one who will ***save you.***

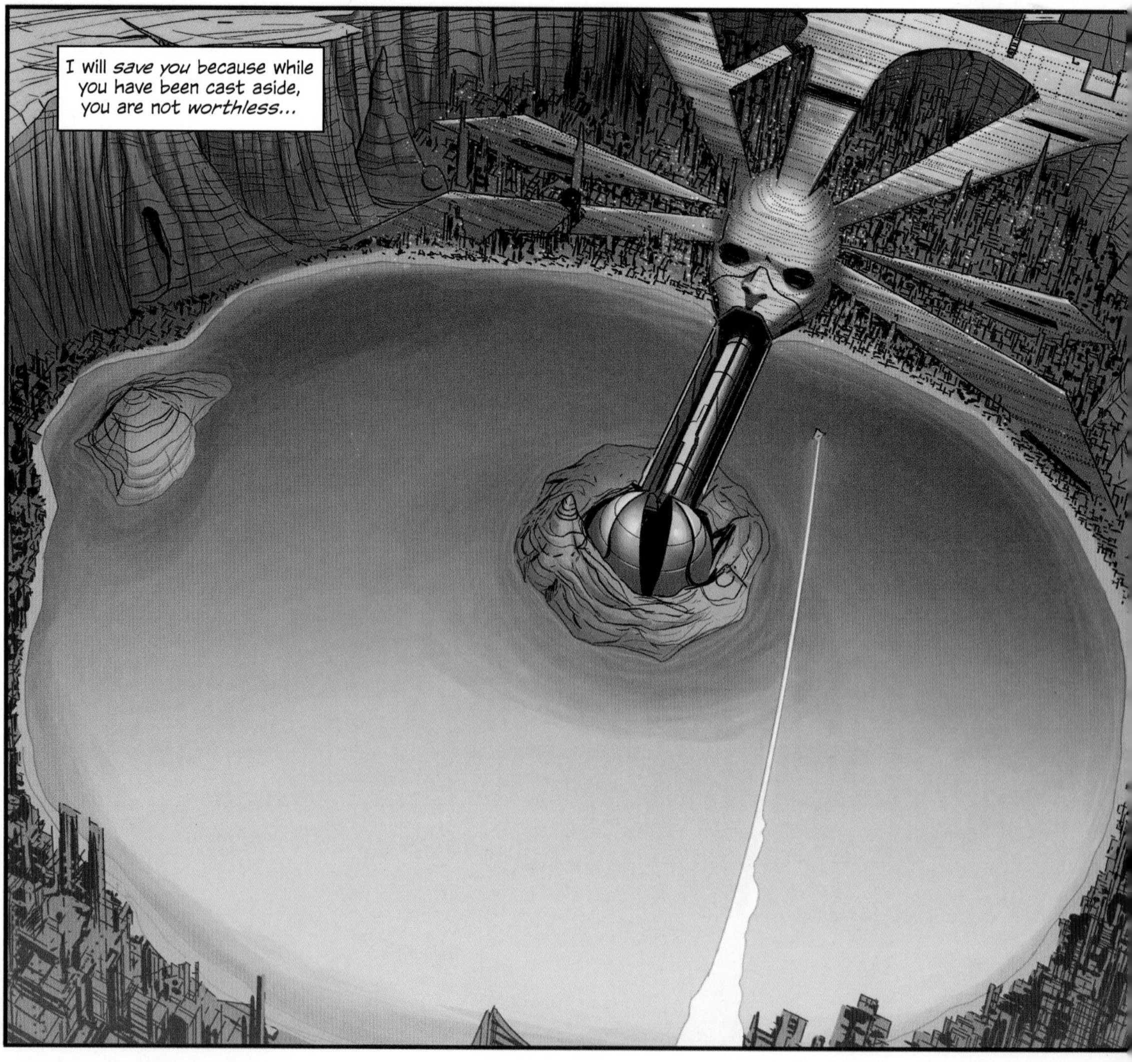
I will *save you* because while you have been cast aside, you are not *worthless...*

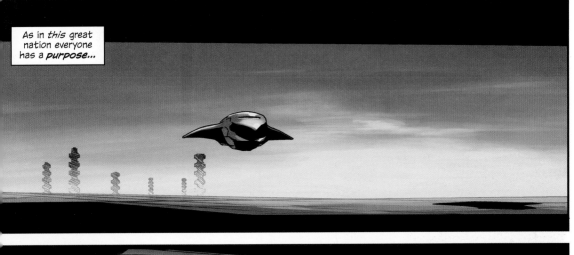

As in *this* great nation everyone has a ***purpose***...

And so shall you.

From this day forward, you are a *treasure* without *peer*...

A Widowmaker.

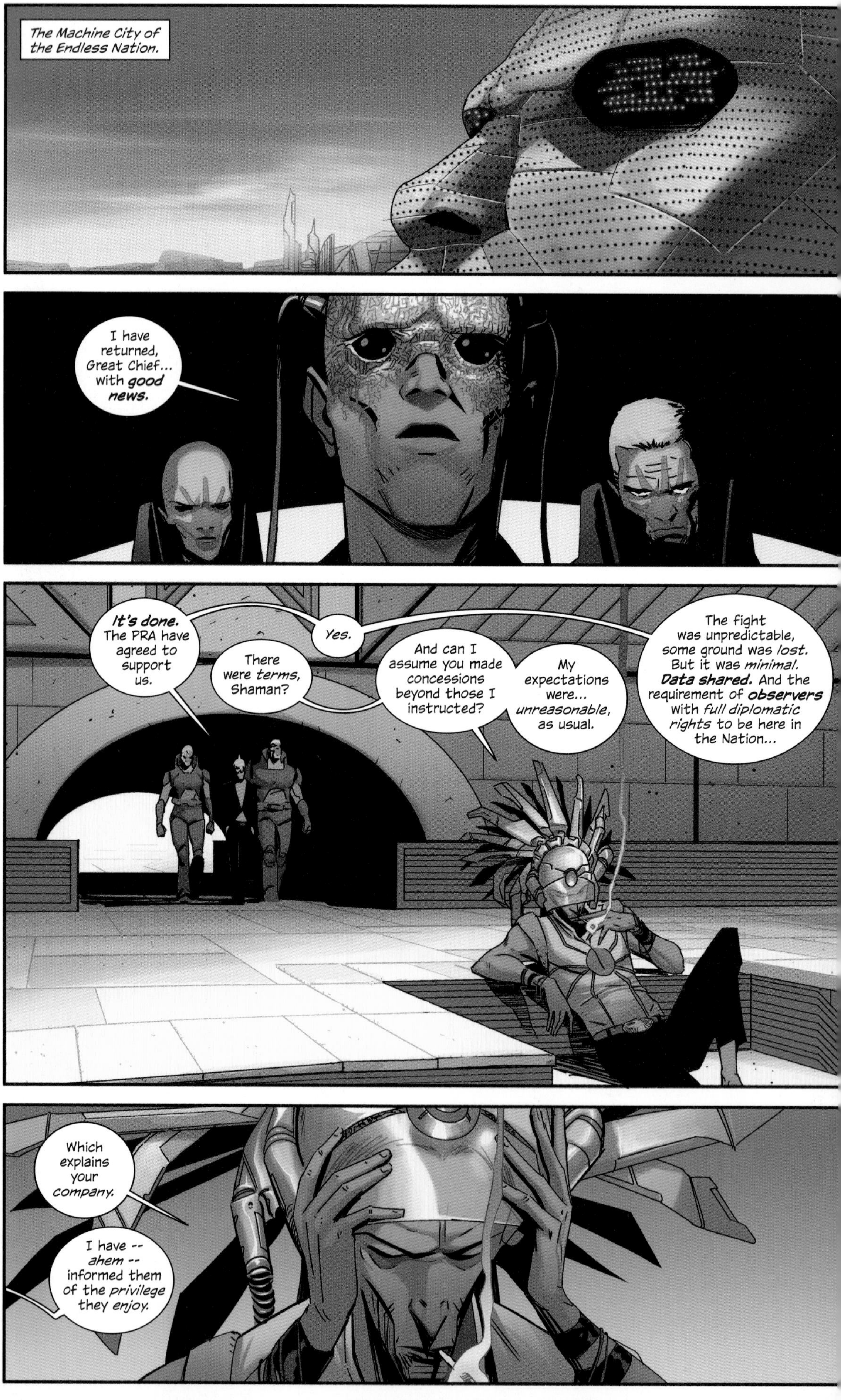
The Machine City of the Endless Nation.
I have returned, Great Chief... with **good news.**
It's done. The PRA have agreed to support us.
There were *terms,* Shaman?
Yes.
And can I assume you made concessions beyond those I instructed?
My expectations were... *unreasonable,* as usual.
The fight was unpredictable, some ground was *lost.* But it was *minimal.* ***Data shared.*** And the requirement of ***observers*** with *full diplomatic rights* to be here in the Nation...
Which explains your *company.*
I have -- *ahem* -- informed them of the *privilege* they *enjoy.*

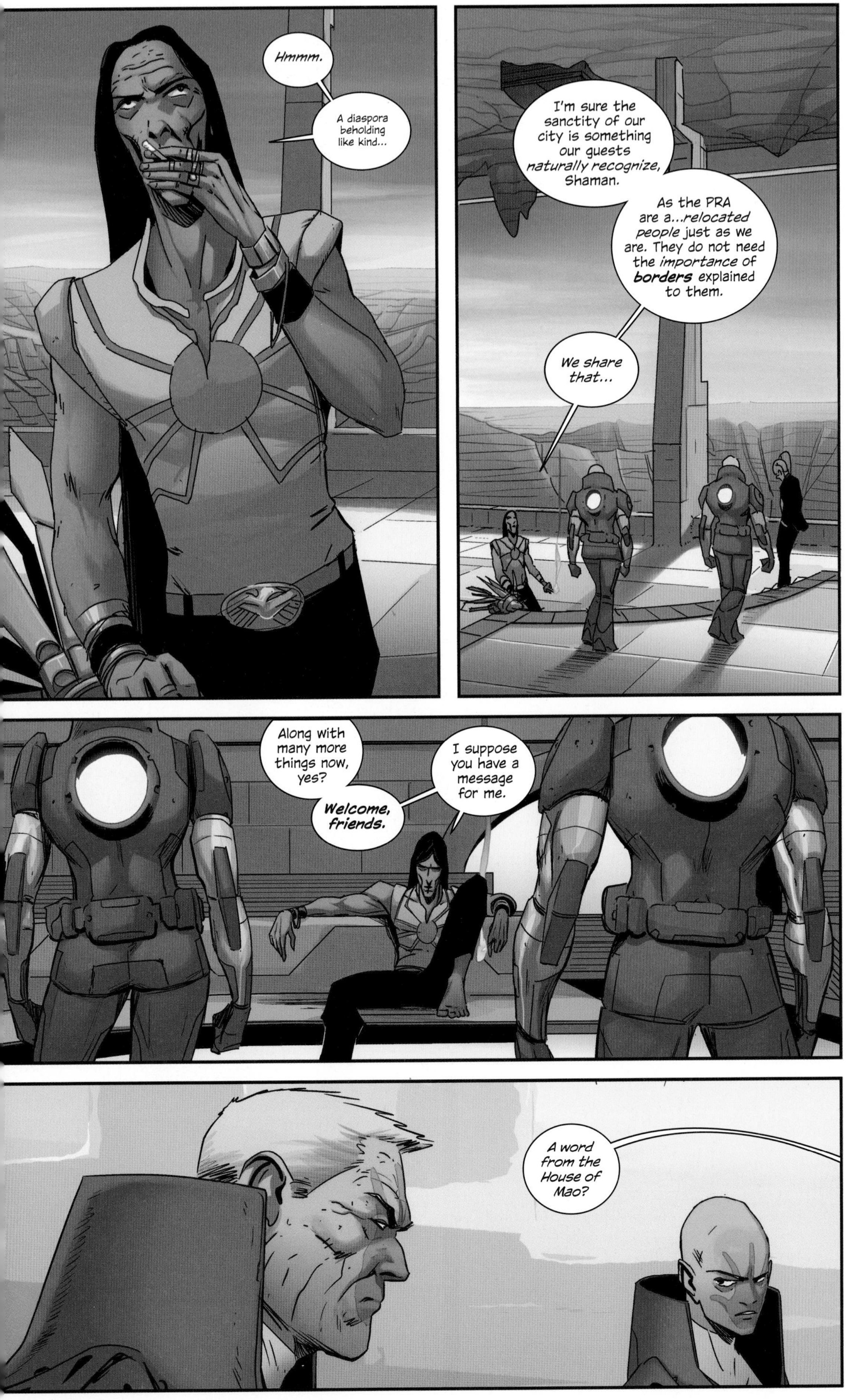
Hmmm.
A diaspora beholding like kind...
I'm sure the sanctity of our city is something our guests naturally recognize, Shaman.
As the PRA are a...relocated people just as we are. They do not need the importance of borders explained to them.
We share that...
Along with many more things now, yes?
Welcome, friends.
I suppose you have a message for me.
A word from the House of Mao?

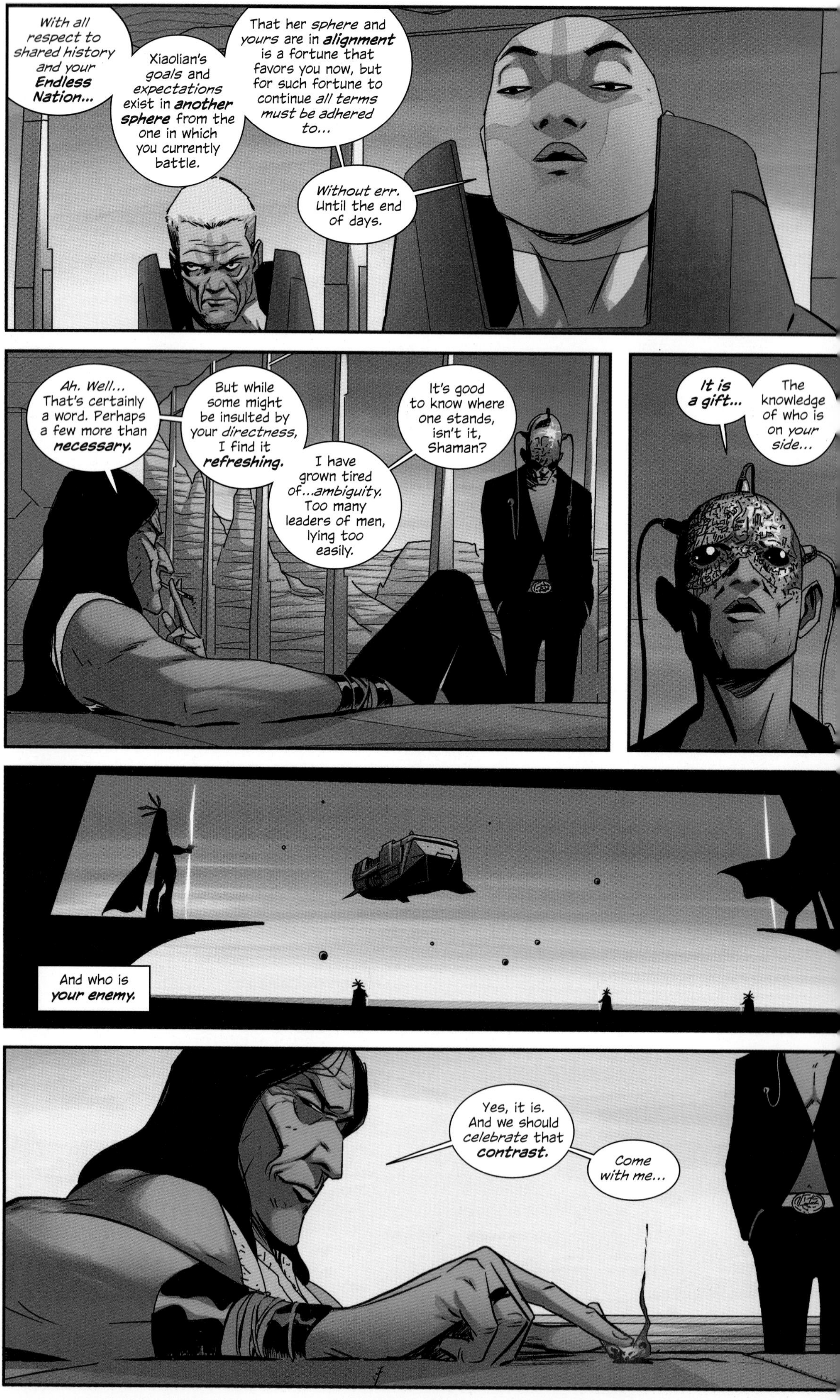
With all respect to shared history and your Endless Nation...
Xiaolian's goals and expectations exist in another sphere from the one in which you currently battle.
That her sphere and yours are in alignment is a fortune that favors you now, but for such fortune to continue all terms must be adhered to...
Without err. Until the end of days.
Ah. Well... That's certainly a word. Perhaps a few more than necessary.
But while some might be insulted by your directness, I find it refreshing.
I have grown tired of...ambiguity. Too many leaders of men, lying too easily.
It's good to know where one stands, isn't it, Shaman?
It is a gift...
The knowledge of who is on your side...
And who is your enemy.
Yes, it is. And we should celebrate that contrast.
Come with me...

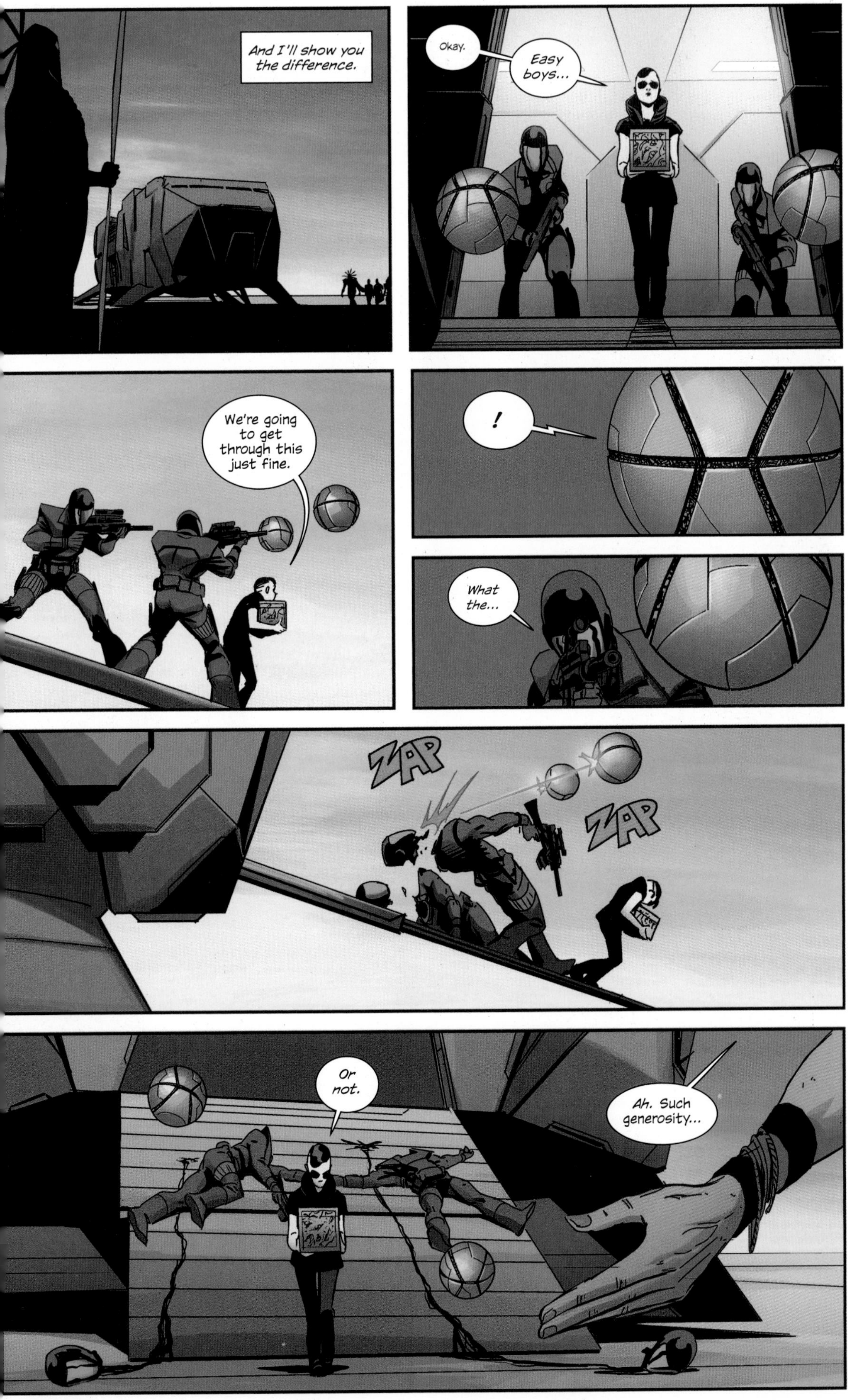
And I'll show you the difference.
Okay.
Easy boys...
We're going to get through this just fine.
!
What the...
ZAP
ZAP
Or not.
Ah. Such generosity...

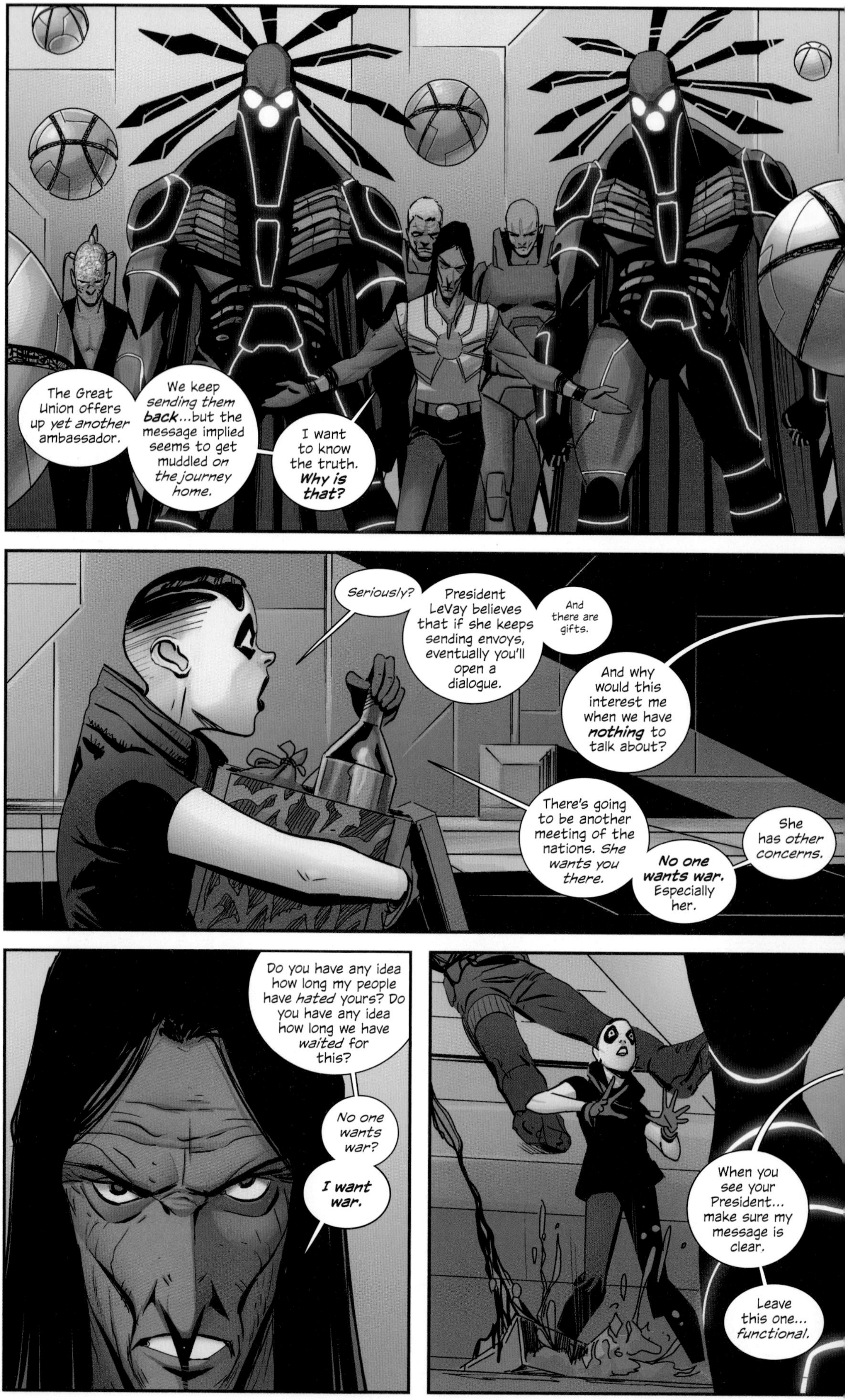
The Great Union offers up *yet another* ambassador.
We keep *sending them* ***back***...but the message implied seems to get muddled *on the journey home.*
I want to know the truth. ***Why is that?***
Seriously?
President LeVay believes that if she keeps sending envoys, eventually you'll open a dialogue.
And there are gifts.
And why would this interest me when we have ***nothing*** to talk about?
There's going to be another meeting of the nations. *She wants you there.*
No one wants war. Especially her.
She has *other concerns.*
Do you have any idea how long my people have *hated* yours? Do you have any idea how long we have *waited* for this?
No one wants war?
I want war.
When you see your President... make sure my message is clear.
Leave this one... *functional.*

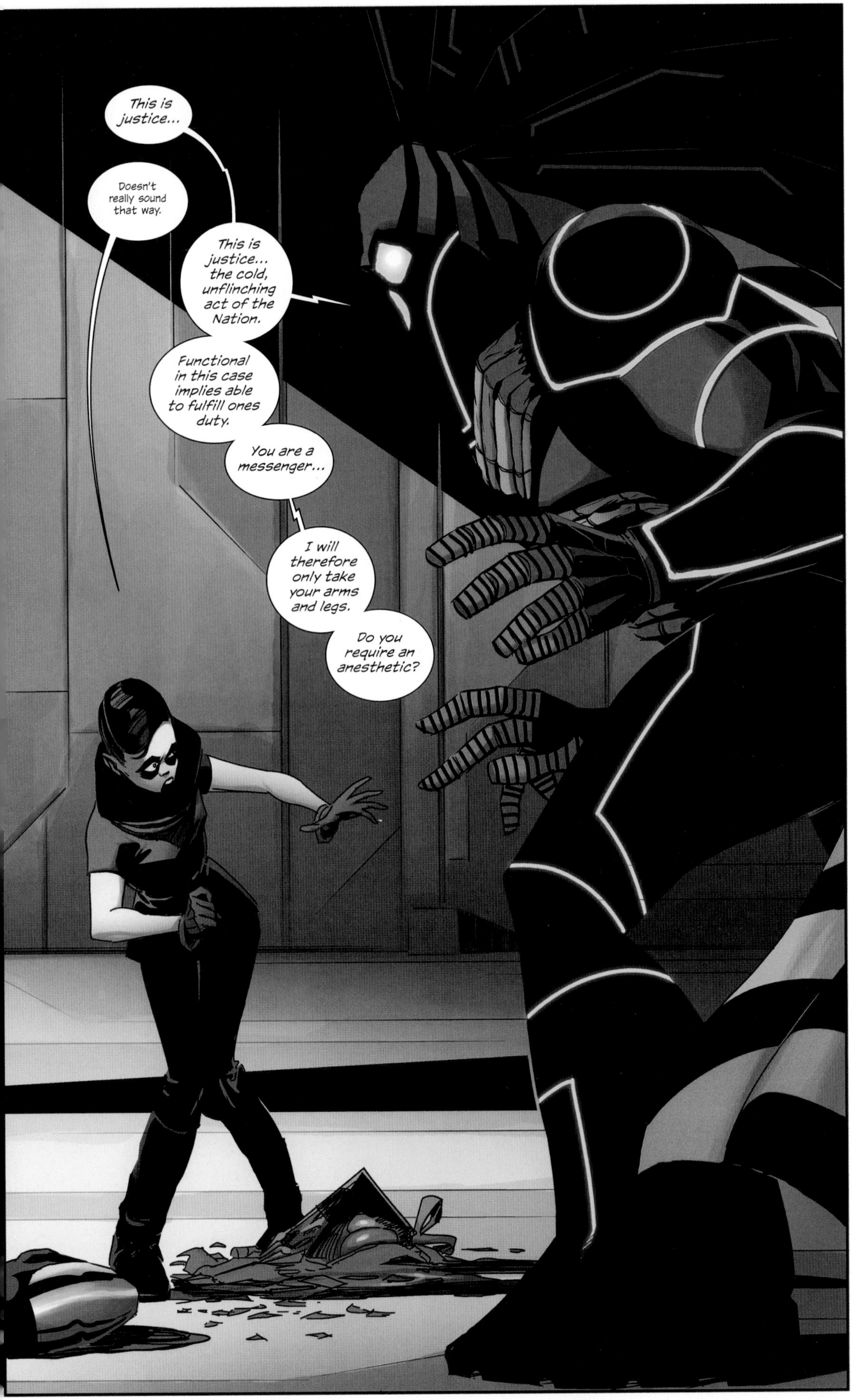
This is justice...
Doesn't really sound that way.
This is justice... the cold, unflinching act of the Nation.
Functional in this case implies able to fulfill ones duty.
You are a messenger...
I will therefore only take your arms and legs.
Do you require an anesthetic?

Go to hell.

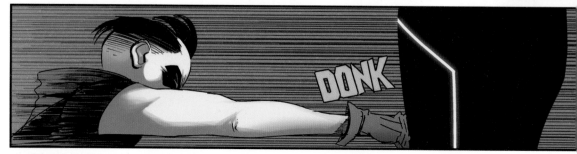

DONK

AIIEE!

≈Huff!≈ Ready to give?

That...

≈Kaff!≈

That... that's all you got?

My father hit harder than that.

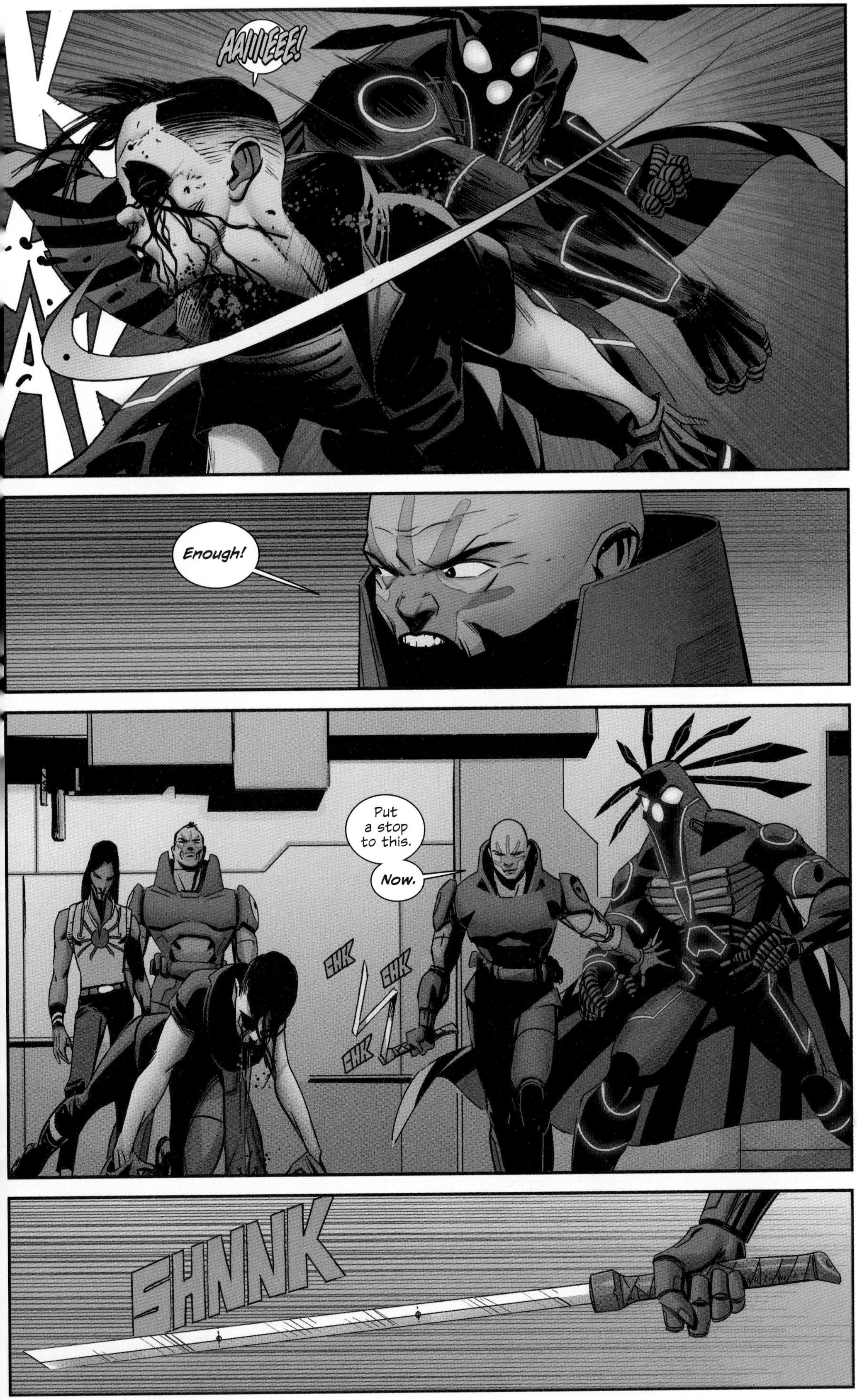
KRAK
AAIIIEEE!
Enough!
Put a stop to this.
Now.
CHK
CHK
CHK
SHNNK

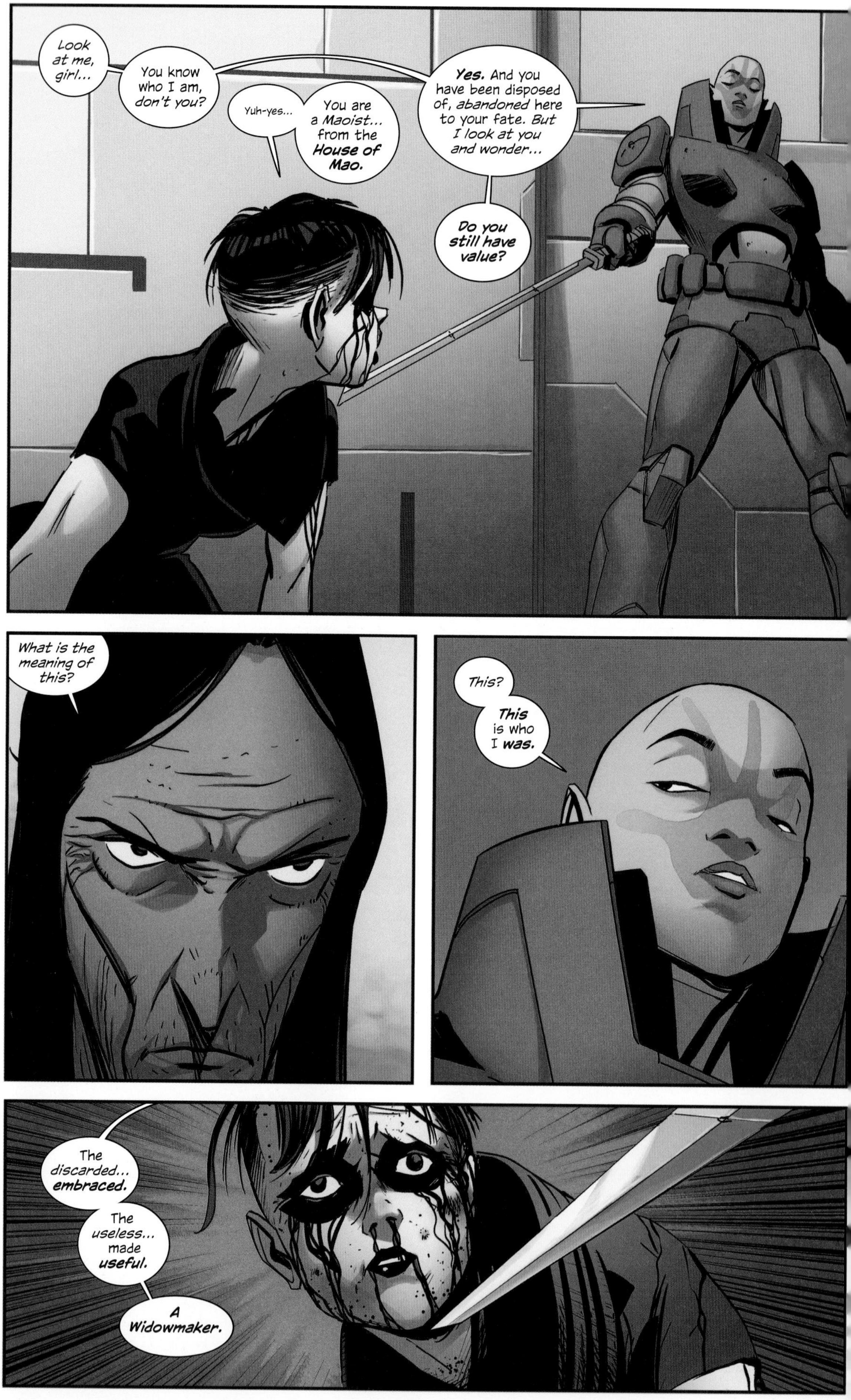
Look at me, girl...
You know who I am, don't you?
Yuh-yes...
You are a Maoist... from the House of Mao.
Yes. And you have been disposed of, abandoned here to your fate. But I look at you and wonder...
Do you still have value?
What is the meaning of this?
This?
This is who I was.
The discarded... embraced.
The useless... made useful.
A Widowmaker.

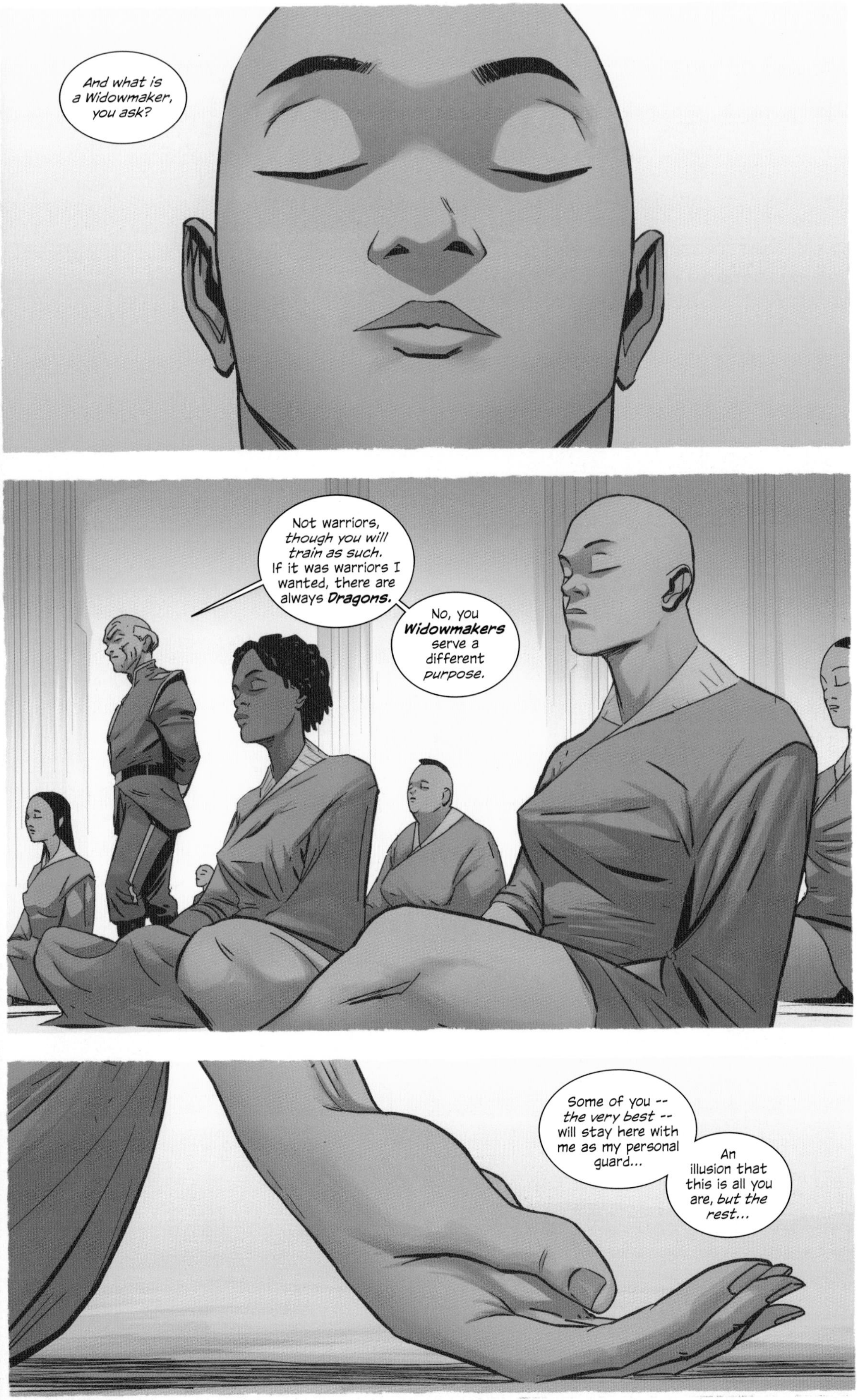
And what is a Widowmaker, you ask?
Not warriors, *though you will train as such.* If it was warriors I wanted, there are always **Dragons.**
No, you **Widowmakers** serve a different *purpose.*
Some of you -- *the very best* -- will stay here with me as my personal guard...
An illusion that this is all you are, *but the rest...*

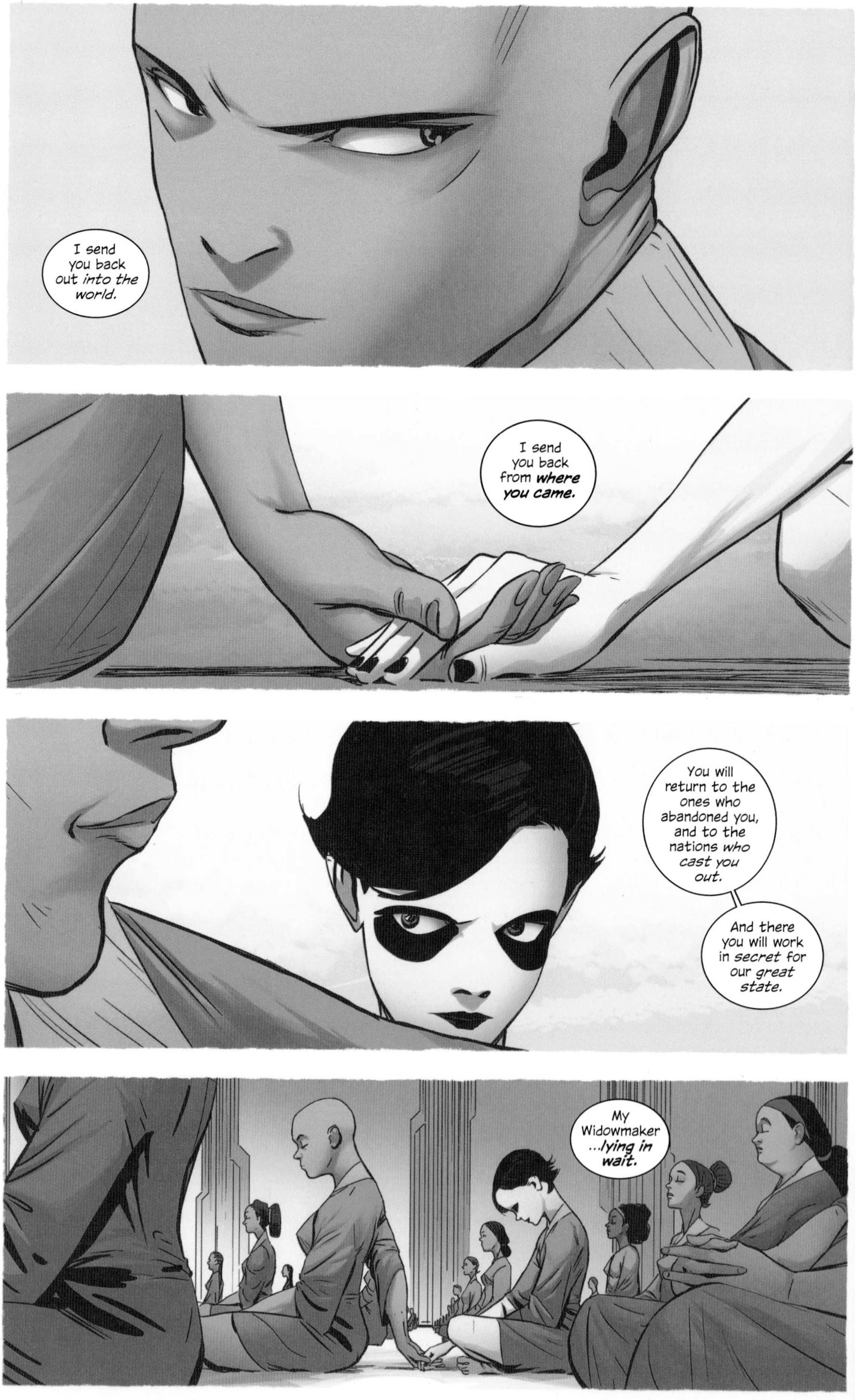
I send you back out *into the world.*
I send you back from ***where you came.***
You will return to the ones who abandoned you, and to the nations *who cast you out.*
And there you will work in *secret* for our *great state.*
My Widowmaker ...***lying in wait.***

YOU HEAR **NOTHING**
BECAUSE YOU DON'T KNOW
WHAT TO **LISTEN FOR.**

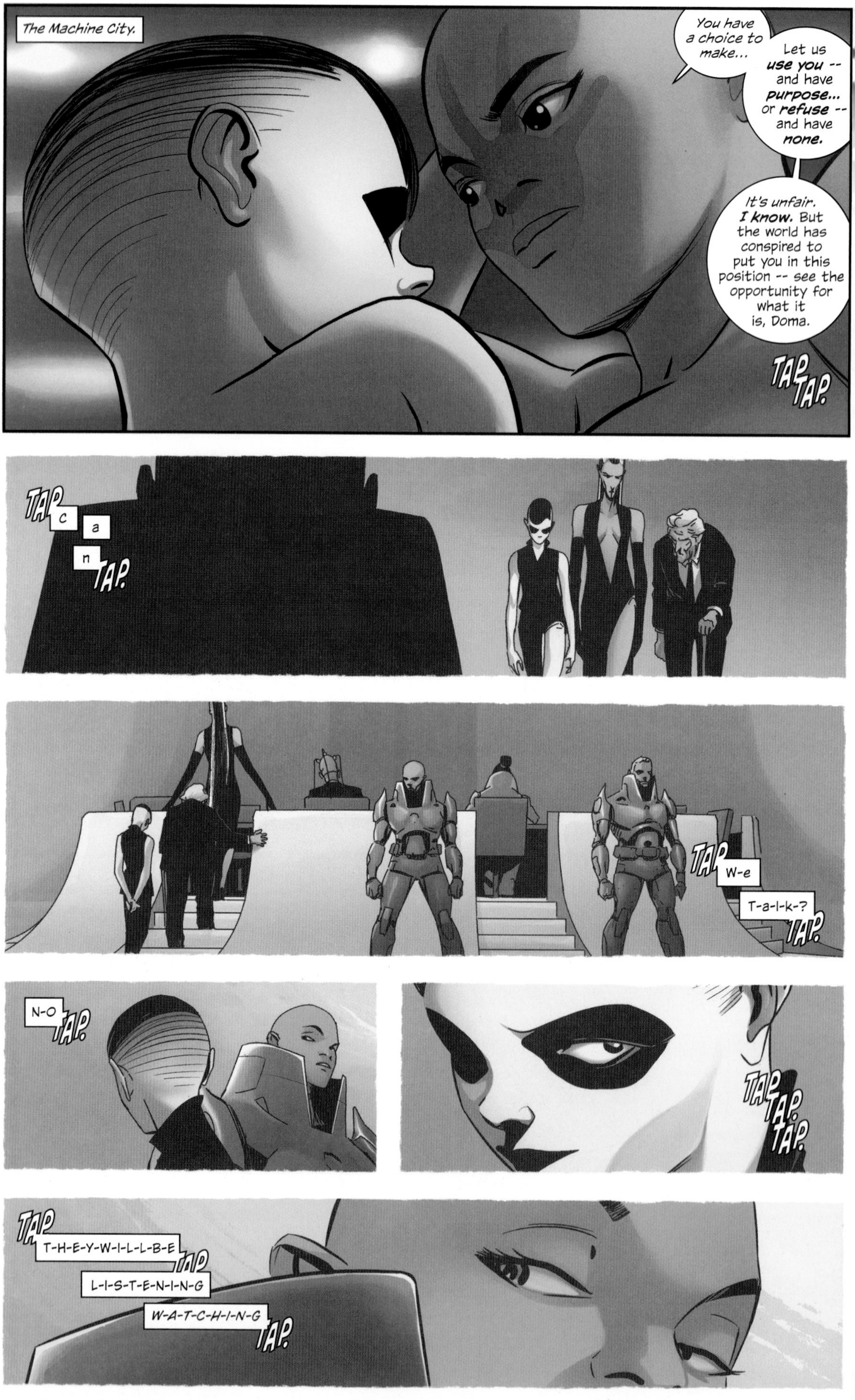

The Machine City.
You have a choice to make...
Let us **use you** -- and have **purpose...** or **refuse** -- and have **none.**
It's unfair. **I know.** But the world has conspired to put you in this position -- see the opportunity for what it is, Doma.
TAP TAP.
TAP
c
a
n
TAP.
TAP
W-e
T-a-l-k-?
TAP.
N-O
TAP.
TAP TAP. TAP.
TAP
T-H-E-Y-W-I-L-L-B-E
TAP
L-I-S-T-E-N-I-N-G
W-A-T-C-H-I-N-G
TAP.

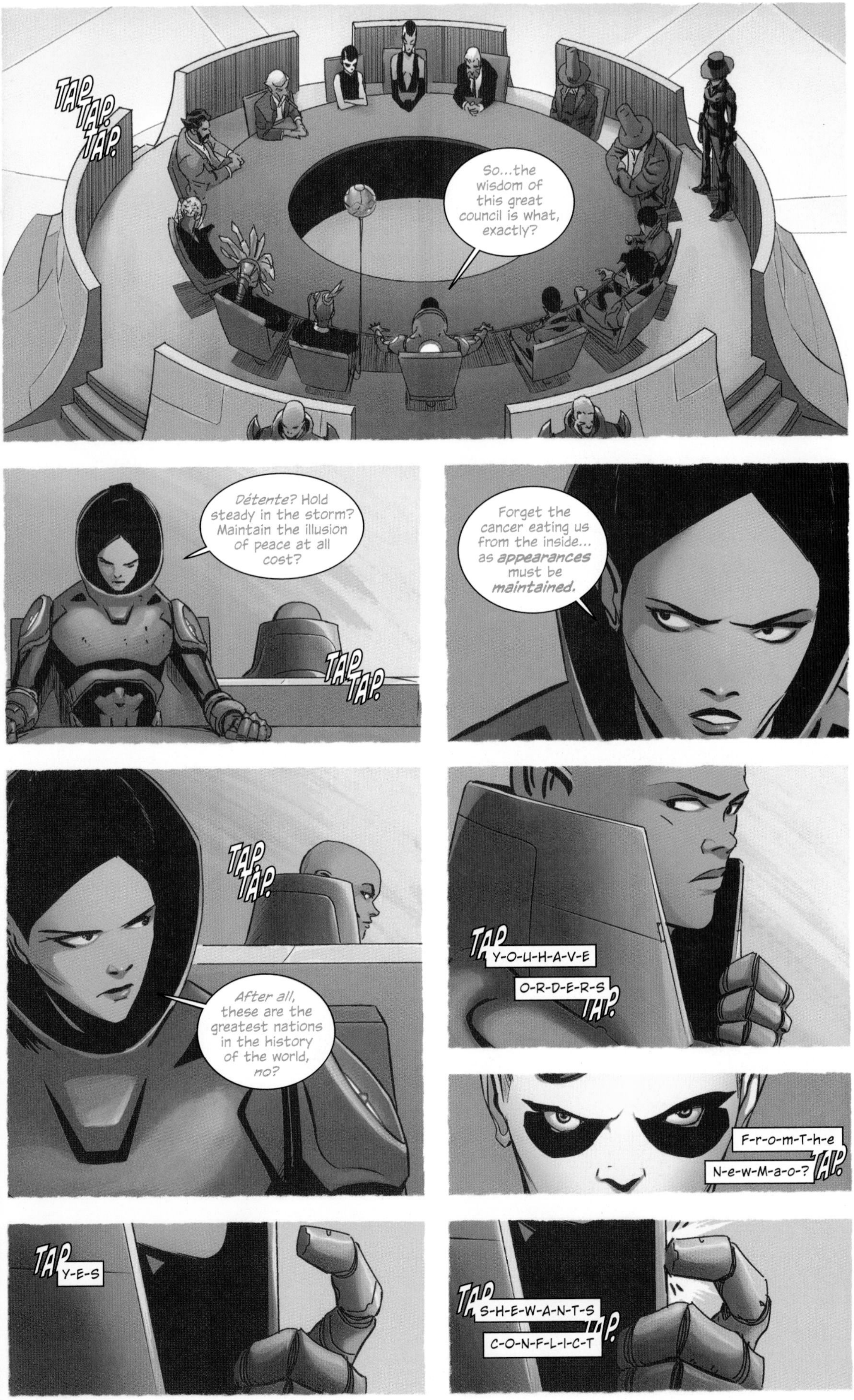
TAP TAP. TAP.
So...the wisdom of this great council is what, exactly?
Détente? Hold steady in the storm? Maintain the illusion of peace at all cost?
TAP TAP.
Forget the cancer eating us from the inside... as appearances must be maintained.
TAP TAP.
After all, these are the greatest nations in the history of the world, no?
TAP
Y-O-U-H-A-V-E
O-R-D-E-R-S
TAP.
F-r-o-m-T-h-e
N-e-w-M-a-o-?
TAP.
TAP
Y-E-S
TAP
S-H-E-W-A-N-T-S
C-O-N-F-L-I-C-T
TAP.

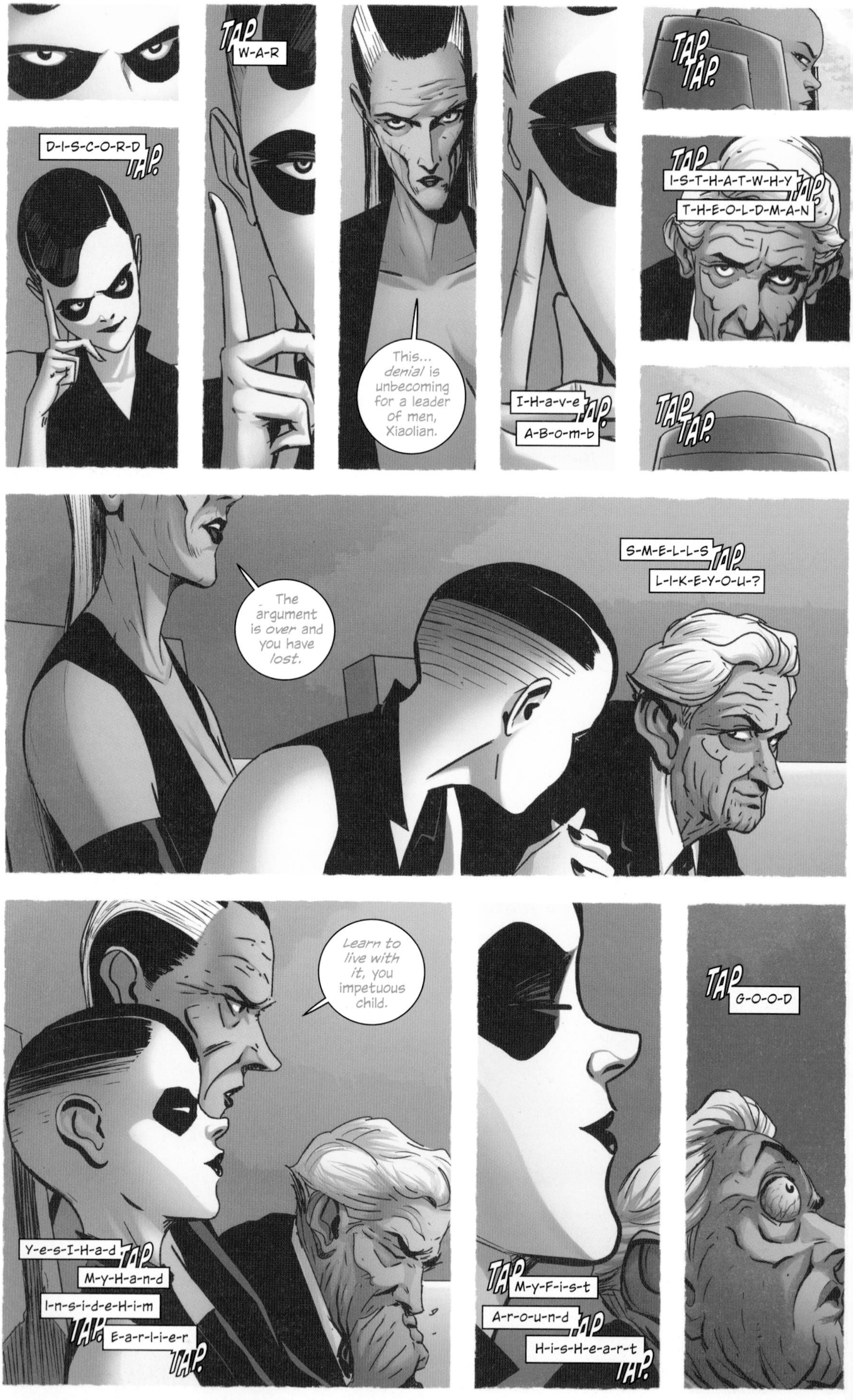
TAP
W-A-R
D-I-S-C-O-R-D
TAP.
This... denial is unbecoming for a leader of men, Xiaolian.
I-H-a-v-e
TAP.
A-B-o-m-b
TAP. TAP.
TAP
I-S-T-H-A-T-W-H-Y
TAP.
T-H-E-O-L-D-M-A-N
TAP. TAP.
The argument is over and you have lost.
S-M-E-L-L-S
TAP.
L-I-K-E-Y-O-U-?
Learn to live with it, you impetuous child.
Y-e-s-I-H-a-d
TAP.
M-y-H-a-n-d
I-n-s-i-d-e-H-i-m
TAP.
E-a-r-l-i-e-r
TAP.
TAP
M-y-F-i-s-t
A-r-o-u-n-d
TAP
H-i-s-H-e-a-r-t
TAP.
TAP
G-O-O-D

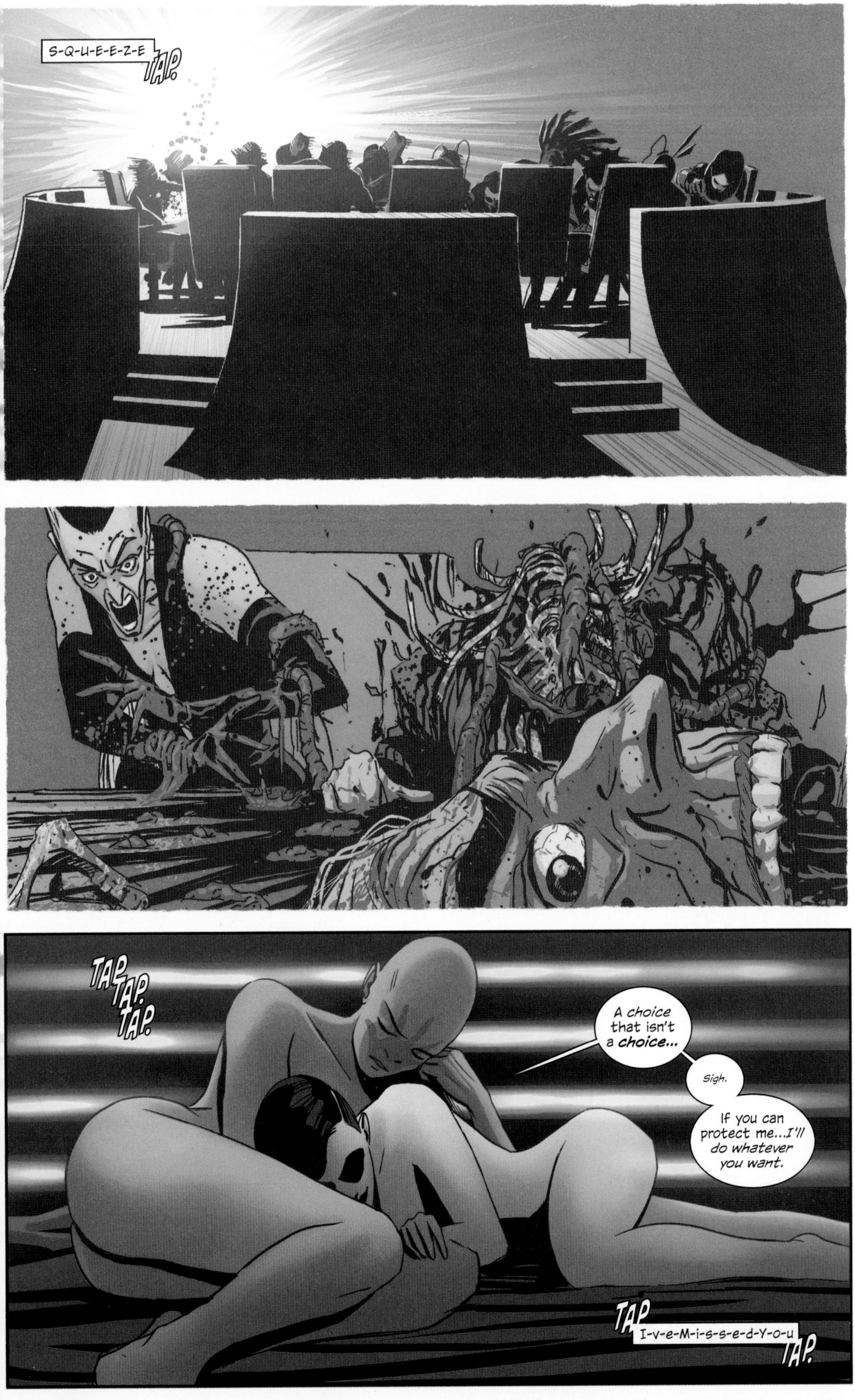
S-Q-U-E-E-Z-E
TAP.
TAP
TAP.
TAP.
A choice that isn't a *choice*...
Sigh.
If you can protect me...*I'll do whatever* you want.
TAP
I-v-e-M-i-s-s-e-d-Y-o-u
TAP.

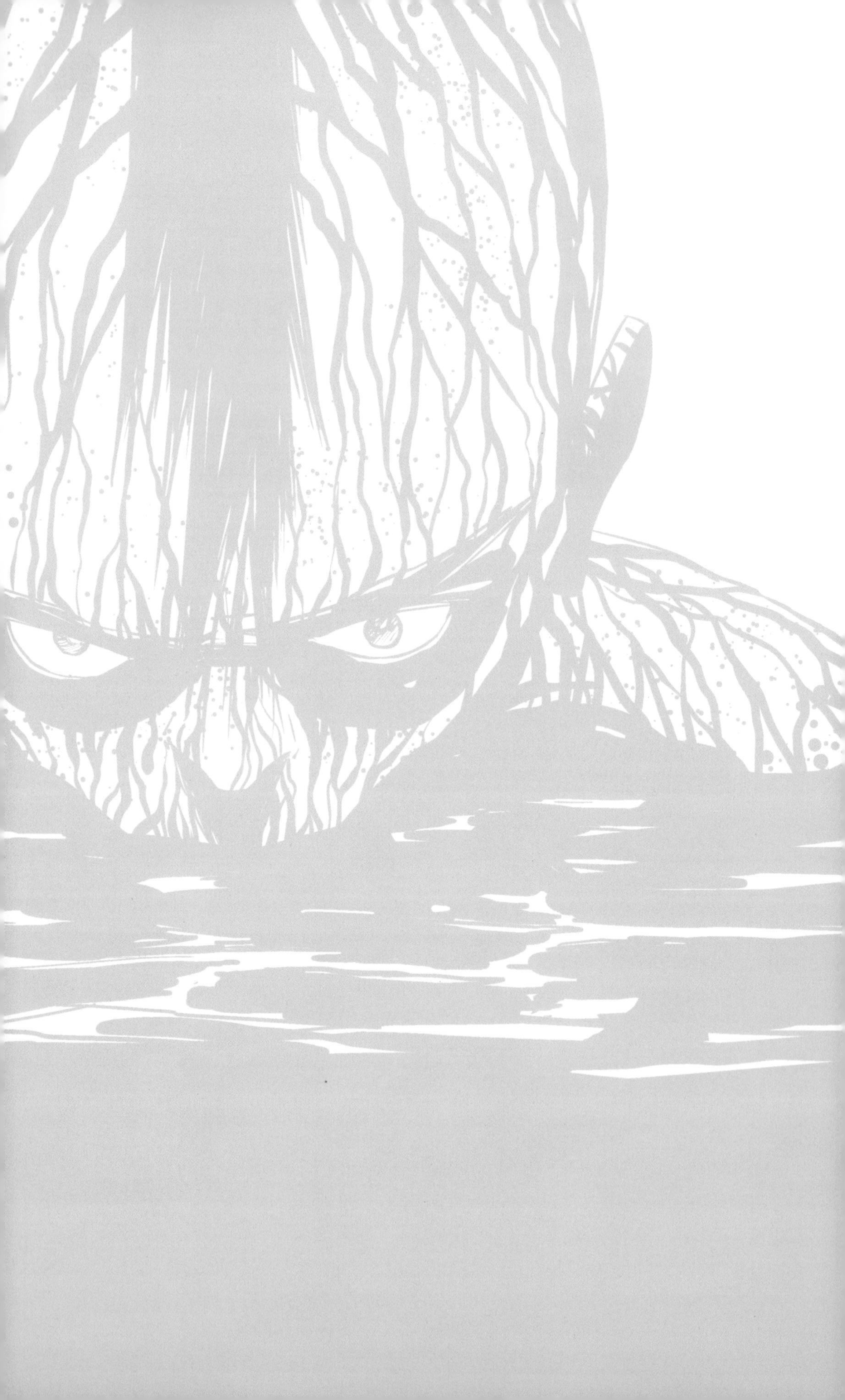

21

TWENTY-ONE:
THIS **GREAT CITY**

YOU HEAR **EVERYTHING**
AND IT REDUCES YOU TO
NOTHING.

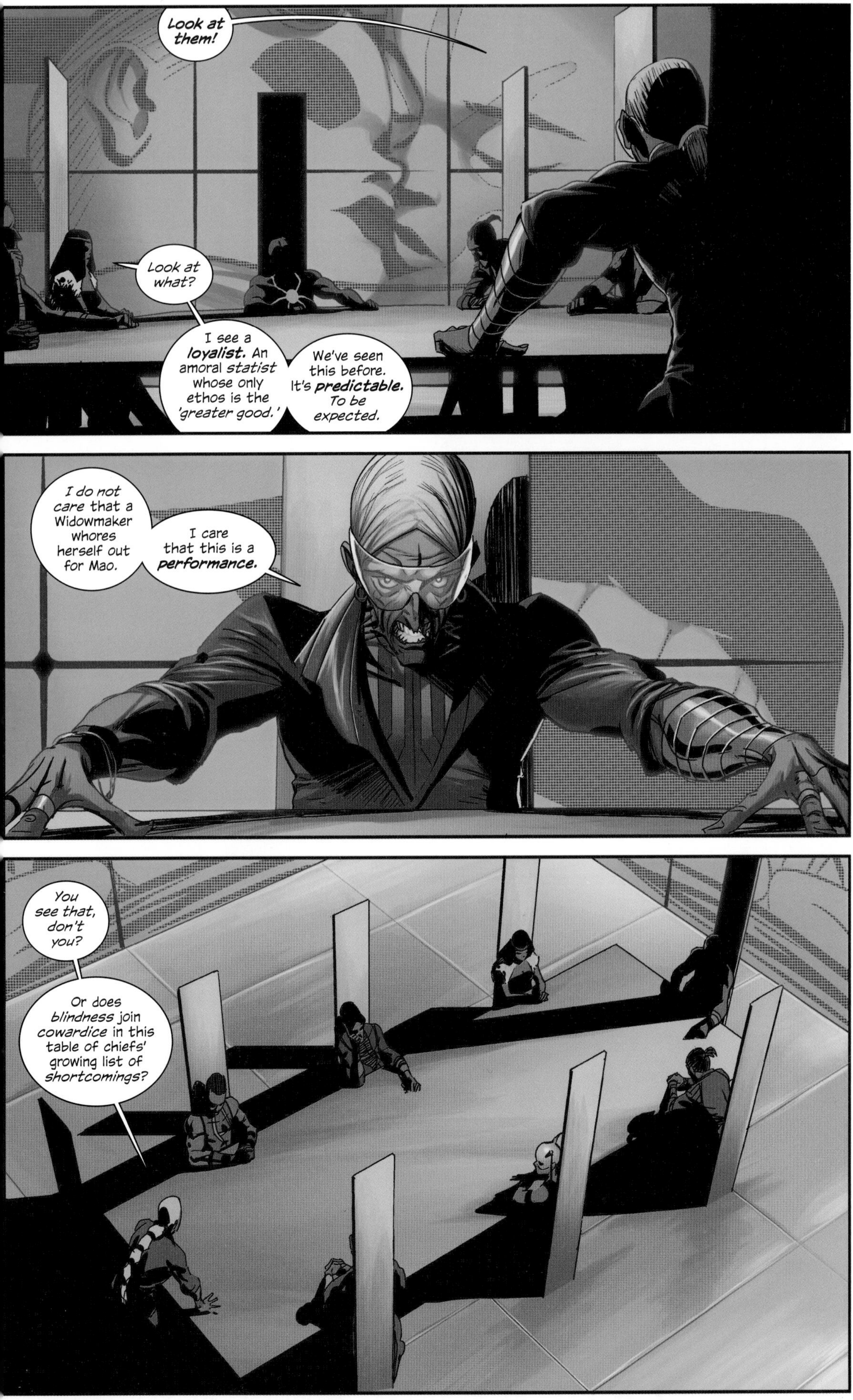
Look at them!
Look at what?
I see a loyalist. An amoral statist whose only ethos is the 'greater good.'
We've seen this before. It's predictable. To be expected.
I do not care that a Widowmaker whores herself out for Mao.
I care that this is a performance.
You see that, don't you?
Or does blindness join cowardice in this table of chiefs' growing list of shortcomings?

Speak for yourself, brother.

All I see is an *agent* turning an *asset.* If the PRA are our allies, how can this be a bad thing?

Bodaway finds affection *suspicious,* Niteesh...

Haven't you heard? The sun also rises in the east.

Tisk.

The horde of Mao is a *long-term* problem.

History is measured in years, not days. It is *unwise* to dismiss any *concerns* regarding the dragon...

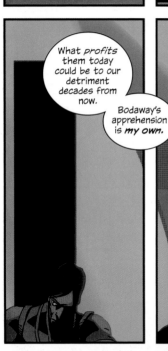

What *profits* them today could be to our detriment decades from now.

Bodaway's apprehension is *my own.*

All of this feels like a mistake.

Agreed!

The data remains *cloudy.*

And yet here we are.

Yes. *Here we are.*

Exactly where we agreed to be *months ago.* Exactly where our chief -- *the chief of chiefs* -- has led us.

Many brothers and sisters have died because we were too aggressive in the south. So we *all agreed* on our alliance with the House of Mao.

All of us. And we also agreed there would be no turning back. What has changed since then?

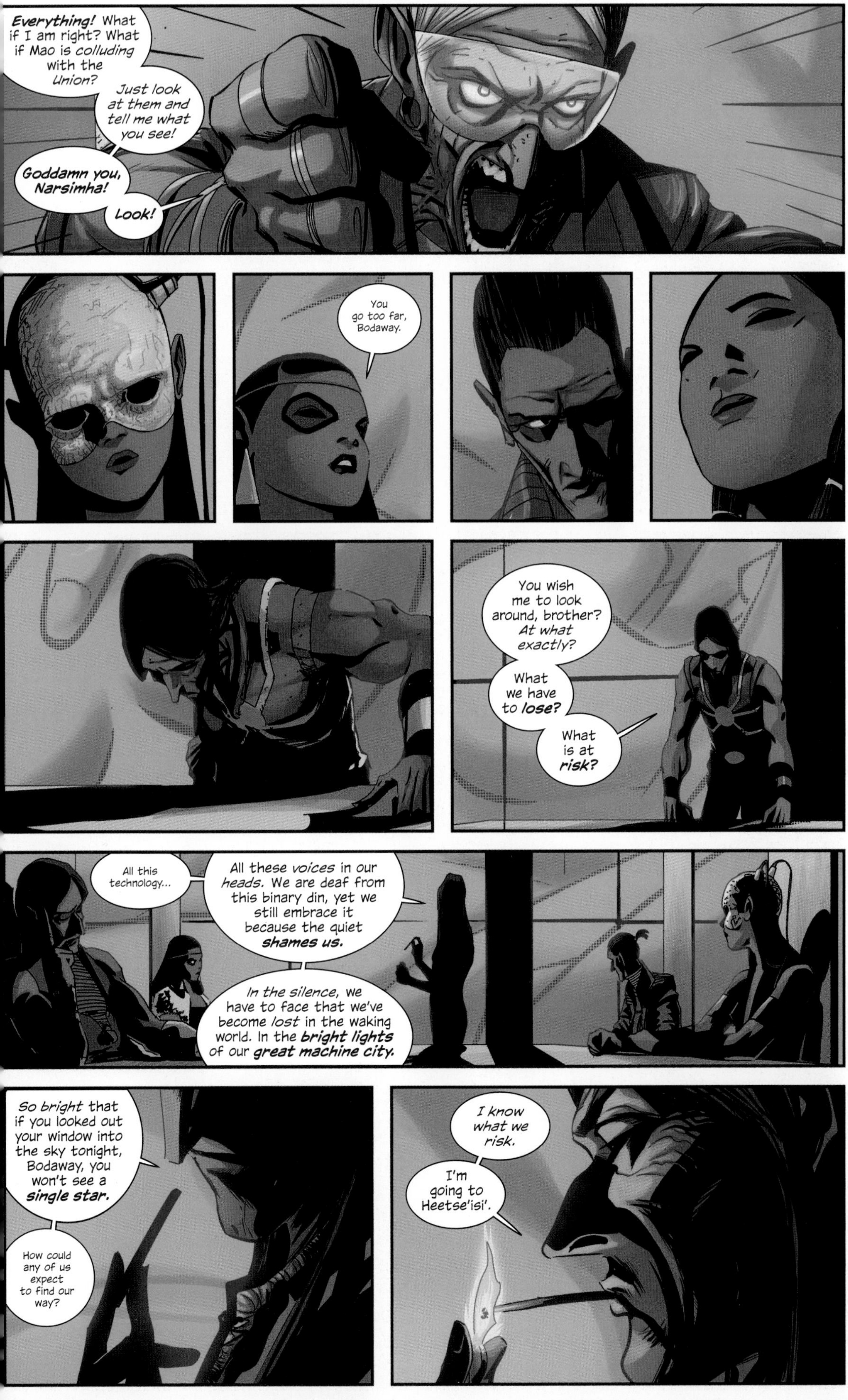

Everything! What if I am right? What if Mao is colluding with the Union?
Just look at them and tell me what you see!
Goddamn you, Narsimha!
Look!
You go too far, Bodaway.
You wish me to look around, brother? At what exactly?
What we have to lose?
What is at risk?
All this technology...
All these voices in our heads. We are deaf from this binary din, yet we still embrace it because the quiet shames us.
In the silence, we have to face that we've become lost in the waking world. In the bright lights of our great machine city.
So bright that if you looked out your window into the sky tonight, Bodaway, you won't see a single star.
How could any of us expect to find our way?
I know what we risk.
I'm going to Heetse'isi'.

Ack! You'll throw *everything* away!

You know *the greater sins:* Never forsake your tribe. Never take life of one of the Nation.

And do not *walk* the *dead lands.*

Have you forgotten even this, Narsimha?

Thirty years.

What?

We've known each other *thirty years,* Bodaway...

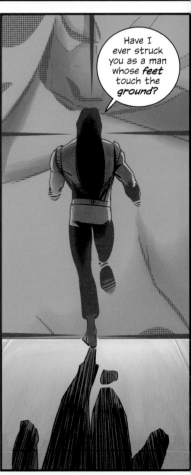

Have I ever struck you as a man whose *feet* touch the *ground?*

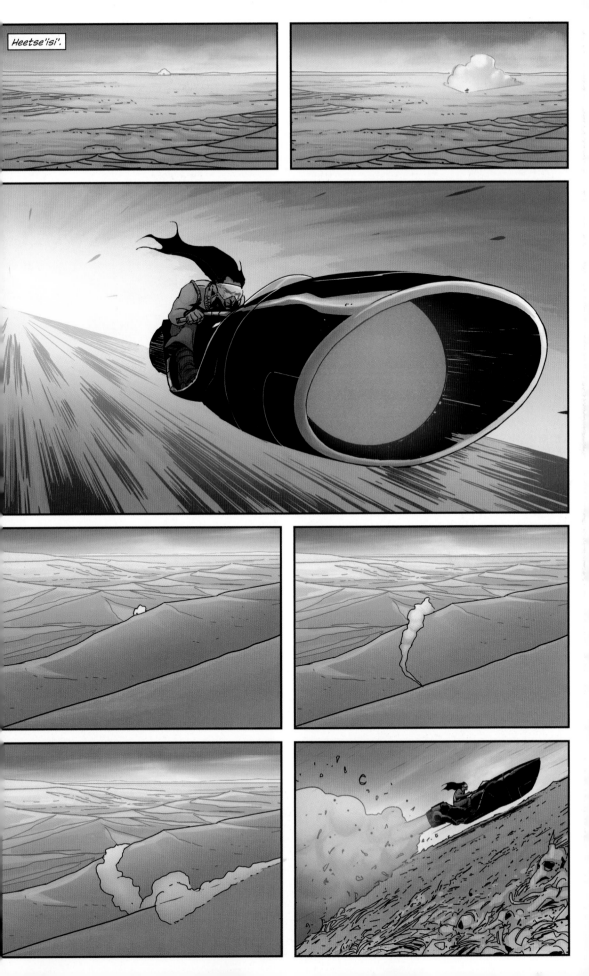

Heetse'isi'.

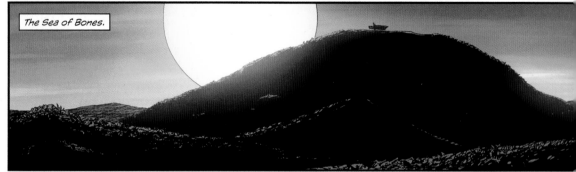

The Sea of Bones.

Hrmpt.

Either show yourself or I'll *summon* you...

I have the *blood* for it.

Hrrrrnnnnn!

Ah!

There you are.

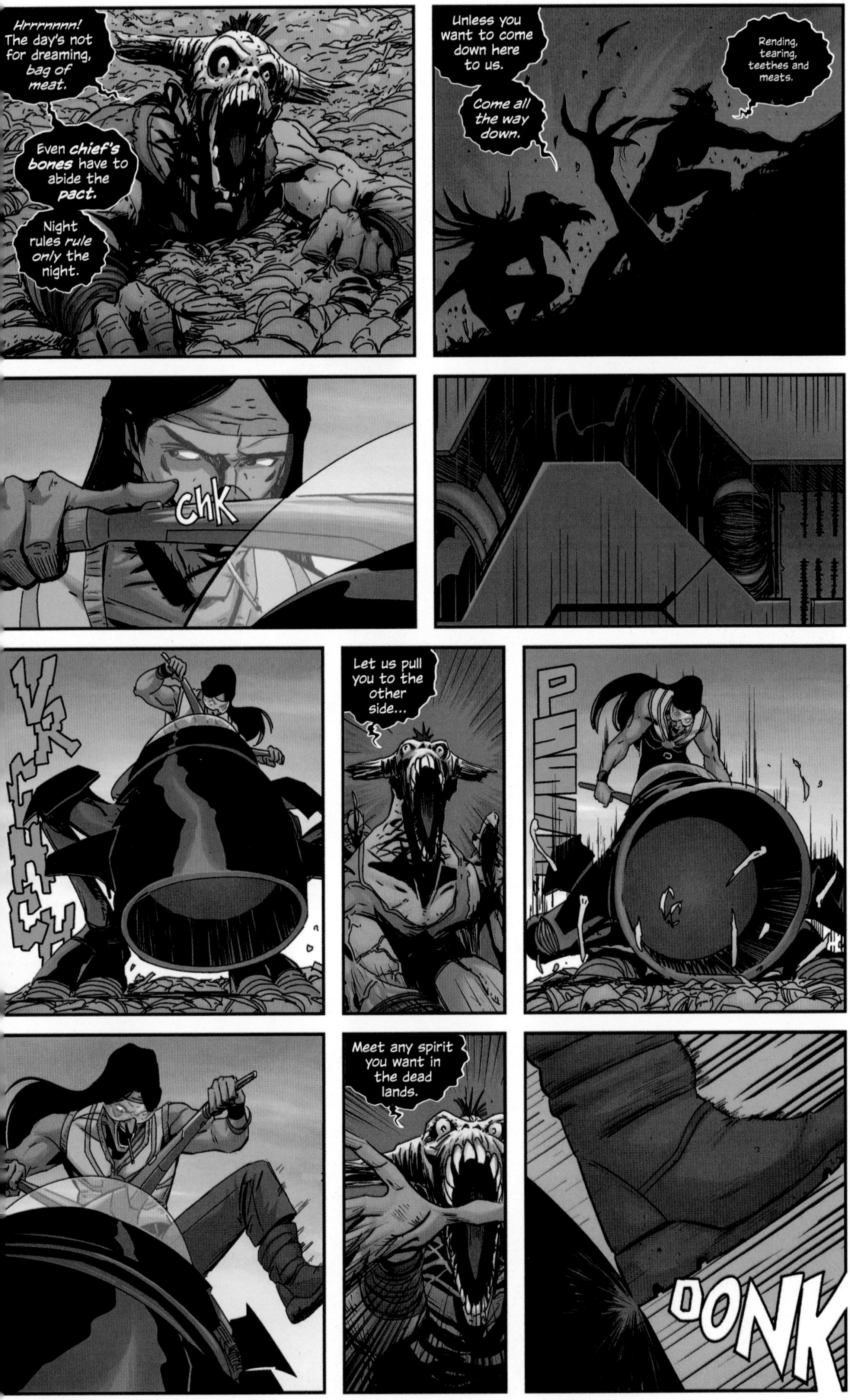
Hrrrnnnn! The day's not for dreaming, bag of meat.
Even chief's bones have to abide the pact.
Night rules rule only the night.
Unless you want to come down here to us.
Come all the way down.
Rending, tearing, teethes and meats.
ChK
VRCHCHCH
Let us pull you to the other side...
PSSH
Meet any spirit you want in the dead lands.
DONK

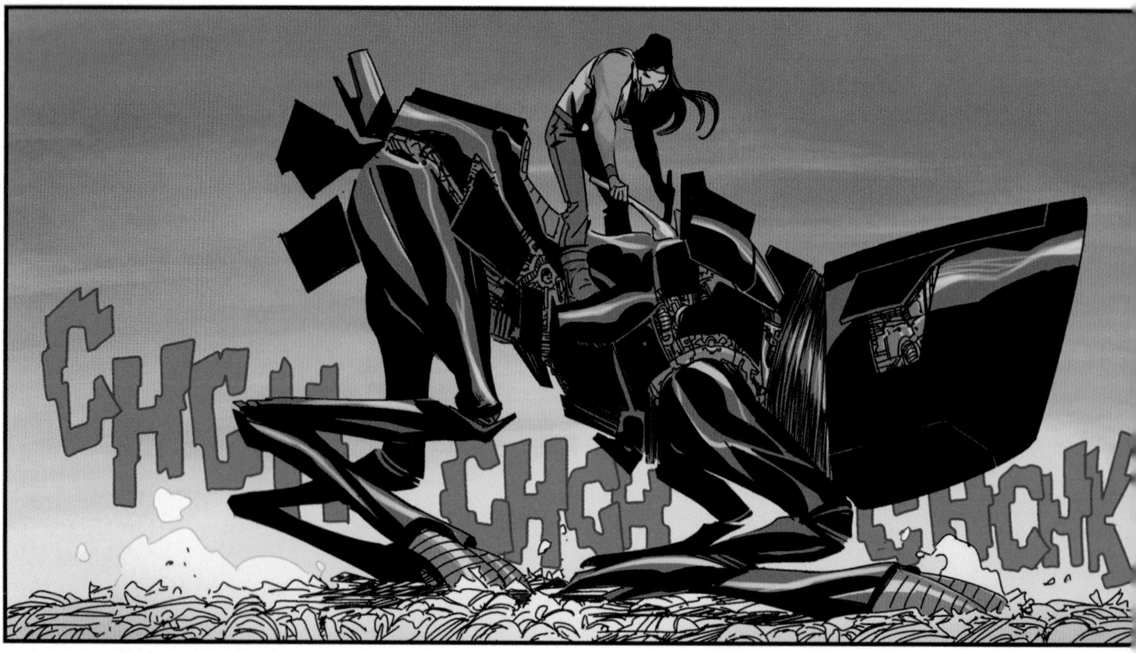
CHCH
CHCH
CHCHK
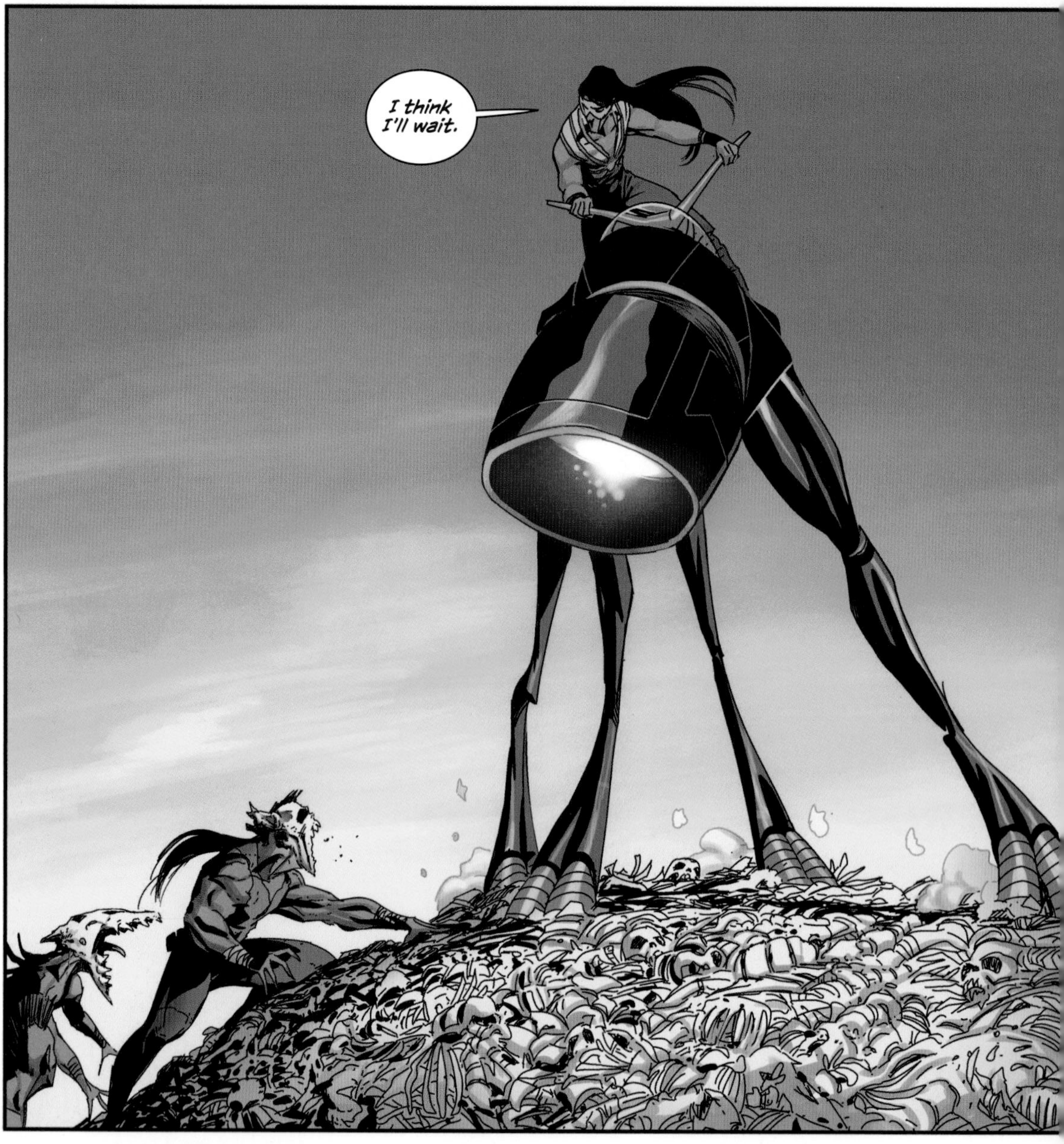
I think I'll wait.

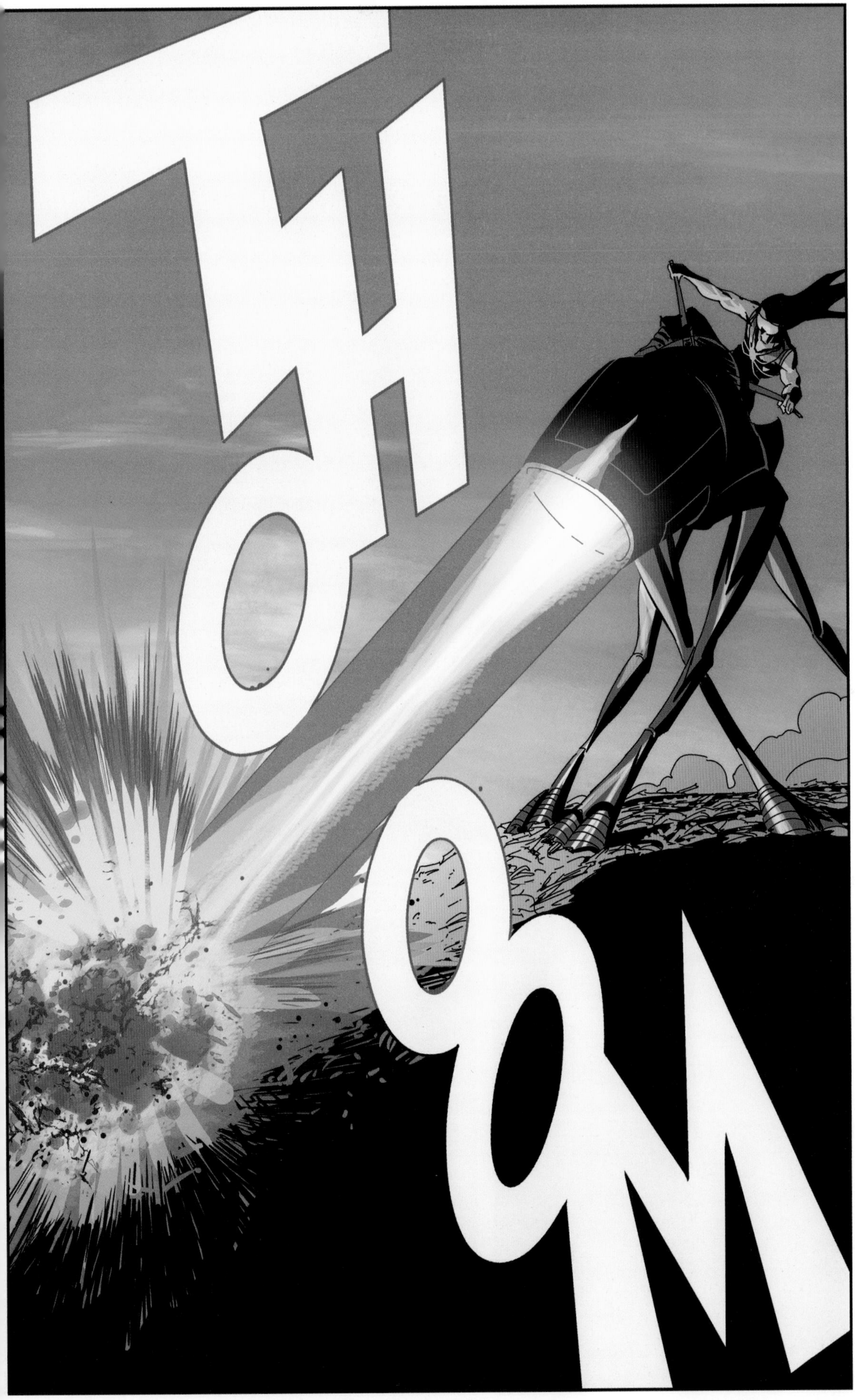
THOOM

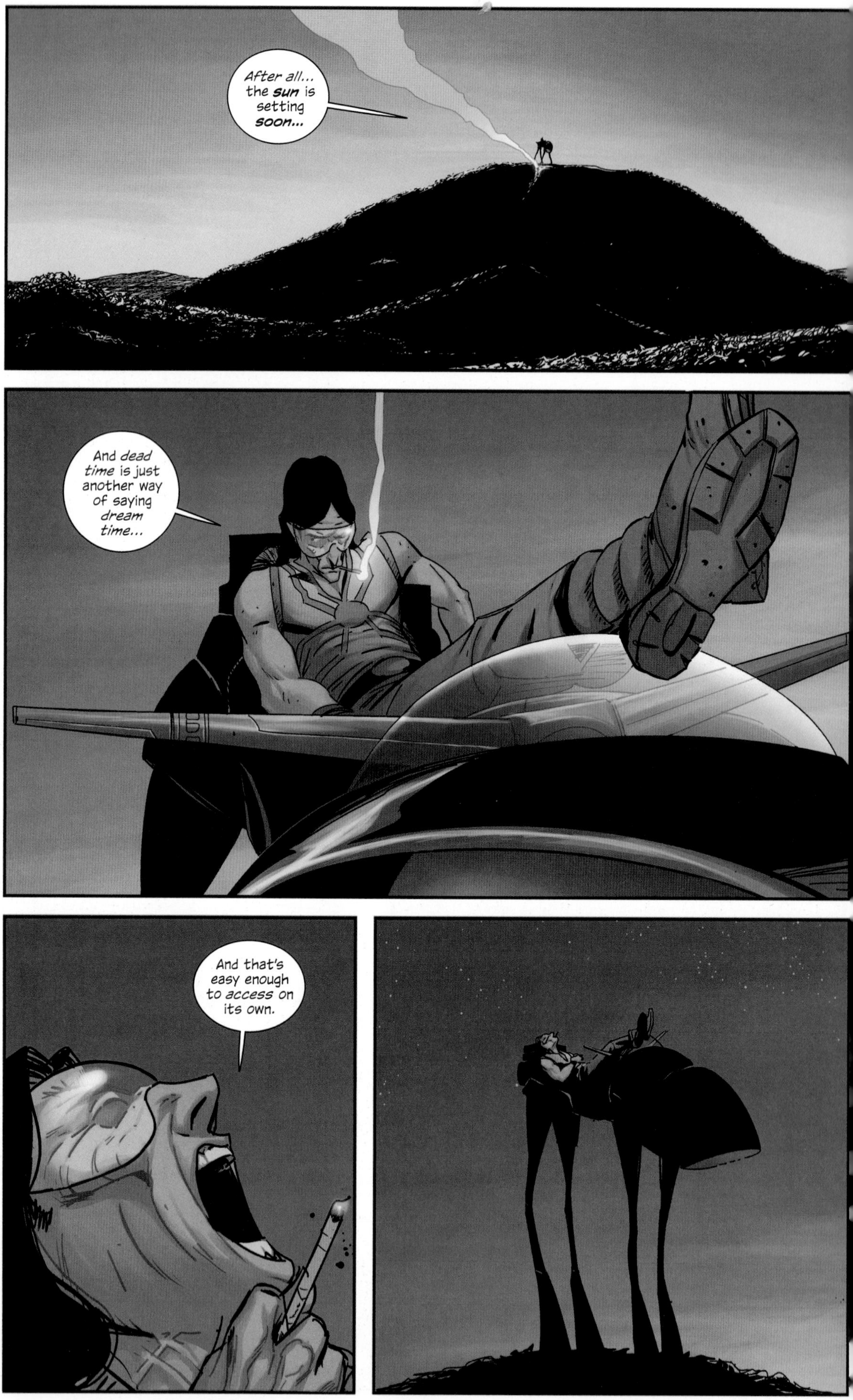
After all... the sun is setting soon...
And dead time is just another way of saying dream time...
And that's easy enough to access on its own.

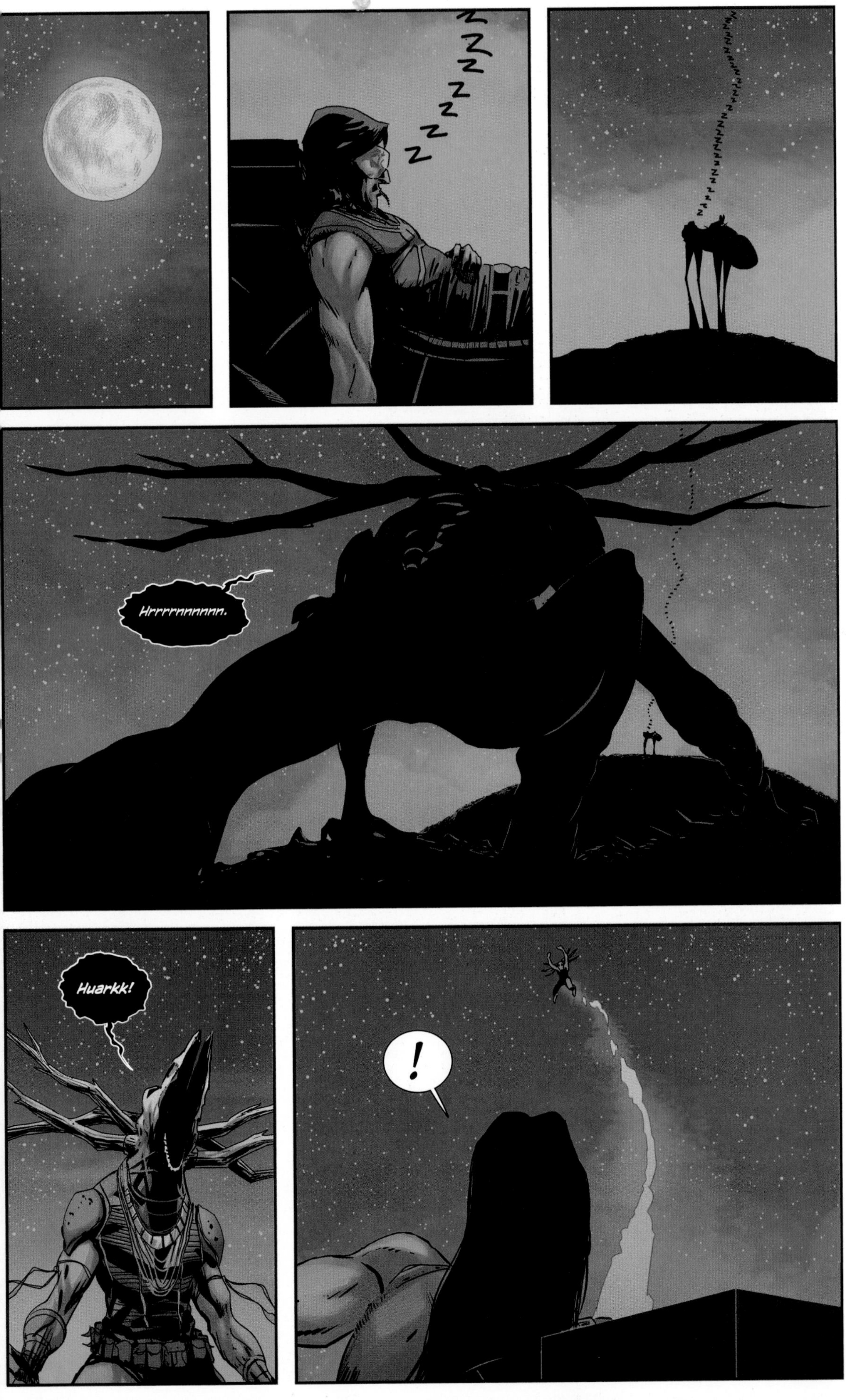
ZZZZZZ
Hrrrrnnnnnnn.
Huarkk!
!

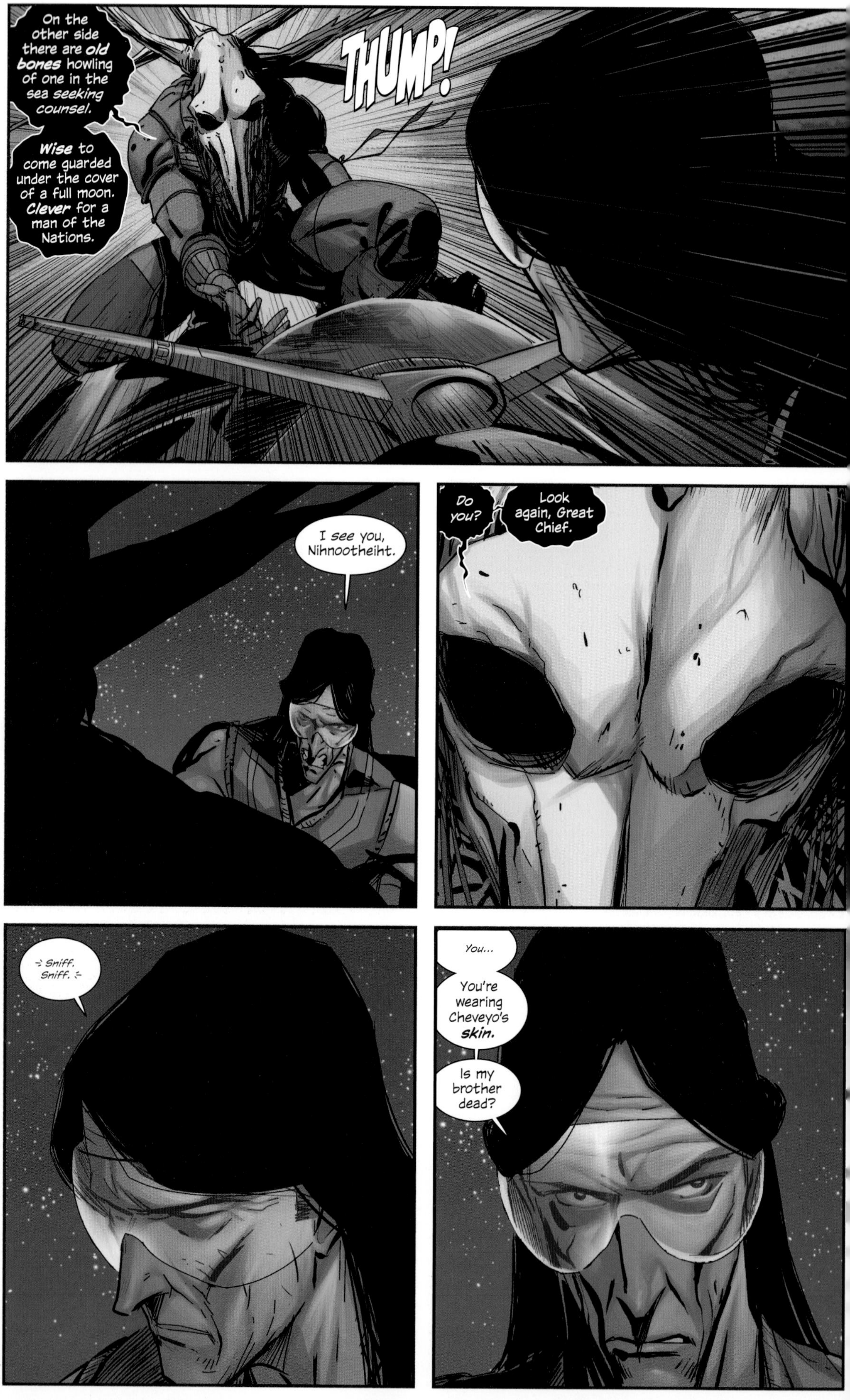
On the other side there are **old bones** howling of one in the sea *seeking* counsel.
Wise to come guarded under the cover of a full moon. ***Clever*** for a man of the Nations.
THUMP!
I *see* you, Nihnootheiht.
Do you?
Look again, Great Chief.
Sniff. Sniff.
You...
You're wearing Cheveyo's ***skin.***
Is my brother dead?

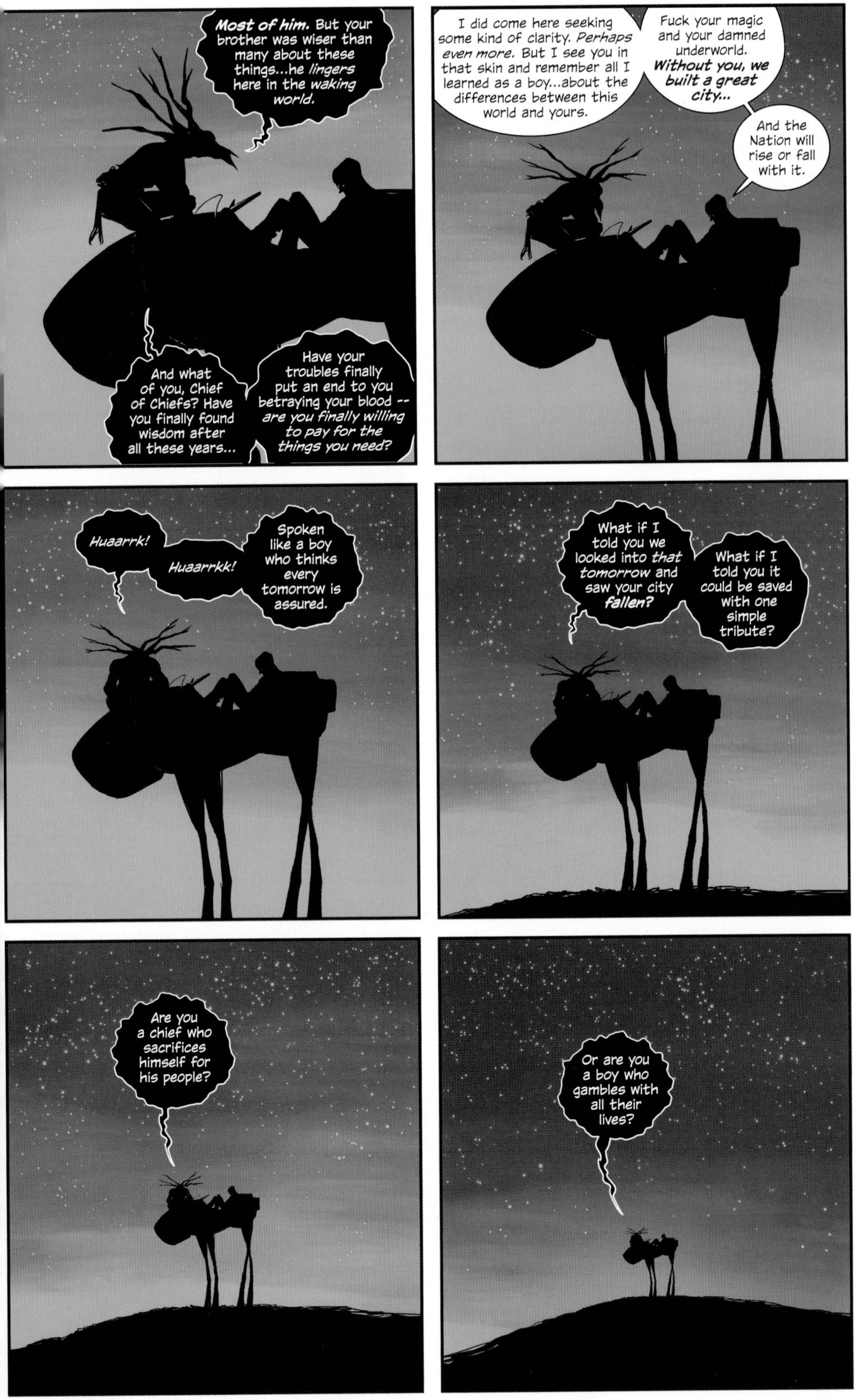

Most of him. But your brother was wiser than many about these things...he lingers here in the waking world.
And what of you, Chief of Chiefs? Have you finally found wisdom after all these years...
Have your troubles finally put an end to you betraying your blood -- are you finally willing to pay for the things you need?
I did come here seeking some kind of clarity. Perhaps even more. But I see you in that skin and remember all I learned as a boy...about the differences between this world and yours.
Fuck your magic and your damned underworld. Without you, we built a great city...
And the Nation will rise or fall with it.
Huaarrk!
Huaarrkk!
Spoken like a boy who thinks every tomorrow is assured.
What if I told you we looked into that tomorrow and saw your city fallen?
What if I told you it could be saved with one simple tribute?
Are you a chief who sacrifices himself for his people?
Or are you a boy who gambles with all their lives?

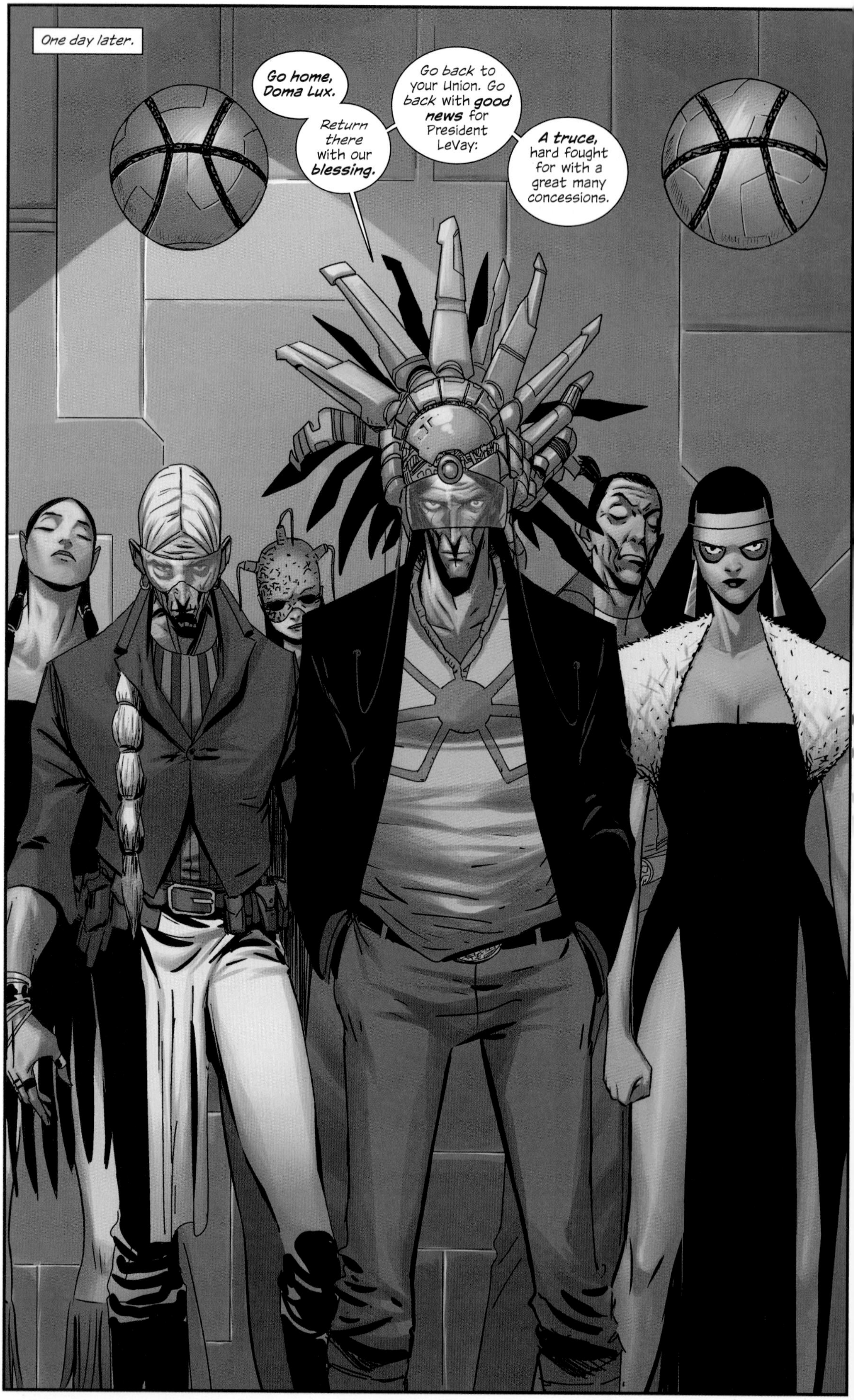
One day later.
Go home, Doma Lux.
Return there with our blessing.
Go back to your Union. Go back with good news for President LeVay:
A truce, hard fought for with a great many concessions.

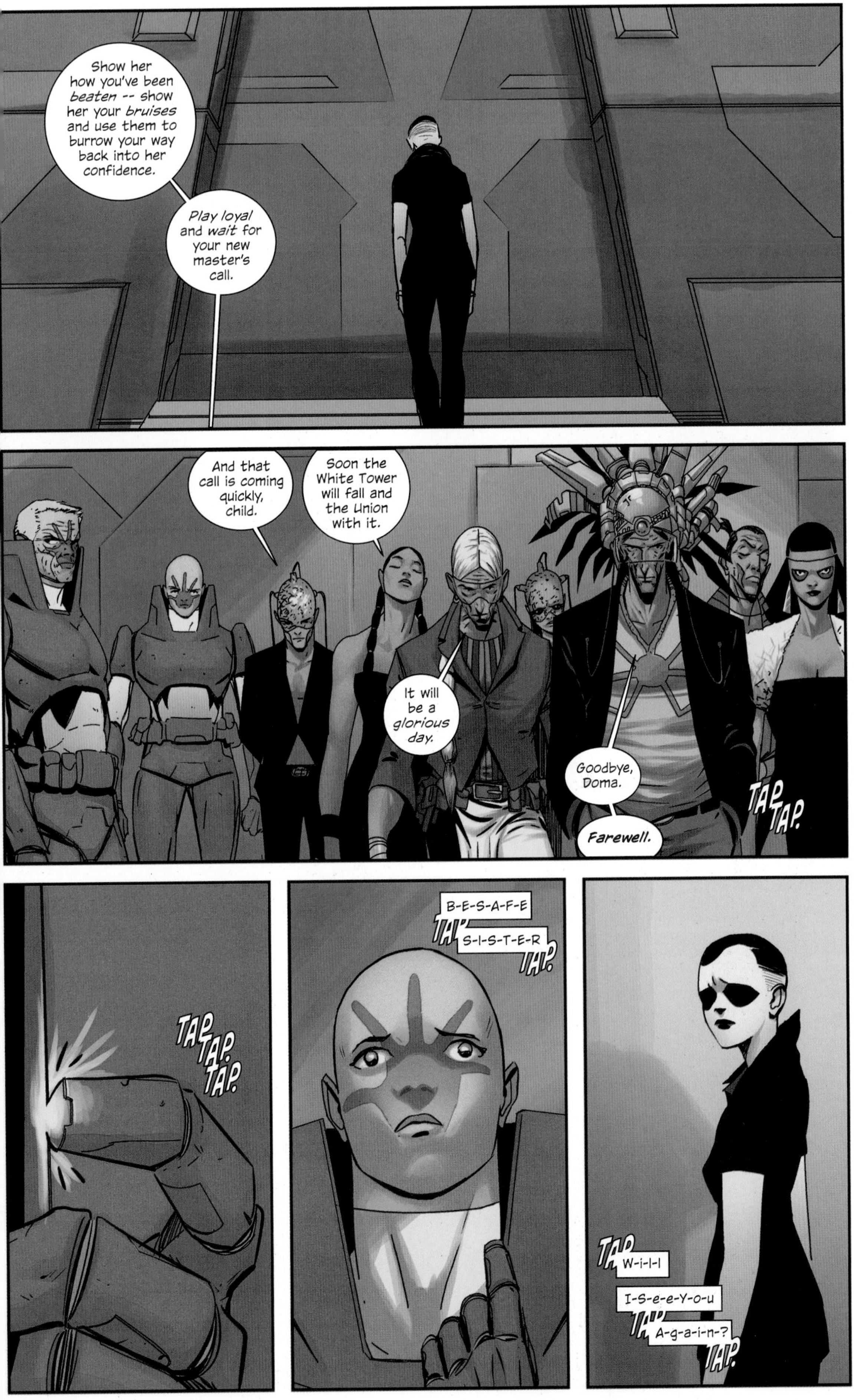
Show her how you've been *beaten* -- show her your *bruises* and use them to burrow your way back into her confidence.
Play loyal and *wait* for your new master's call.
And that call is coming quickly, child.
Soon the White Tower will fall and the Union with it.
It will be a *glorious* day.
Goodbye, Doma.
Farewell.
TAP TAP.
TAP TAP. TAP.
B-E-S-A-F-E
TAP
S-I-S-T-E-R
TAP.
TAP
W-i-l-l
I-S-e-e-Y-o-u
TAP
A-g-a-i-n-?
TAP.

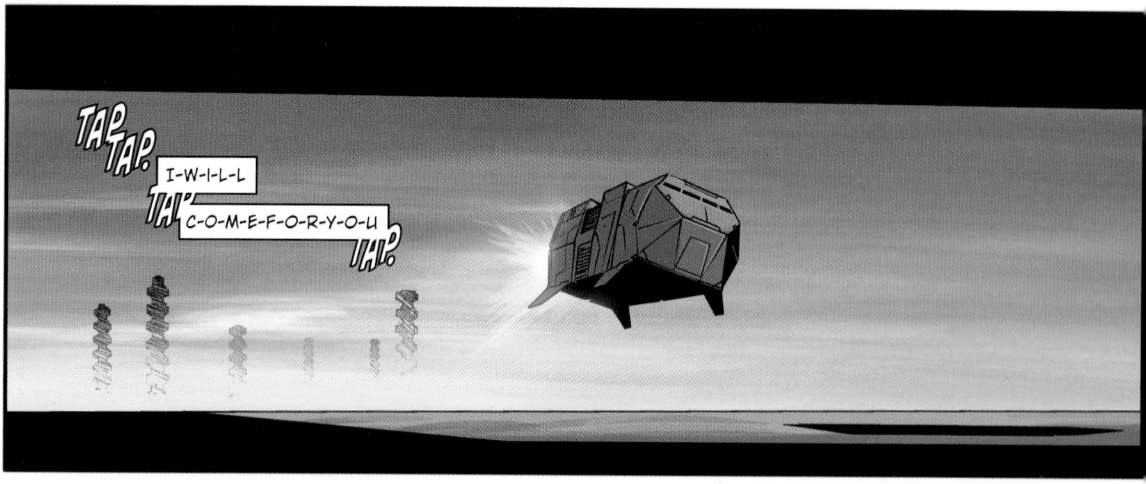
TAP TAP.
I-W-I-L-L
TAP
C-O-M-E-F-O-R-Y-O-U
TAP.

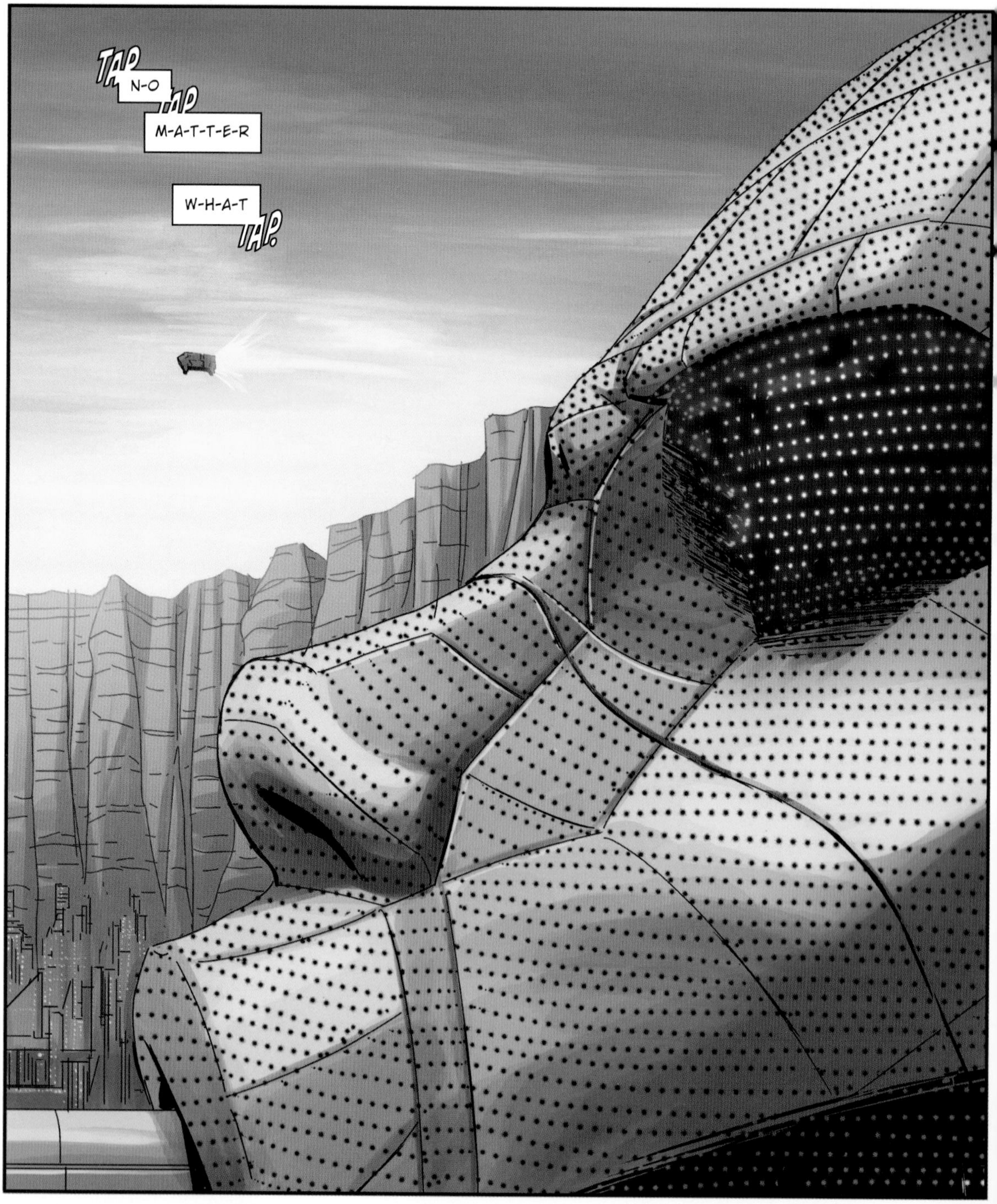
TAP
N-O
TAP
M-A-T-T-E-R
W-H-A-T
TAP.

IT NEVER STOPS.

THE CYCLE OF **POWER, GREED** AND **REVENGE.**

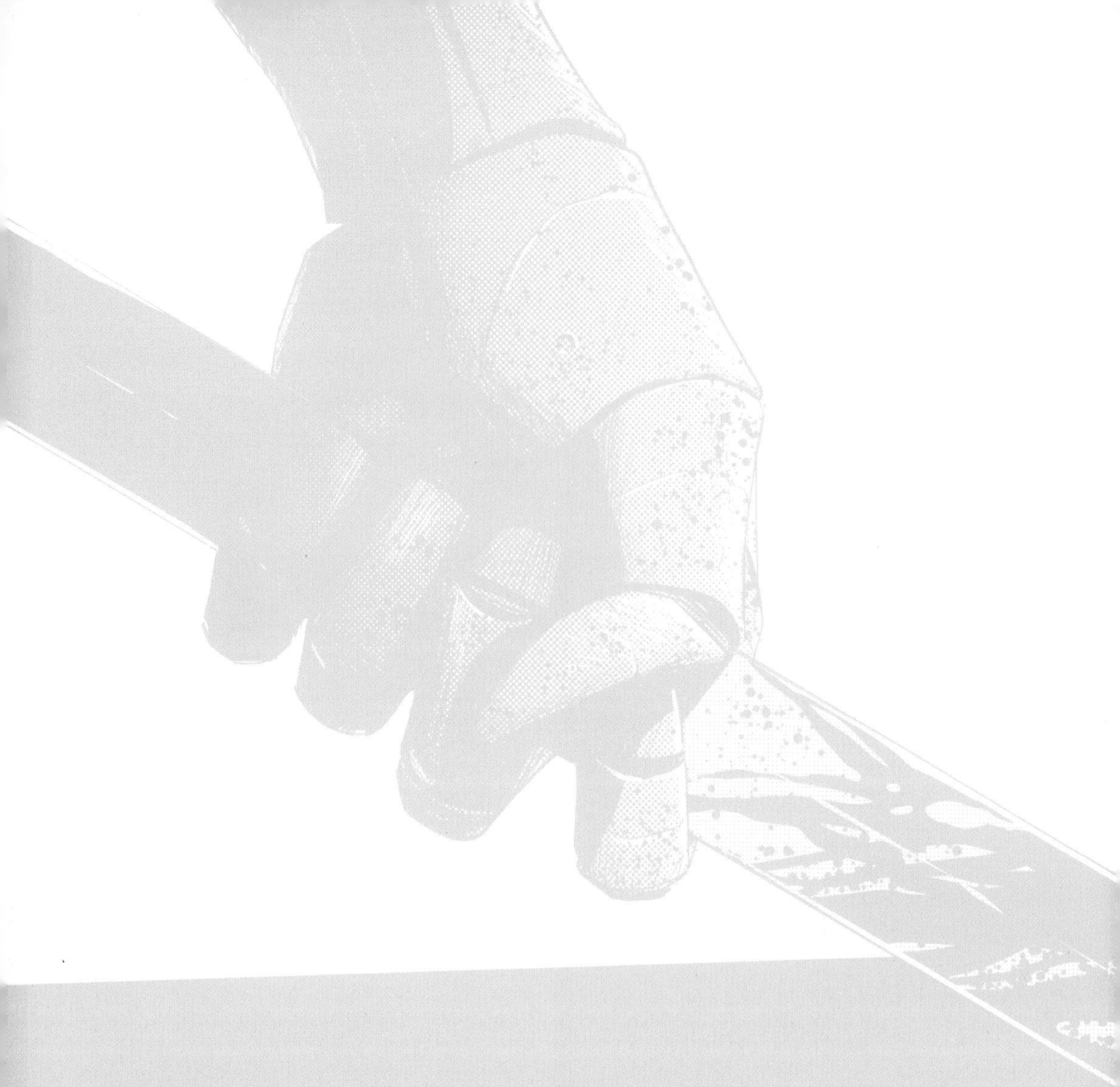

TWENTY-TWO:
A MOMENT OF
SILENCE

WHEN THEY COME FOR YOU,
IT WILL BE WHERE YOU FEEL
SAFEST.

IN YOUR **HOME.** IN YOUR **BED.**
IN YOUR **SLEEP.**

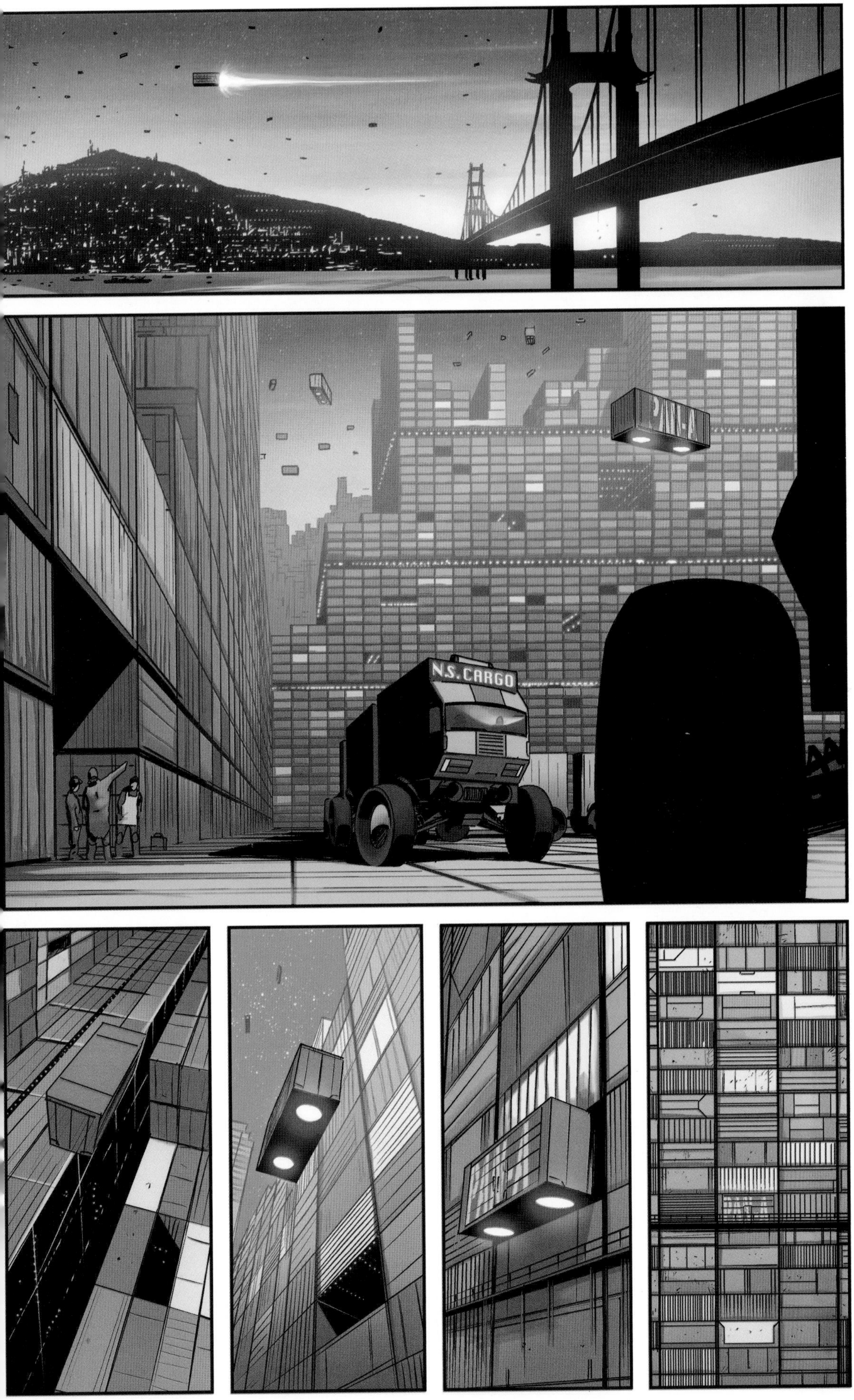
N.S. CARGO

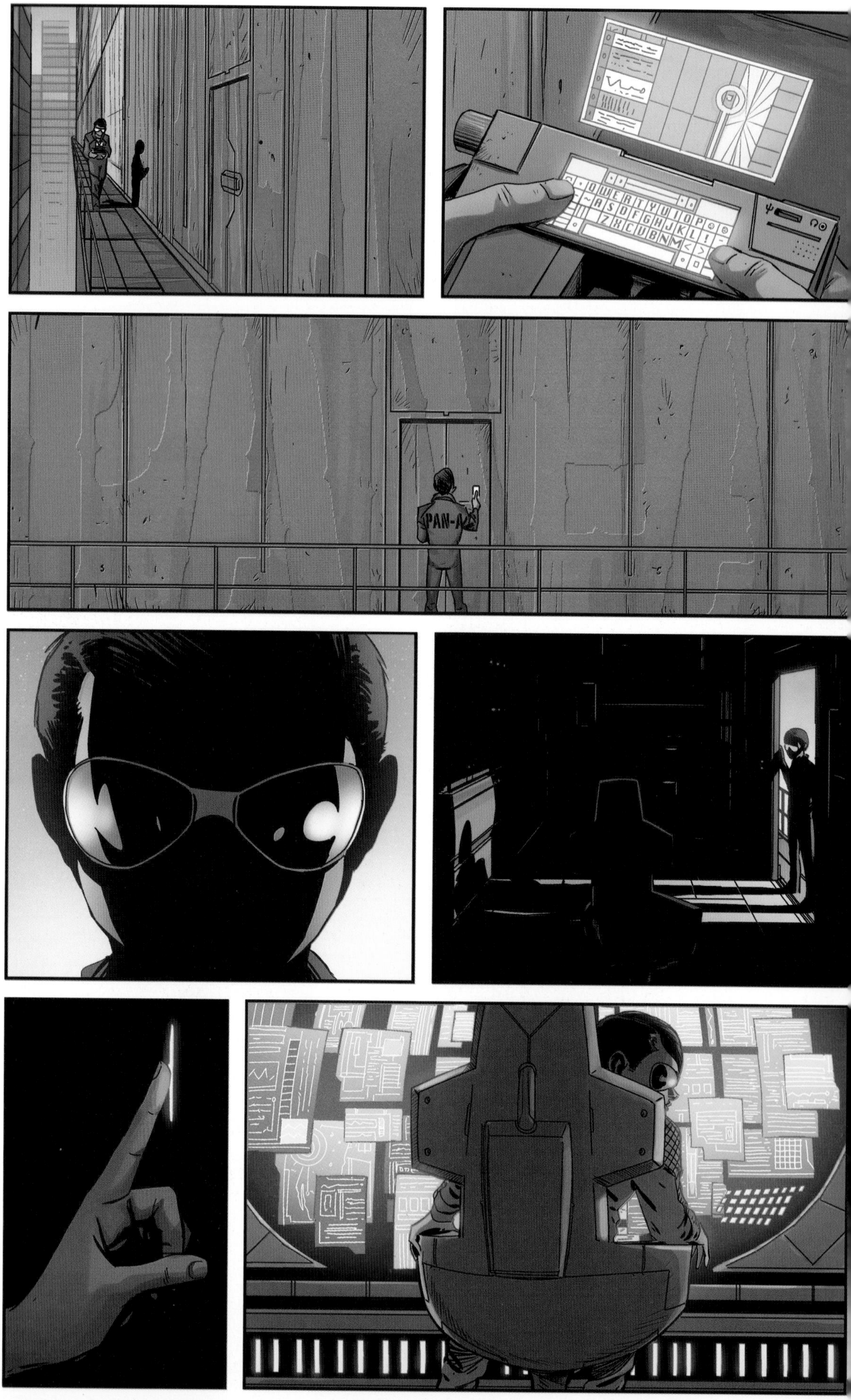
PAN-A

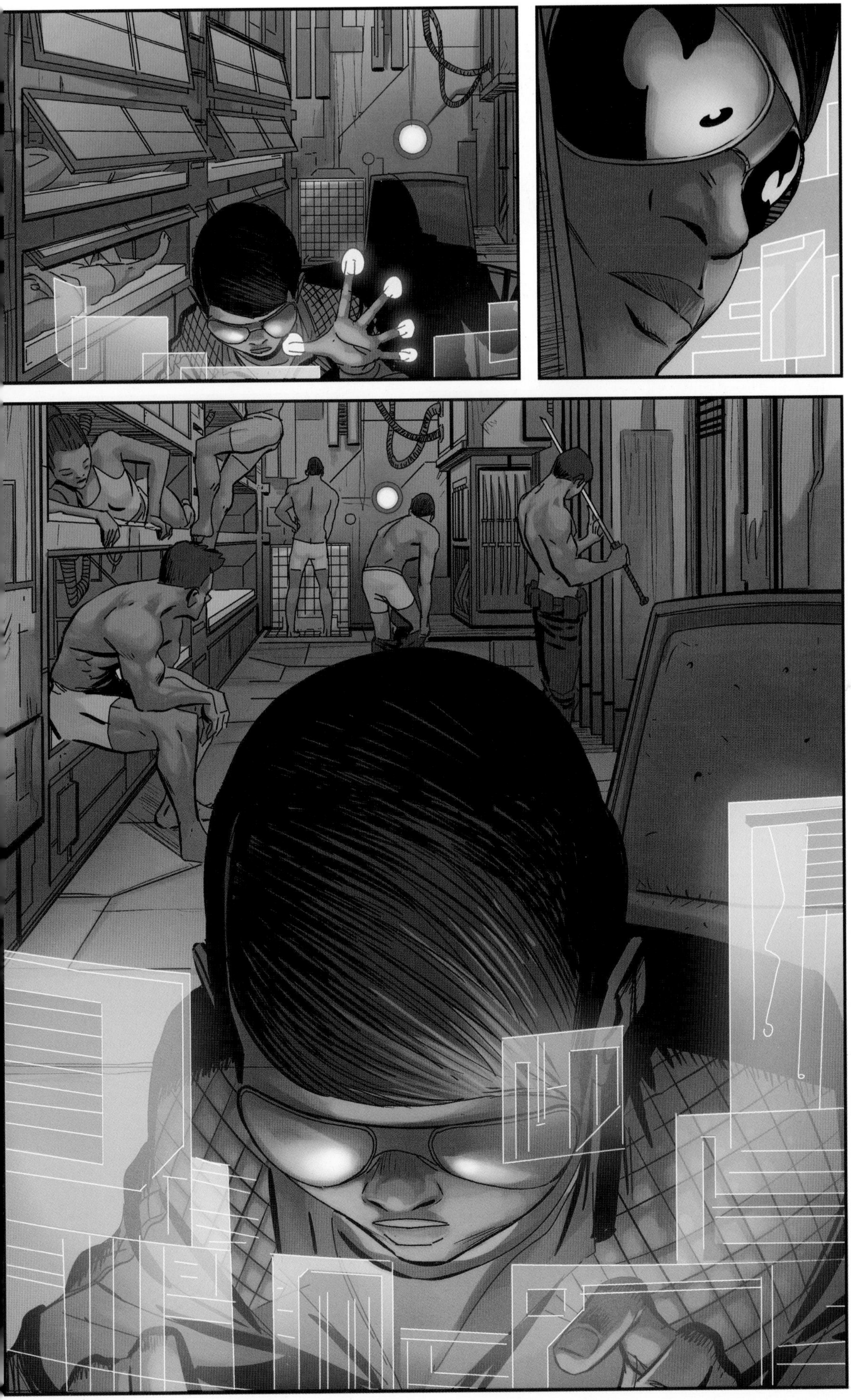

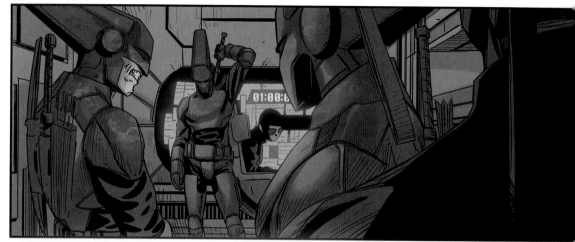

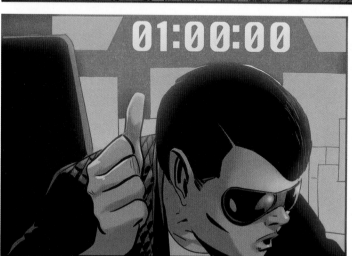

00:59:59

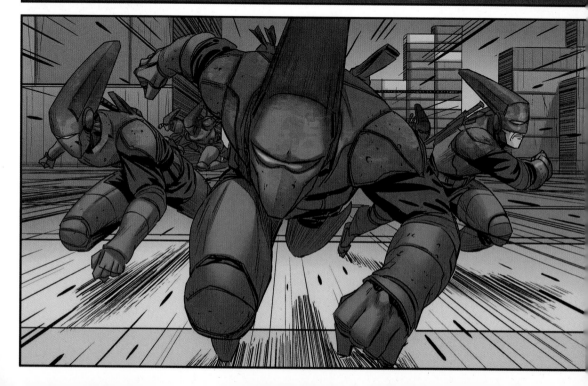

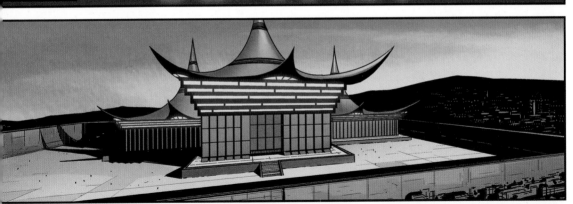

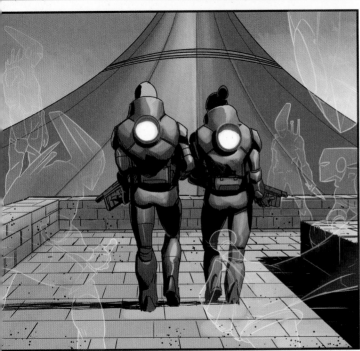

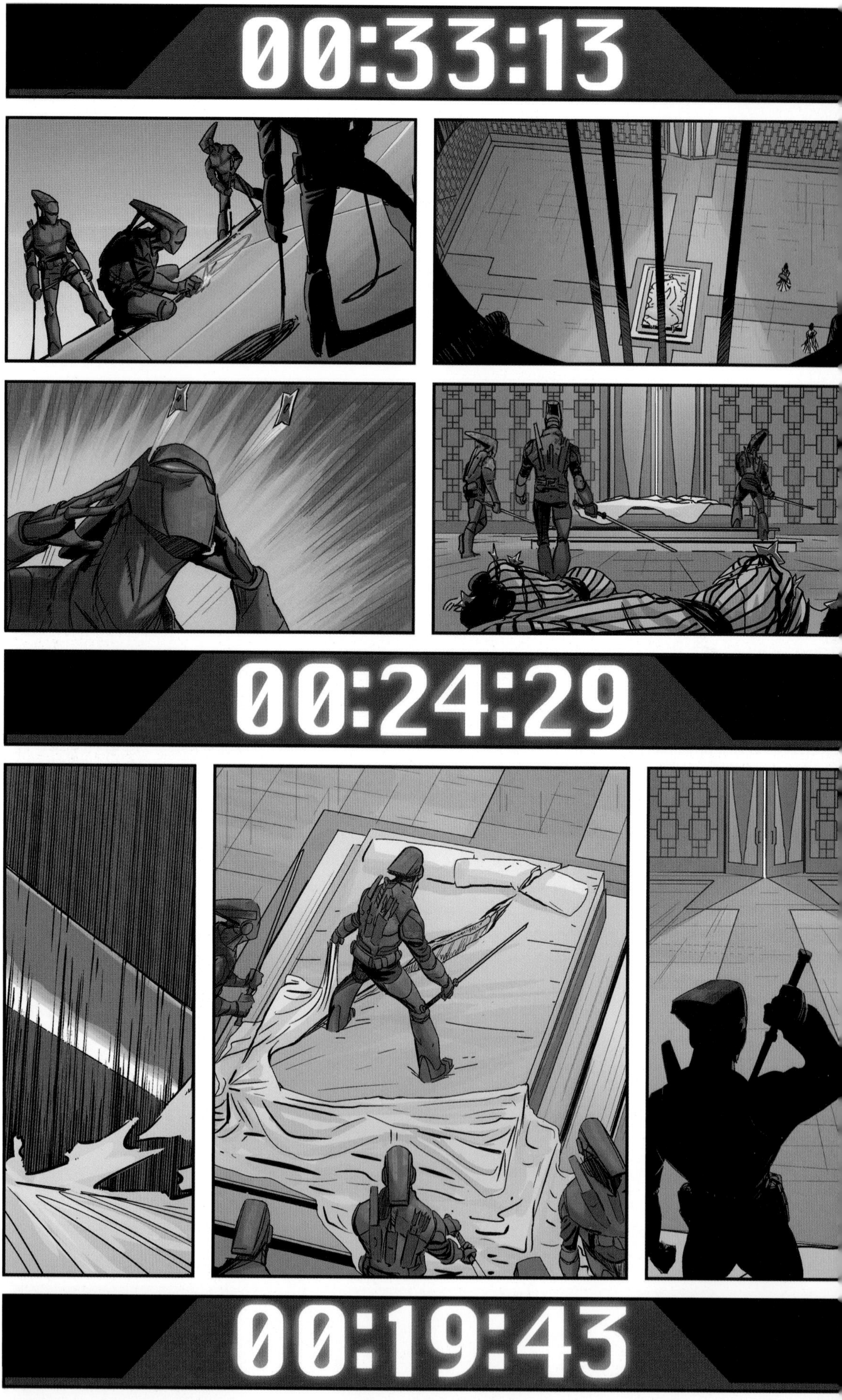
00:33:13
00:24:29
00:19:43

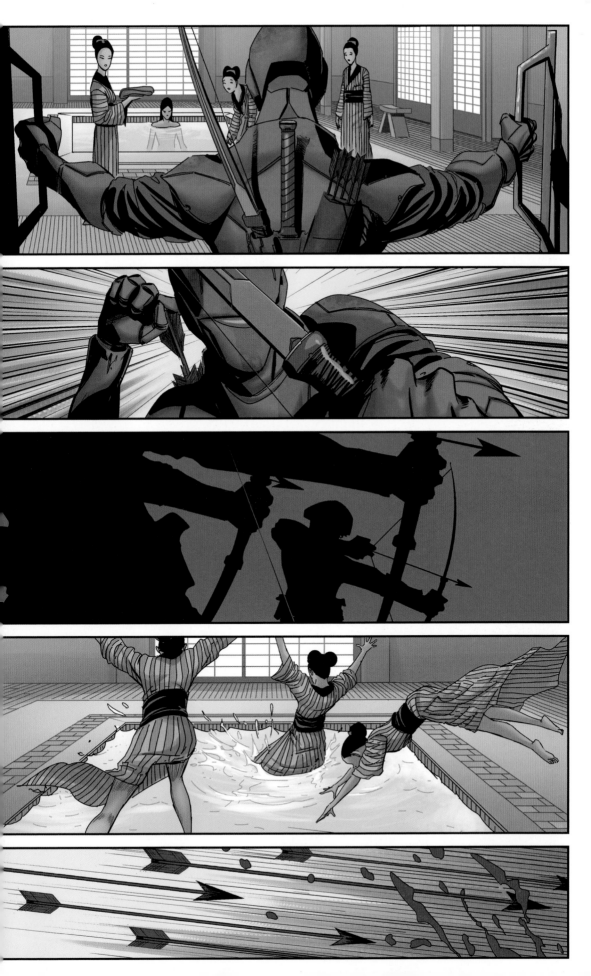

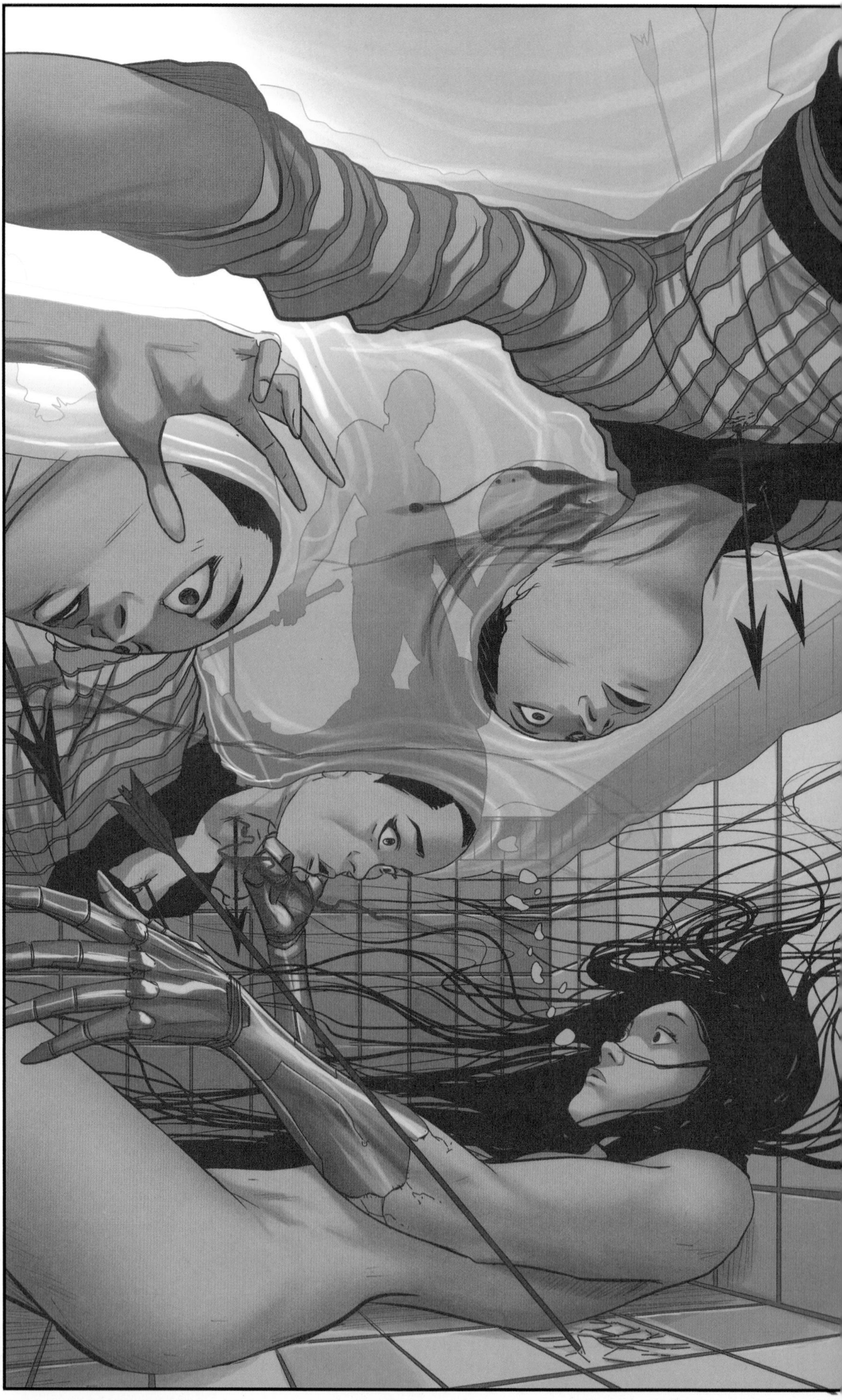

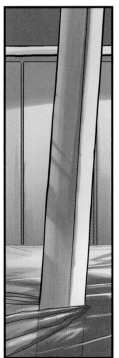

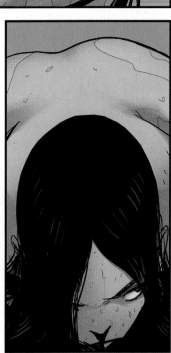

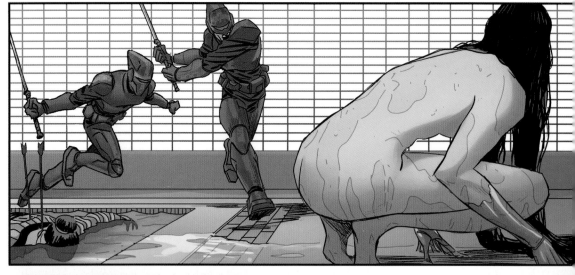

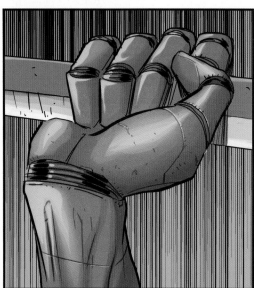

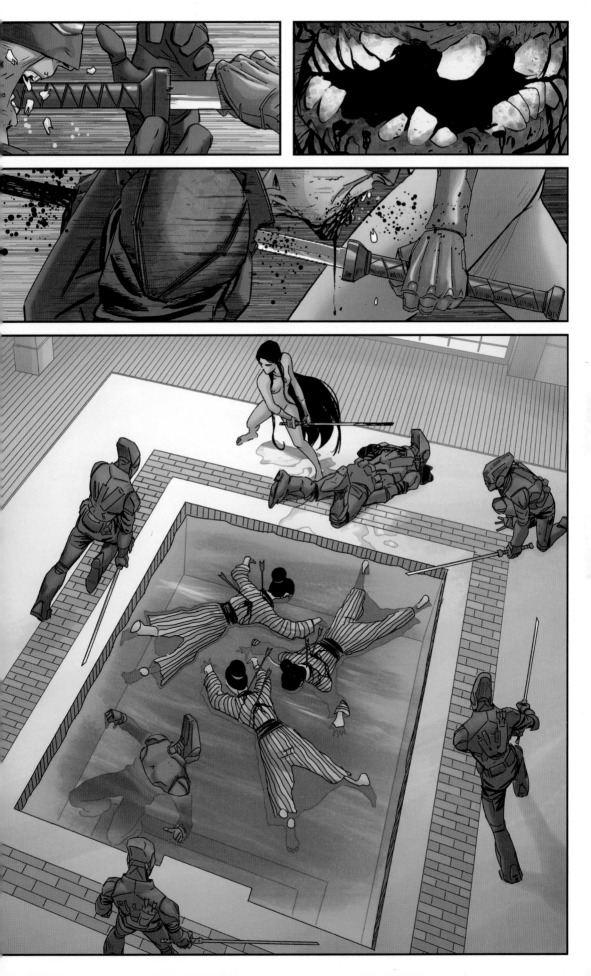

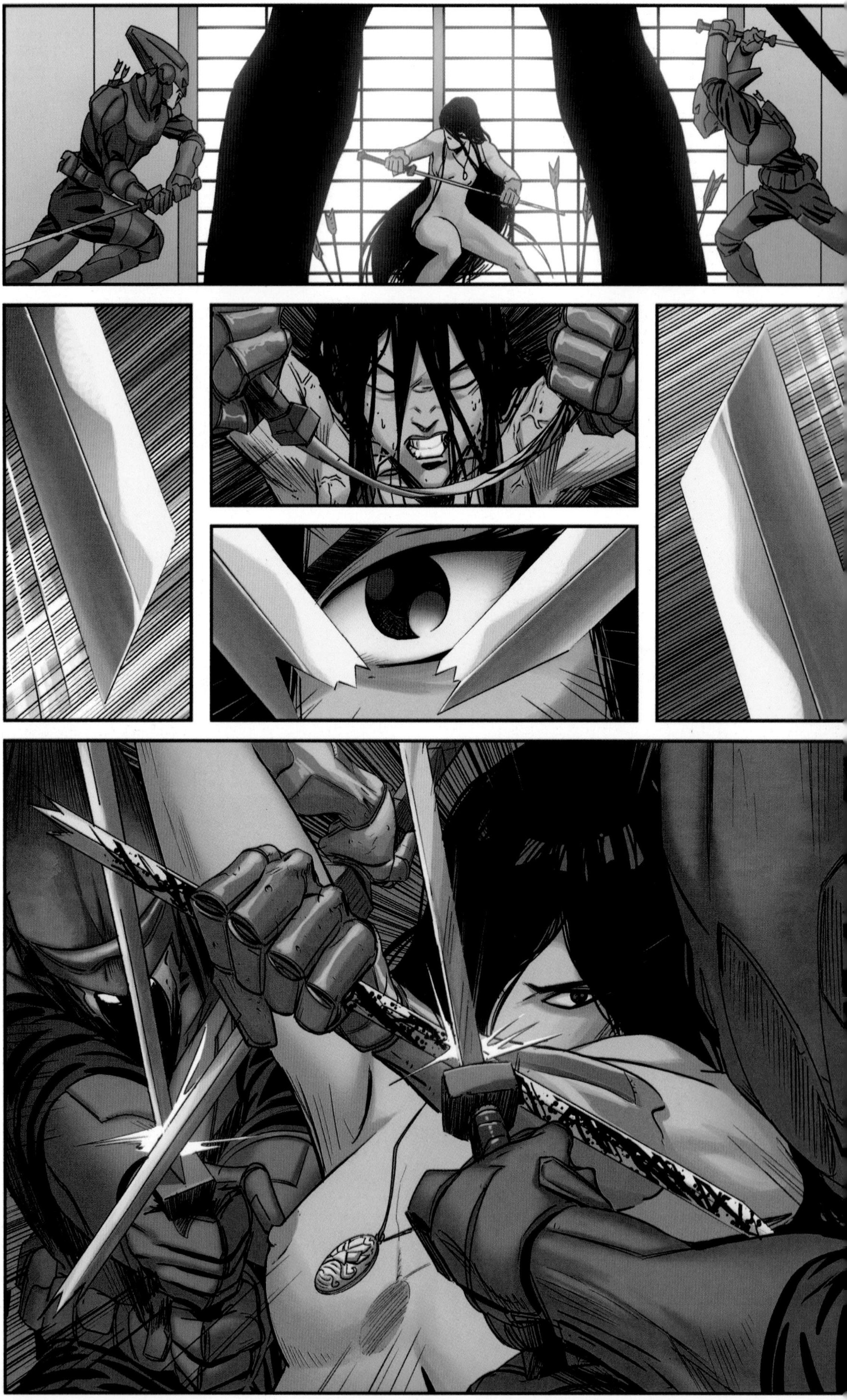

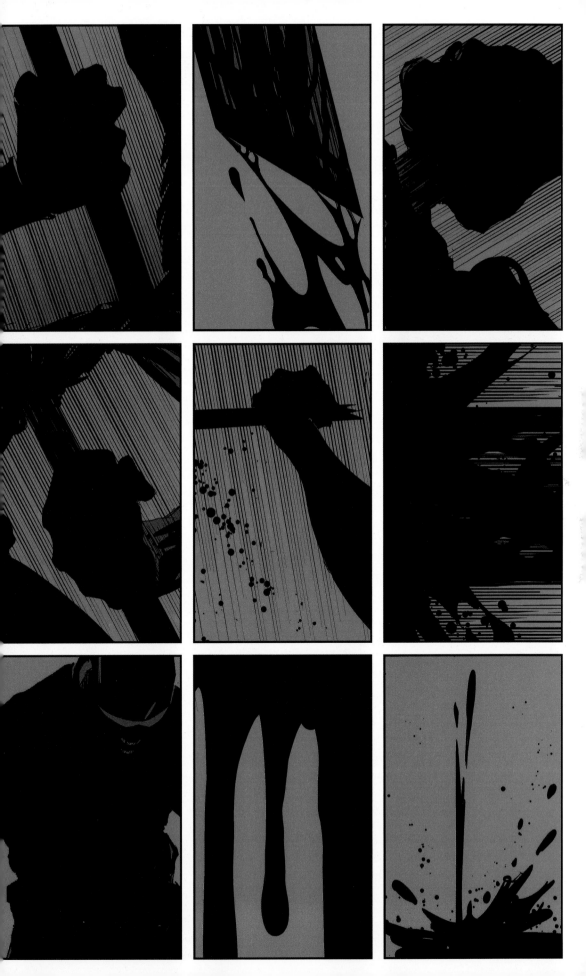

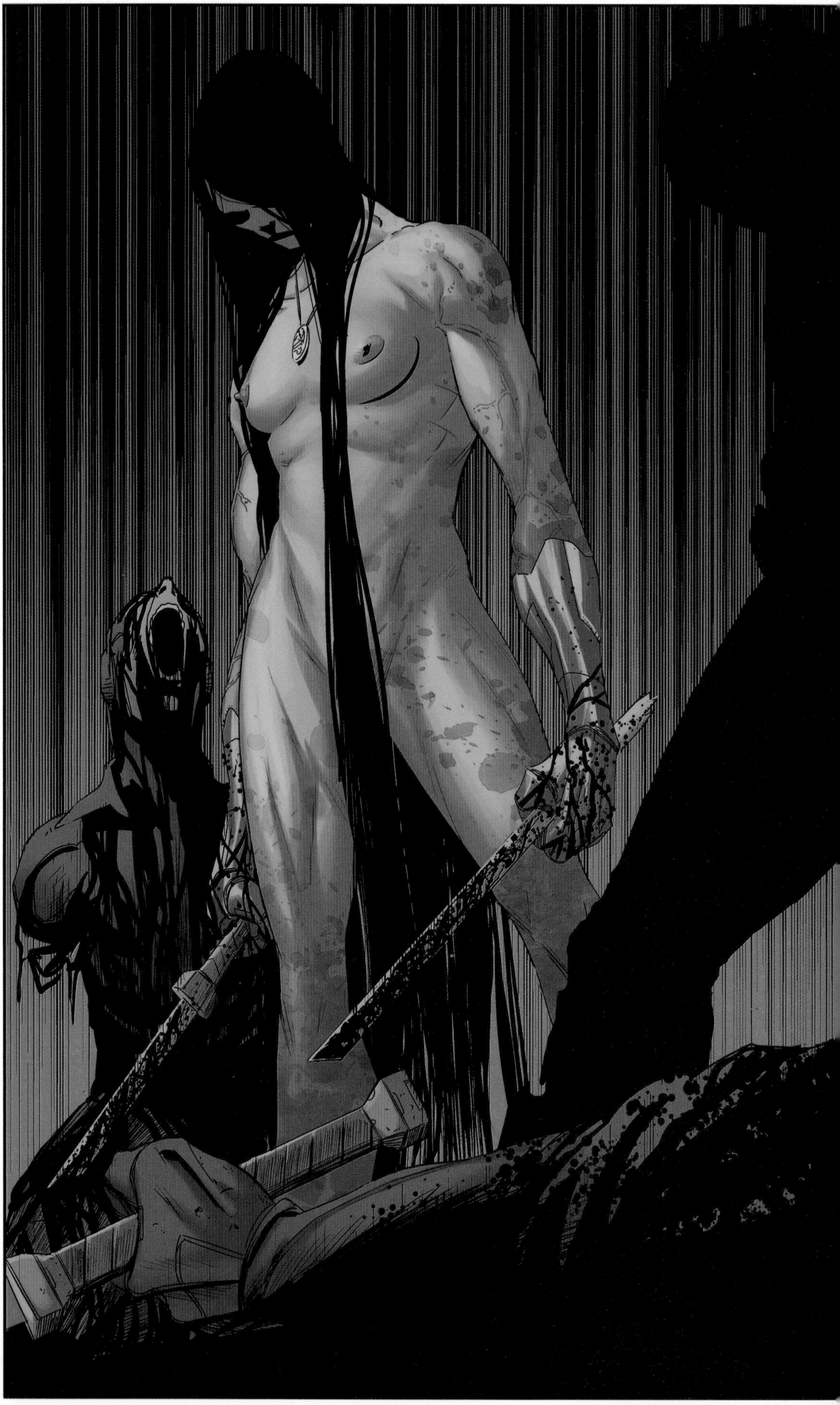

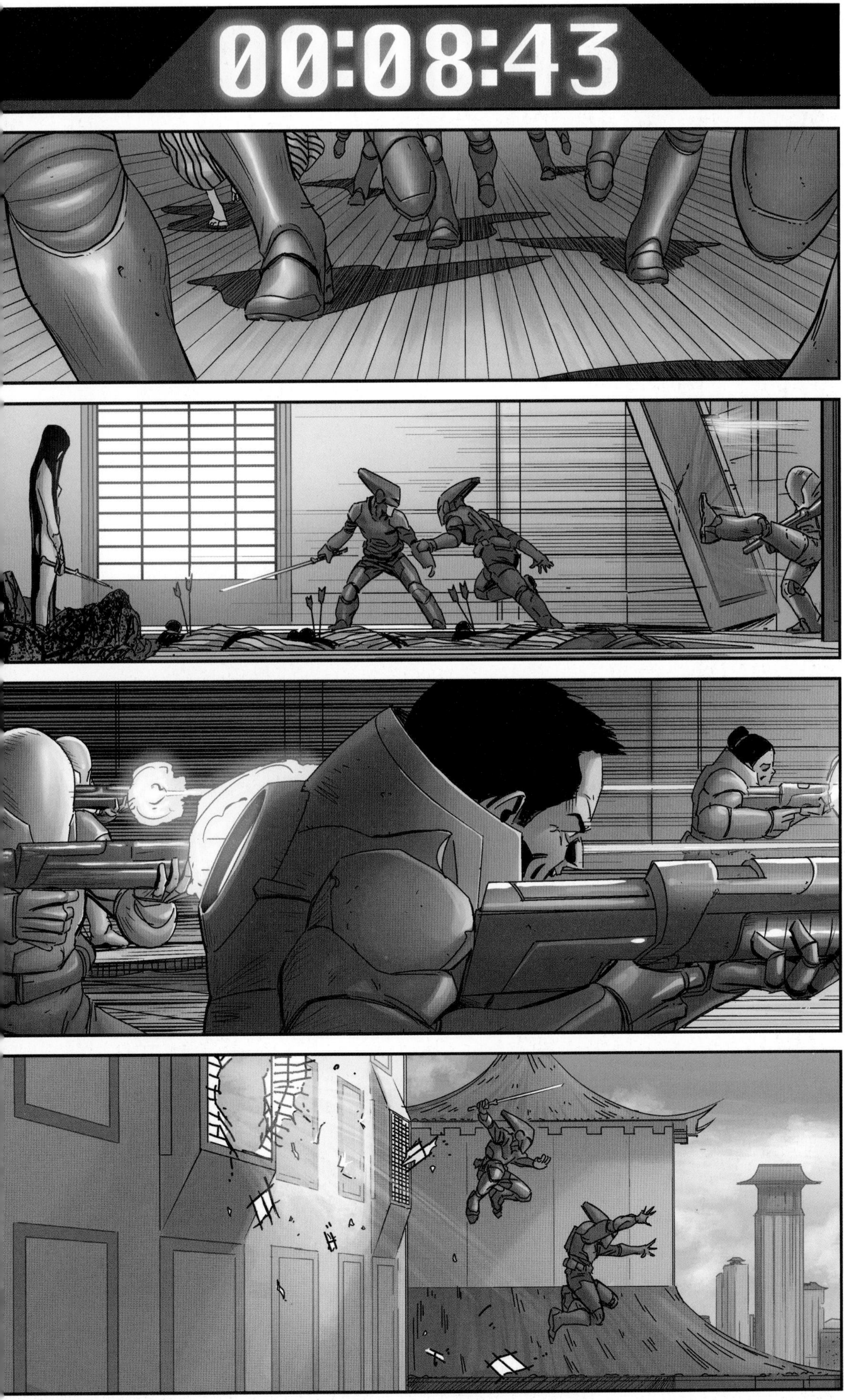
00:08:43

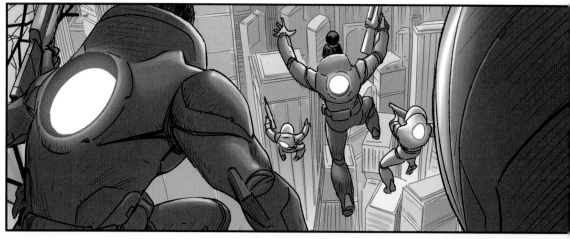

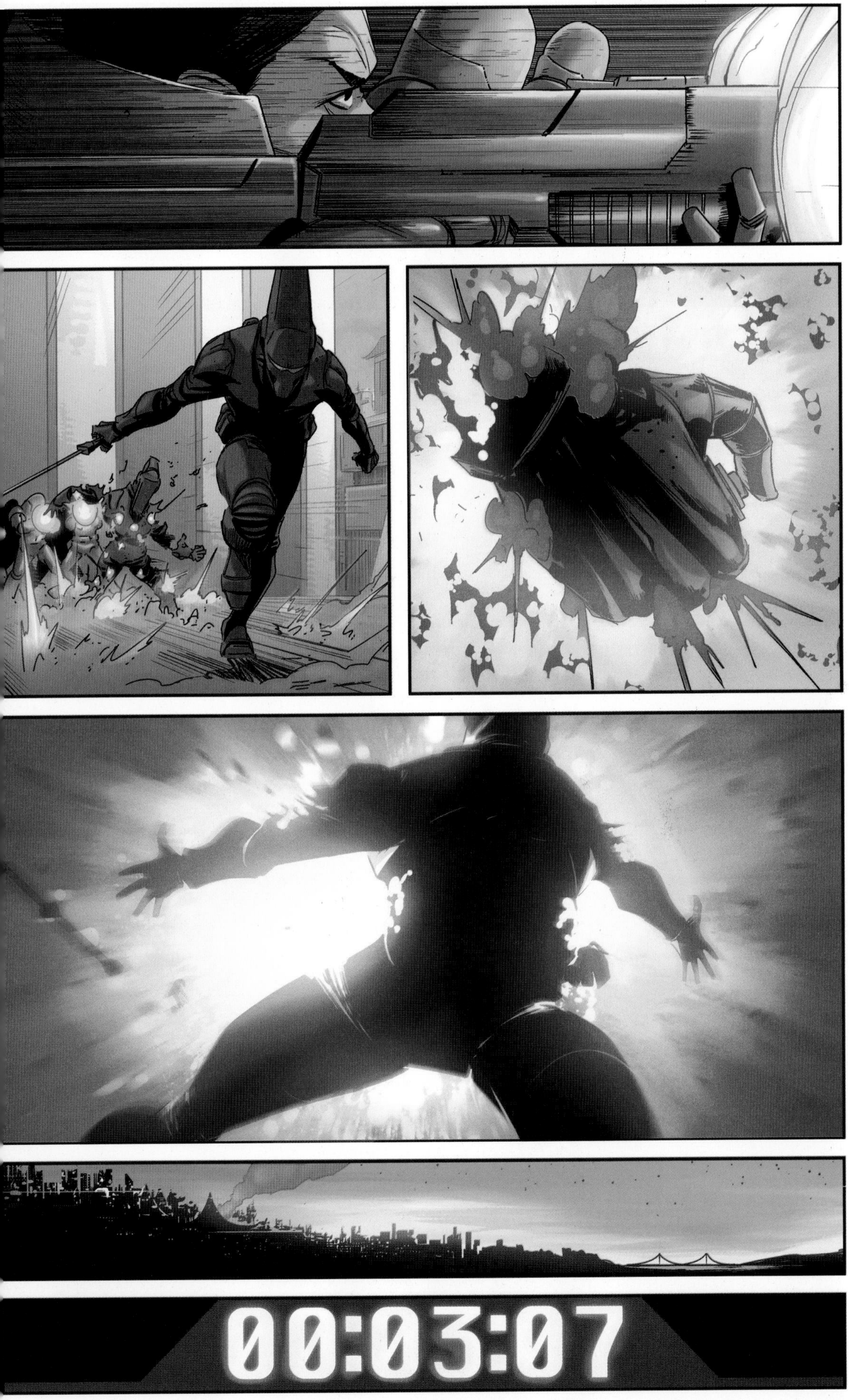
00:03:07

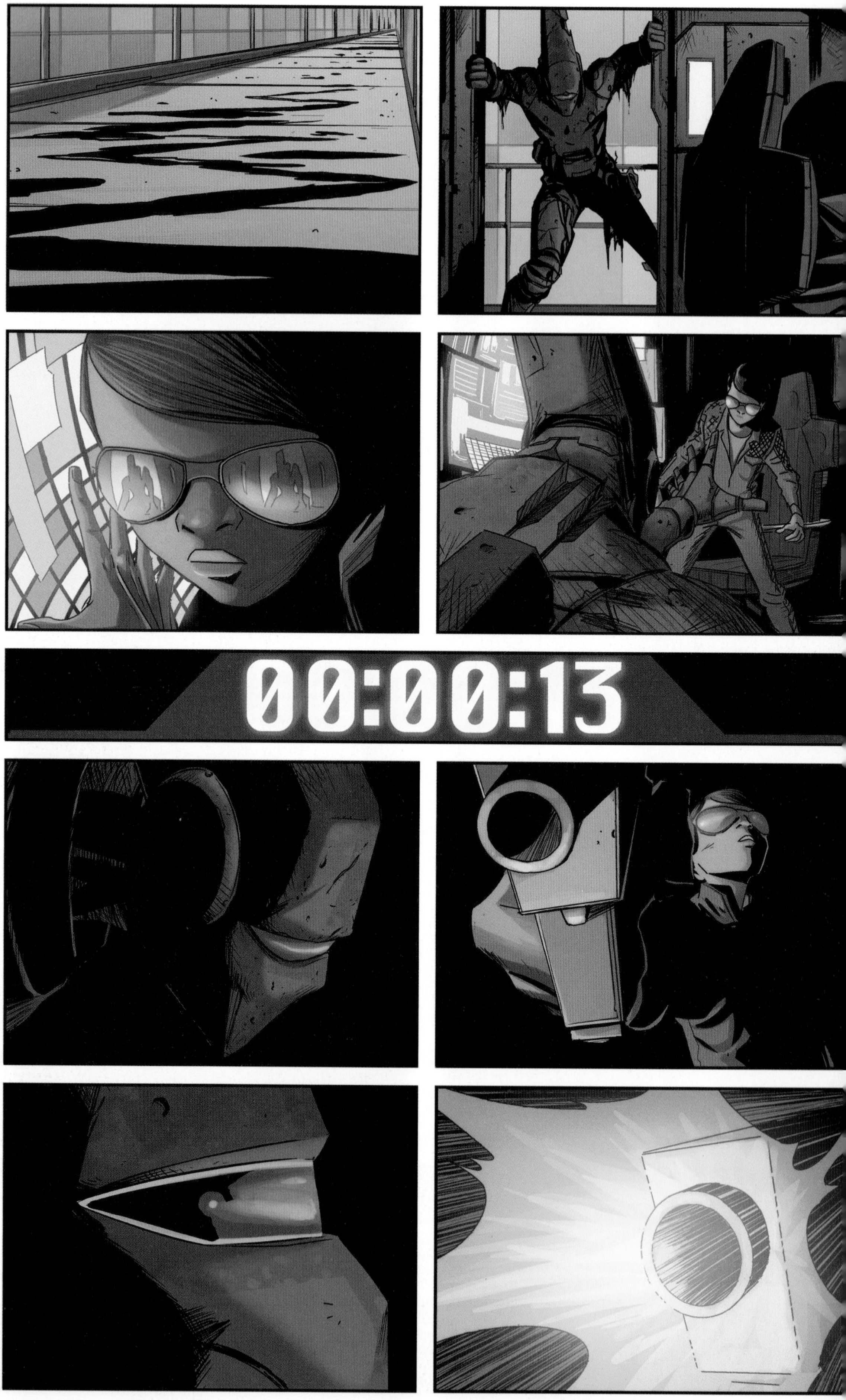
00:00:13

FAI

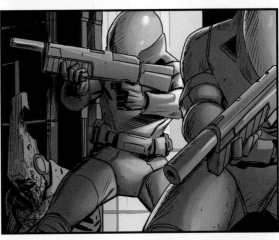

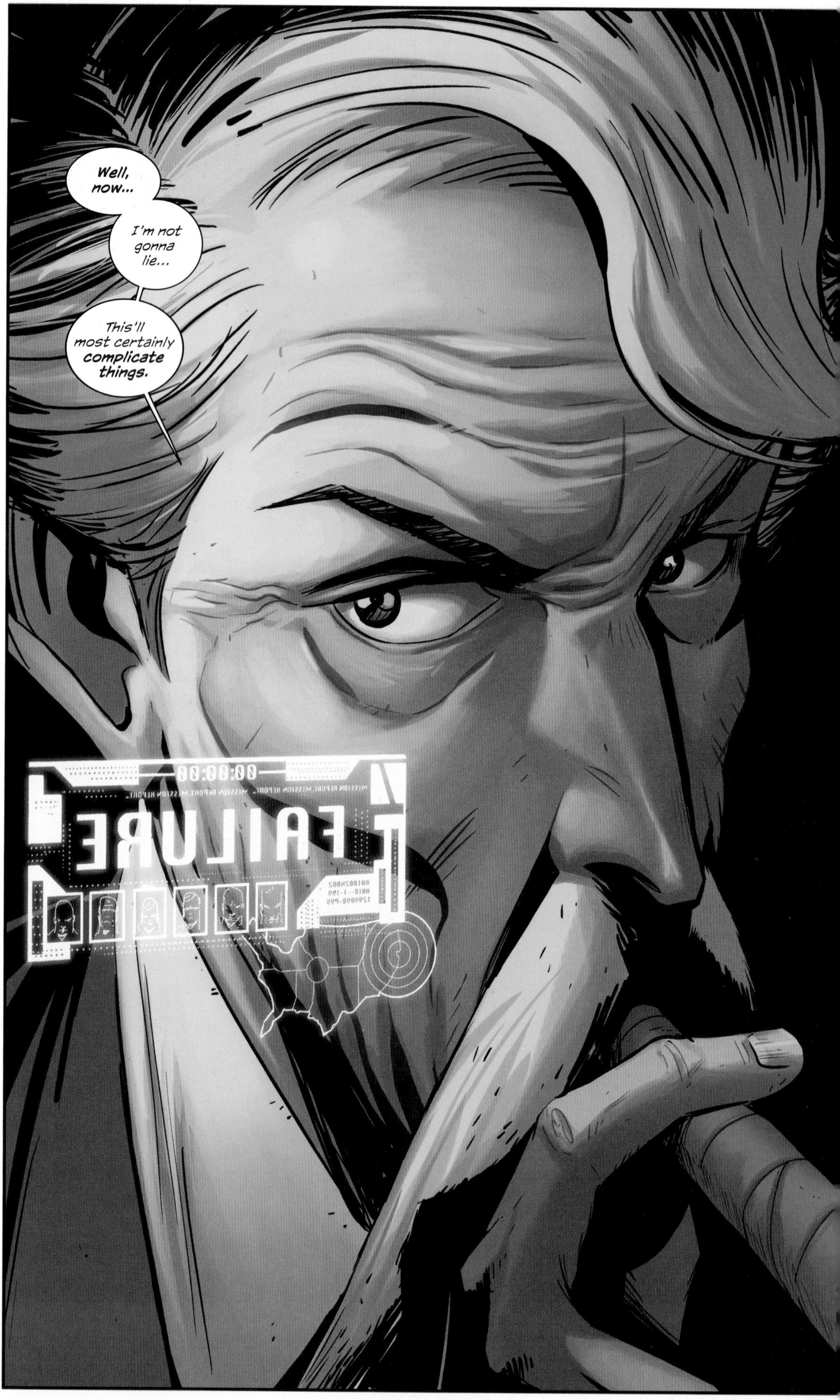

Well, now...
I'm not gonna lie...
This'll most certainly **complicate things.**
FAILURE

ONE BAD **LIE** AND THE WHOLE
WEB **UNRAVELS.**

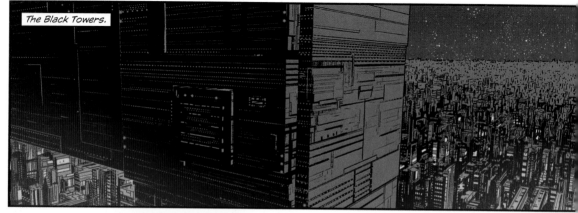

The Black Towers.

Normally, I don't like to tell tales of *days gone by*... especially when those days are *my own*...

Which isn't to say I find it *cumbersome* to enrich my own *personal mythology*.

I *clearly* do.

And, *frankly*, given my reputation, if I were to imply otherwise, then you would know I was a *liar* -- and a *poor one* at that.

For what a frail and fallen creature is man. And how can I -- *being man* -- appear before you now, the much-ballyhooed, resplendent sum of both *staggering intellect* and *flawless breeding*?

It's not possible is it? For one to be so *blessed*?

No. Of course not. But then again, I think we spiders all appreciate the fine craftsmanship and beauty of a well-spun web.

Don't we now?

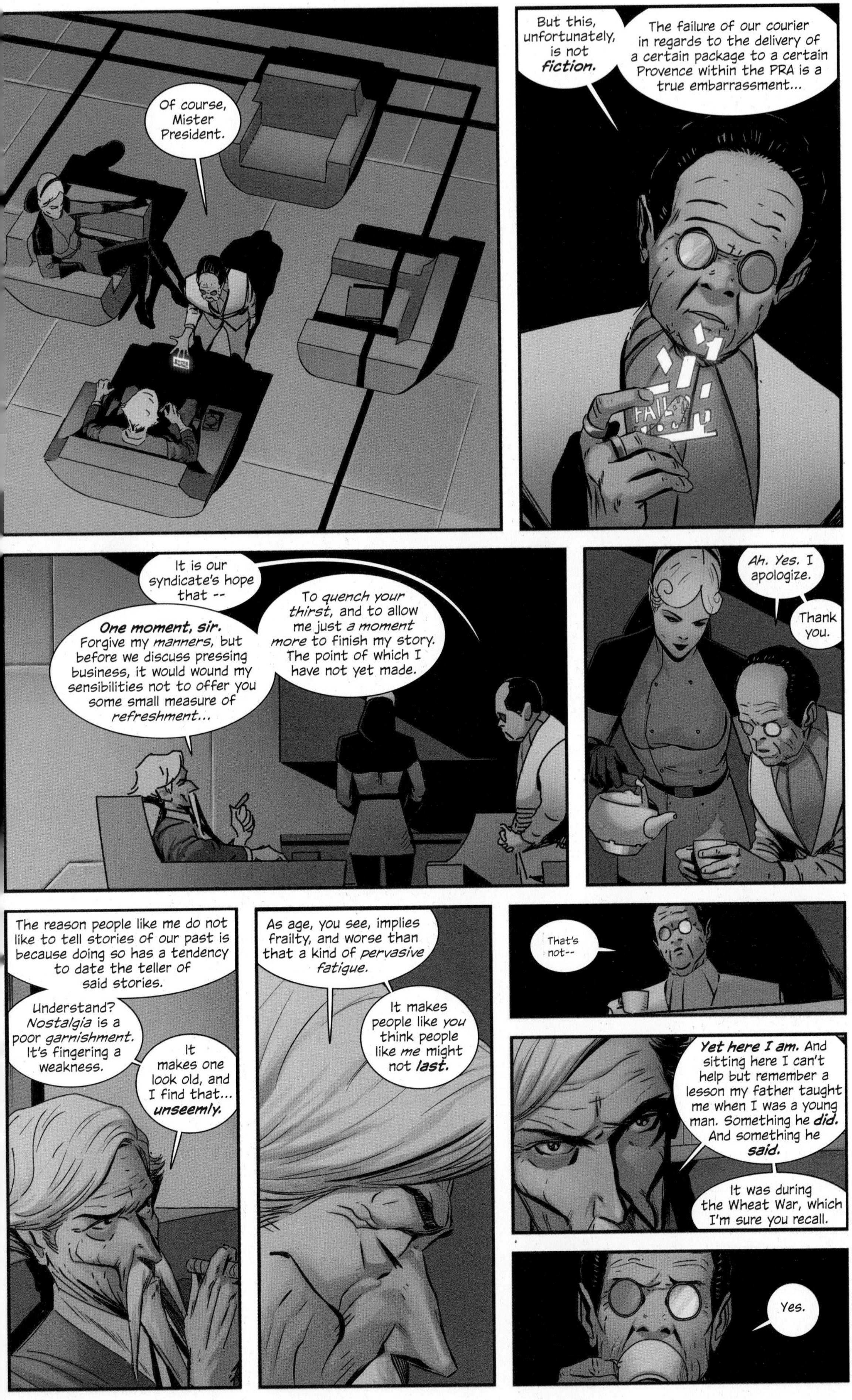
Of course, Mister President.
But this, unfortunately, is not *fiction.*
The failure of our courier in regards to the delivery of a certain package to a certain Provence within the PRA is a true embarrassment...
It is our syndicate's hope that --
One moment, sir. Forgive my *manners,* but before we discuss pressing business, it would wound my sensibilities not to offer you some small measure of *refreshment...*
To *quench your thirst,* and to allow me just *a moment more* to finish my story. The point of which I have not yet made.
Ah. Yes. I apologize.
Thank you.
The reason people like me do not like to tell stories of our past is because doing so has a tendency to date the teller of said stories.
Understand? *Nostalgia* is a poor *garnishment.* It's fingering a weakness.
It makes one look old, and I find that... ***unseemly.***
As age, you see, implies frailty, and worse than that a kind of *pervasive fatigue.*
It makes people like *you* think people like *me* might not ***last.***
That's not--
Yet here I am. And sitting here I can't help but remember a lesson my father taught me when I was a young man. Something he ***did.*** And something he ***said.***
It was during the Wheat War, which I'm sure you recall.
Yes.

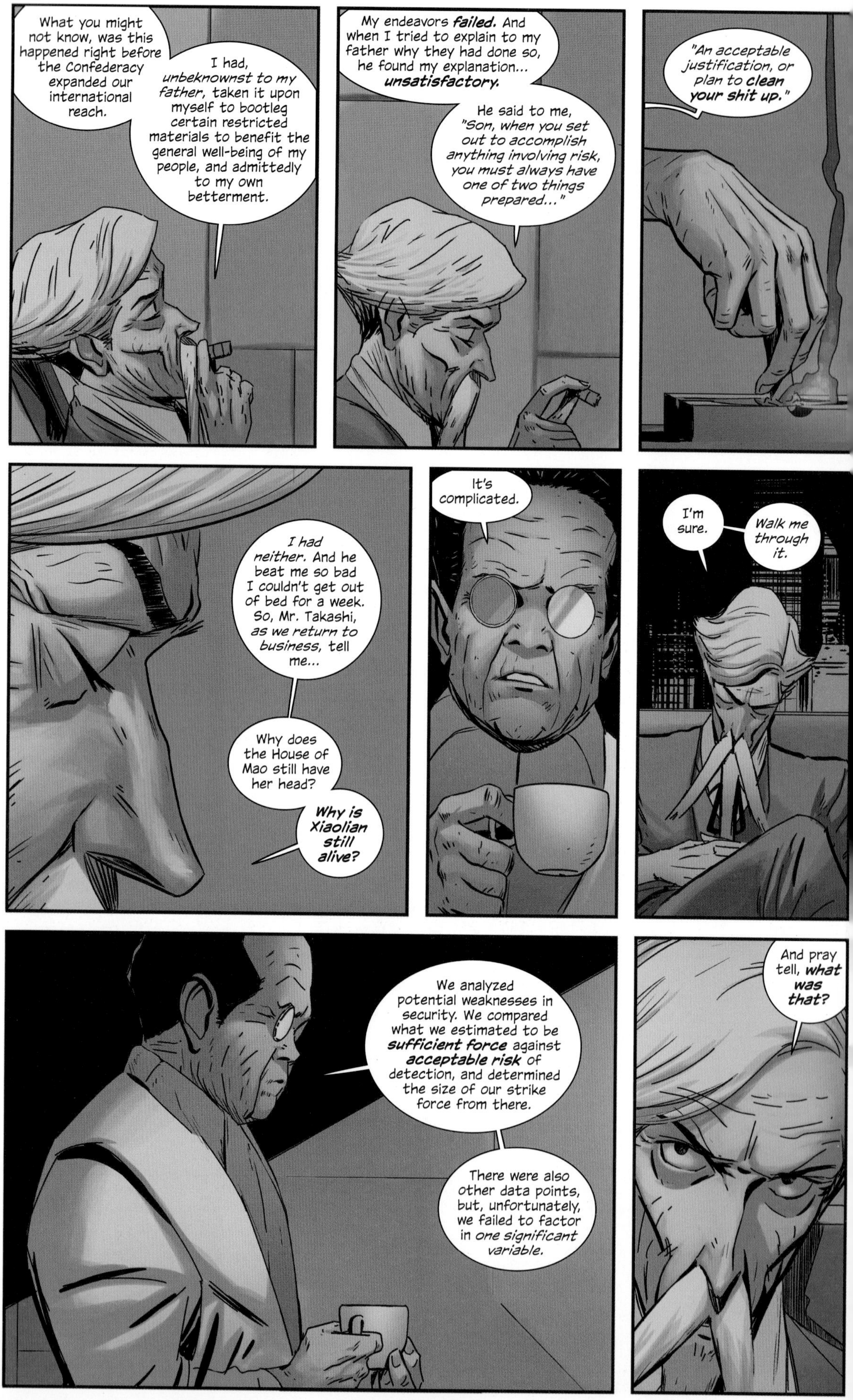
What you might not know, was this happened right before the Confederacy expanded our international reach.
I had, *unbeknownst to my father*, taken it upon myself to bootleg certain restricted materials to benefit the general well-being of my people, and admittedly to my own betterment.
My endeavors ***failed.*** And when I tried to explain to my father why they had done so, he found my explanation... ***unsatisfactory.***
He said to me, *"Son, when you set out to accomplish anything involving risk, you must always have one of two things prepared..."*
"An acceptable justification, or plan to ***clean your shit up."***
I had neither. And he beat me so bad I couldn't get out of bed for a week. So, Mr. Takashi, *as we return to business*, tell me...
Why does the House of Mao still have her head?
Why is Xiaolian still alive?
It's complicated.
I'm sure.
Walk me through it.
We analyzed potential weaknesses in security. We compared what we estimated to be ***sufficient force*** against ***acceptable risk*** of detection, and determined the size of our strike force from there.
There were also other data points, but, unfortunately, we failed to factor in *one significant variable.*
And pray tell, ***what was that?***

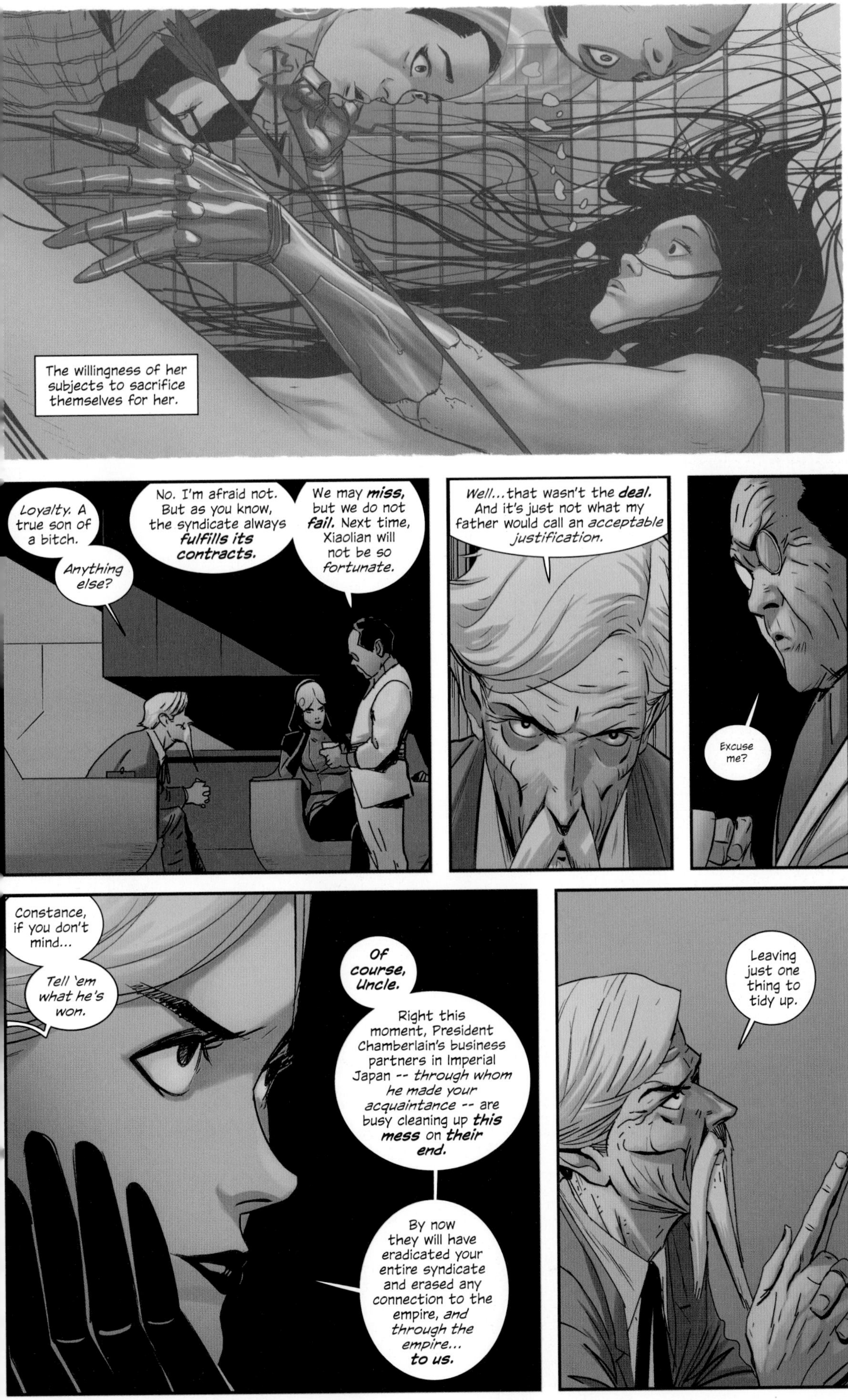
The willingness of her subjects to sacrifice themselves for her.
Loyalty. A true son of a bitch.
Anything else?
No. I'm afraid not. But as you know, the syndicate always fulfills its contracts.
We may miss, but we do not fail. Next time, Xiaolian will not be so fortunate.
Well...that wasn't the deal. And it's just not what my father would call an acceptable justification.
Excuse me?
Constance, if you don't mind...
Tell 'em what he's won.
Of course, Uncle.
Right this moment, President Chamberlain's business partners in Imperial Japan -- through whom he made your acquaintance -- are busy cleaning up this mess on their end.
By now they will have eradicated your entire syndicate and erased any connection to the empire, and through the empire... to us.
Leaving just one thing to tidy up.

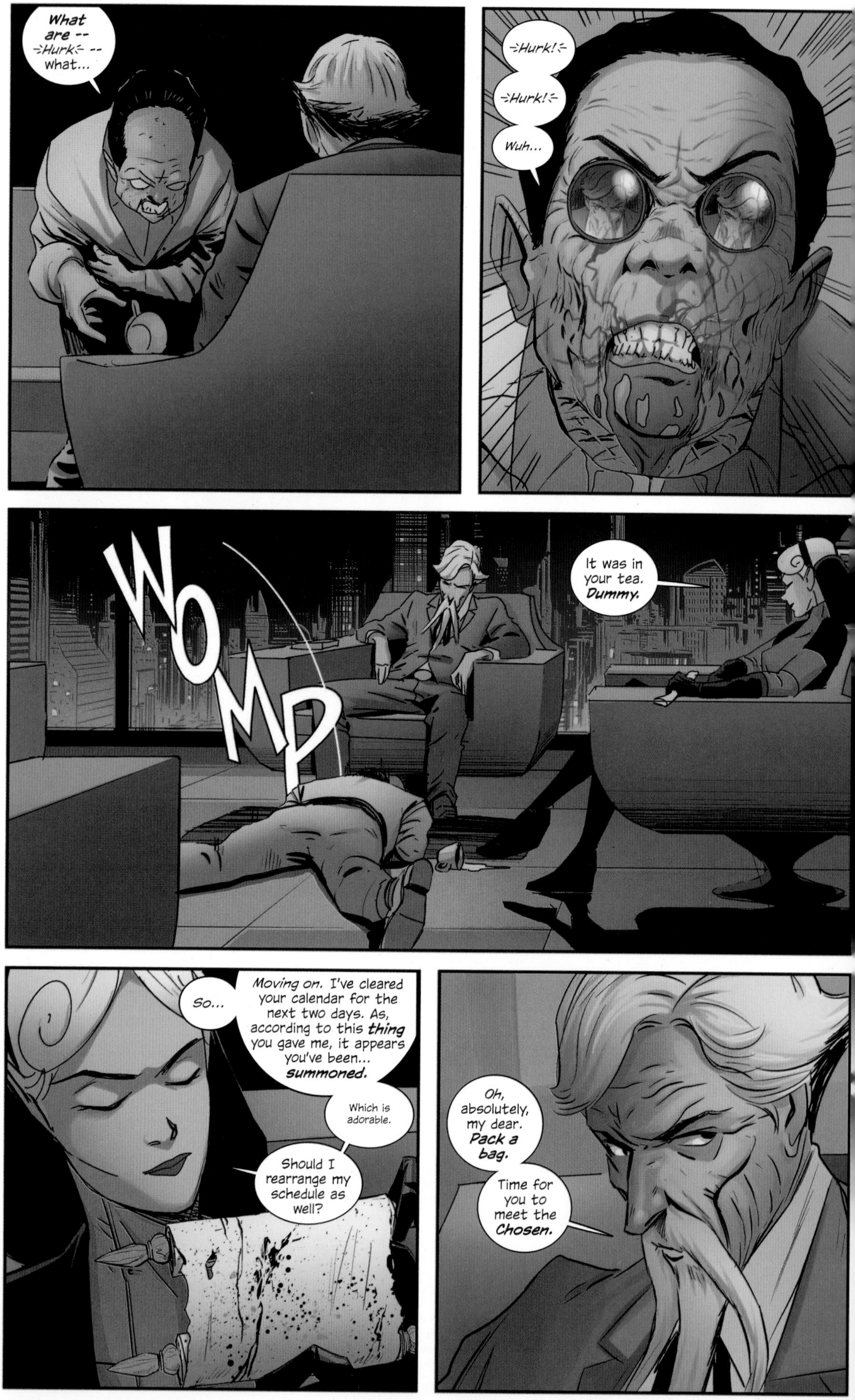

What are -- -Hurk- -- what...
-Hurk!-
-Hurk!-
Wuh...
WOMP
It was in your tea. Dummy.
So...
Moving on. I've cleared your calendar for the next two days. As, according to this thing you gave me, it appears you've been... summoned.
Which is adorable.
Should I rearrange my schedule as well?
Oh, absolutely, my dear. Pack a bag.
Time for you to meet the Chosen.

FEAR NOT.

DEAD MEN DO NOT **LIE.**

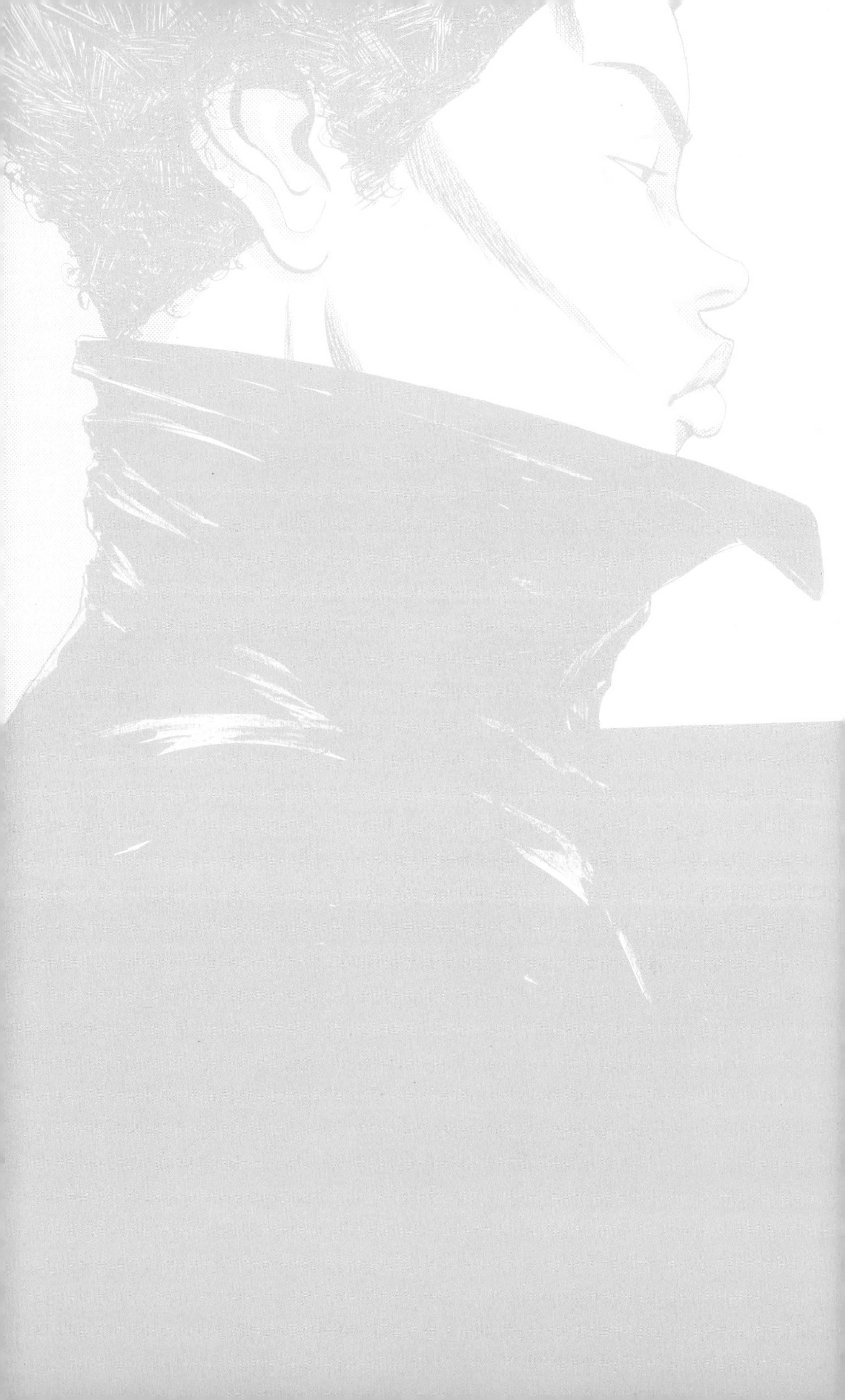

23

TWENTY-THREE:
A **SON** OF THE
KINGDOM

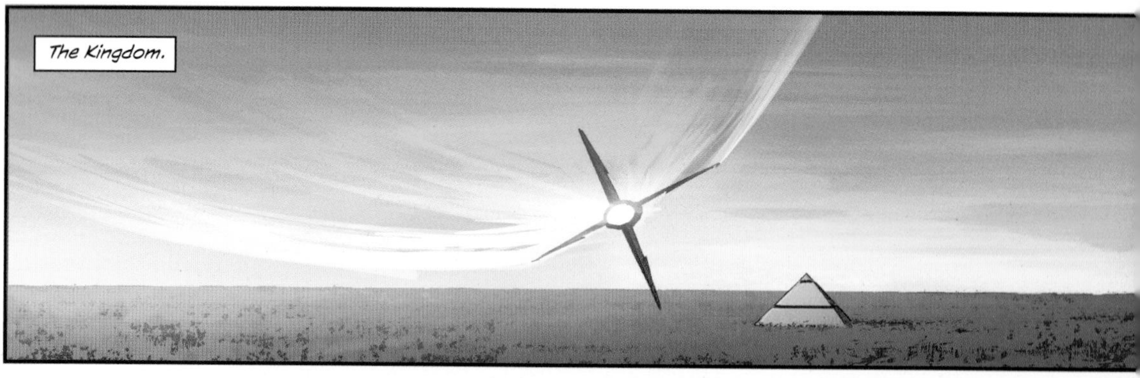
The Kingdom.

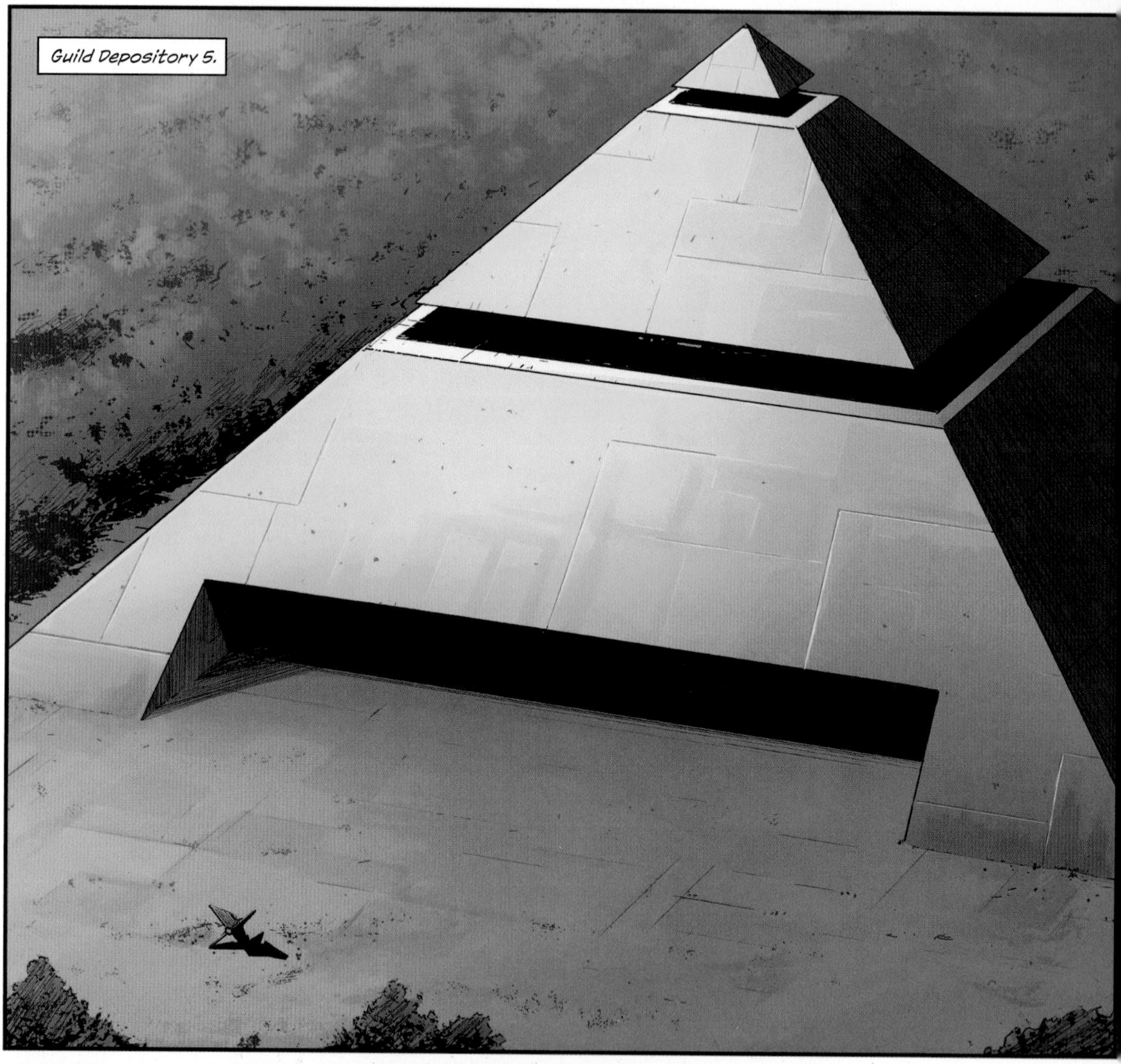
Guild Depository 5.

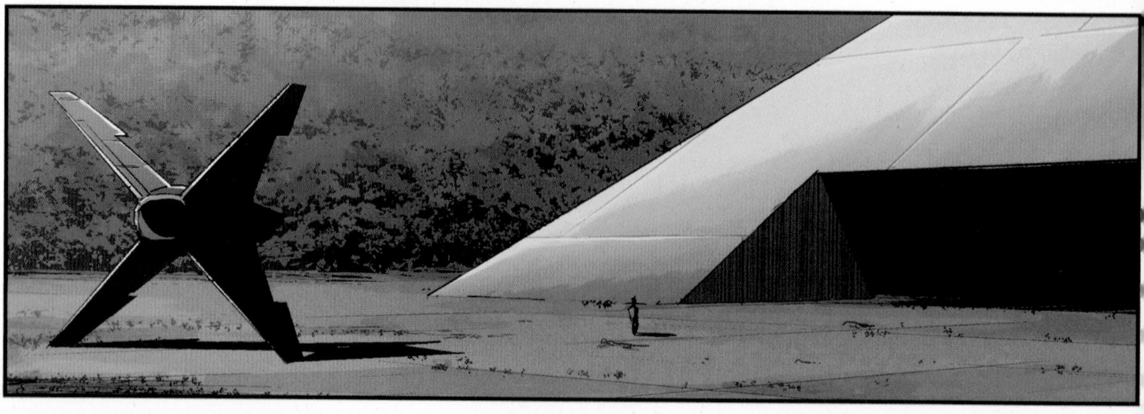

PSSHH

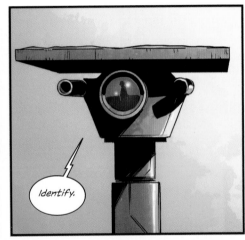

Identify.

Pfftt. Do it yourself.

Scanning...

Freeman, John. Crown Prince. First of fourteen. Security level: 2.

Access... granted.

Awaiting instructions.

Shut down the grid and all recording devices.

Go to sleep.

Acknowledged.

Shutting down.

It's disarmed. You can approach.

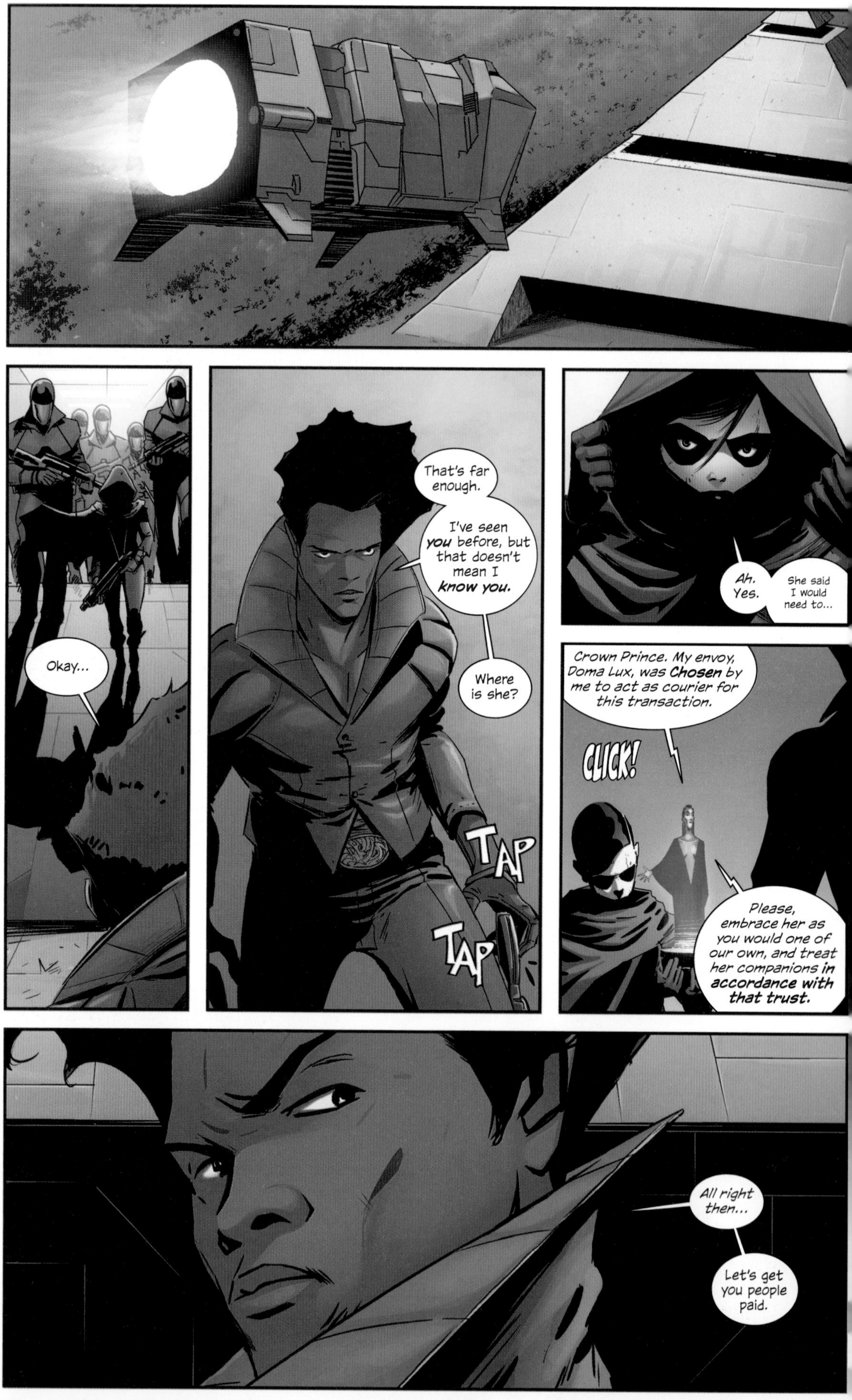
Okay...
That's far enough.
I've seen **you** before, but that doesn't mean I **know you.**
Where is she?
TAP
TAP
Ah. Yes.
She said I would need to...
*Crown Prince. My envoy, Doma Lux, was **Chosen** by me to act as courier for this transaction.*
CLICK!
*Please, embrace her as you would one of our own, and treat her companions **in accordance with that trust.***
All right then...
Let's get you people paid.

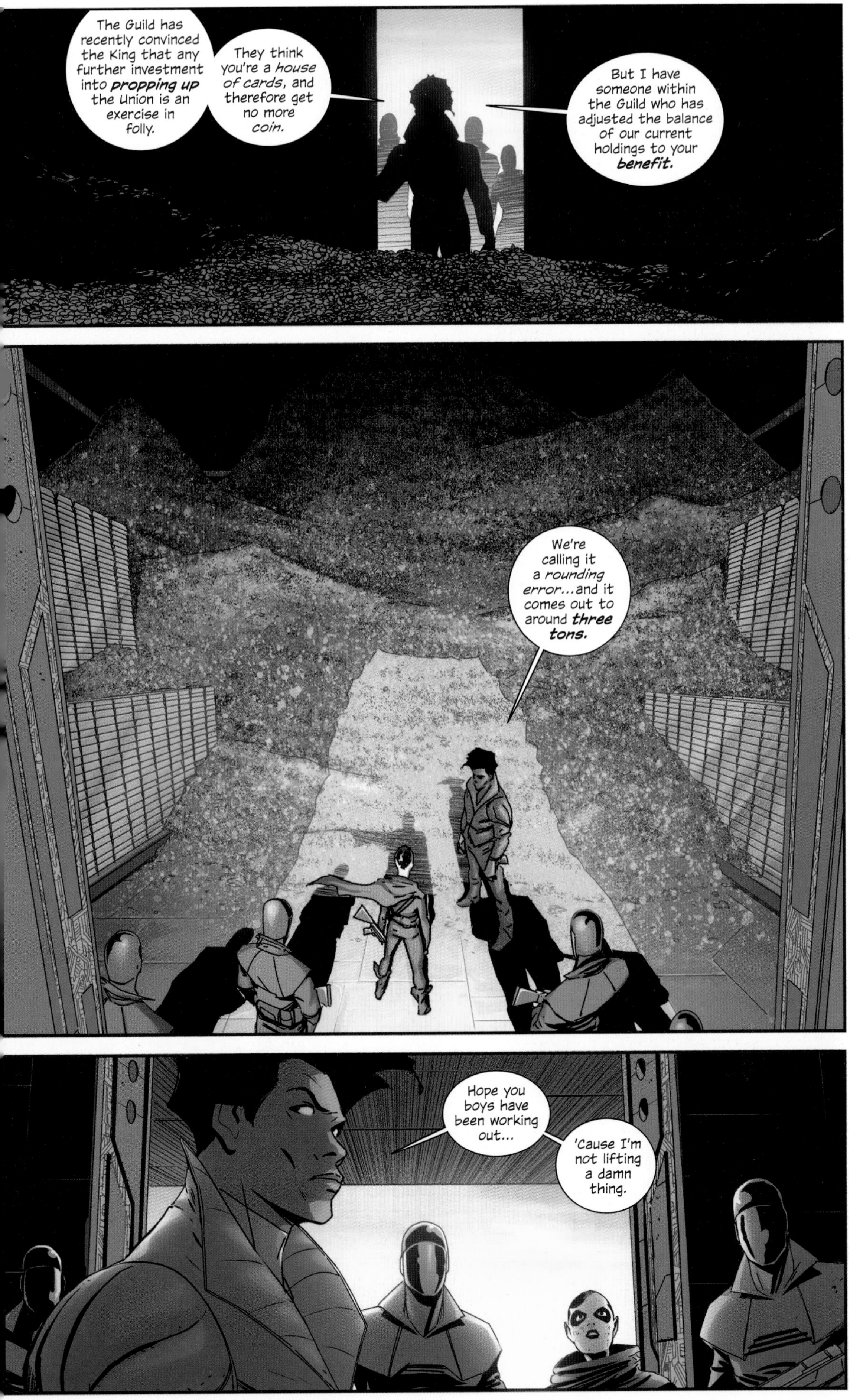
The Guild has recently convinced the King that any further investment into ***propping up*** the Union is an exercise in folly.
They think you're a *house of cards*, and therefore get no more *coin.*
But I have someone within the Guild who has adjusted the balance of our current holdings to your ***benefit.***
We're calling it a *rounding error*...and it comes out to around ***three tons.***
Hope you boys have been working out...
'Cause I'm not lifting a damn thing.

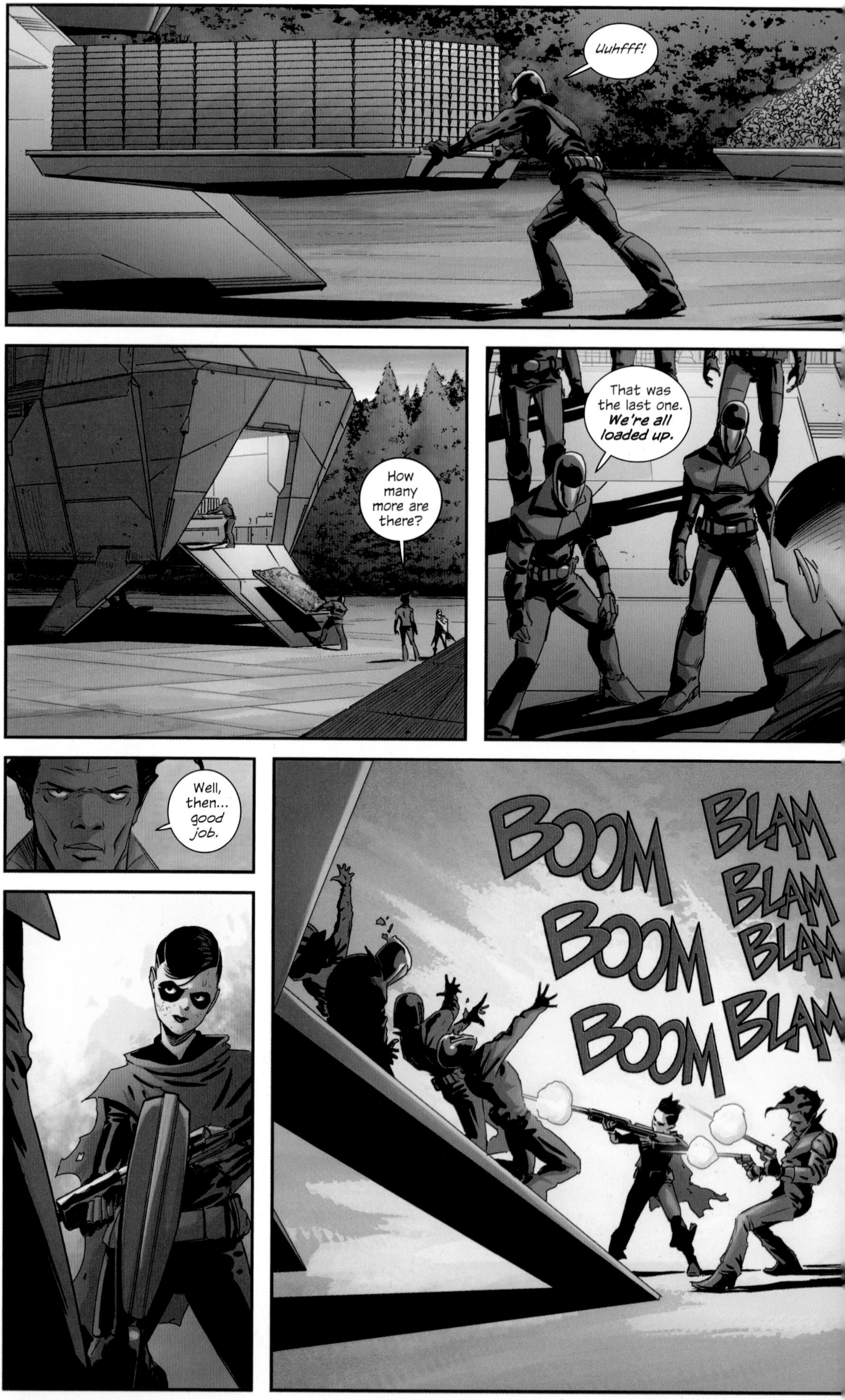

Uuhfff!
How many more are there?
That was the last one. *We're all loaded up.*
Well, then... good job.
BOOM BOOM BOOM
BLAM BLAM BLAM BLAM

"...in accordance with that trust," huh?

Exactly.

Either you are one of us...or you are not.

I'd tell you to remember that, but you don't strike me as the sort who would *take* it to heart.

Now run home to mommy.

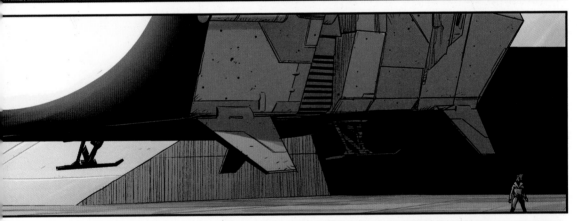

You can come out now.

I know you're there.

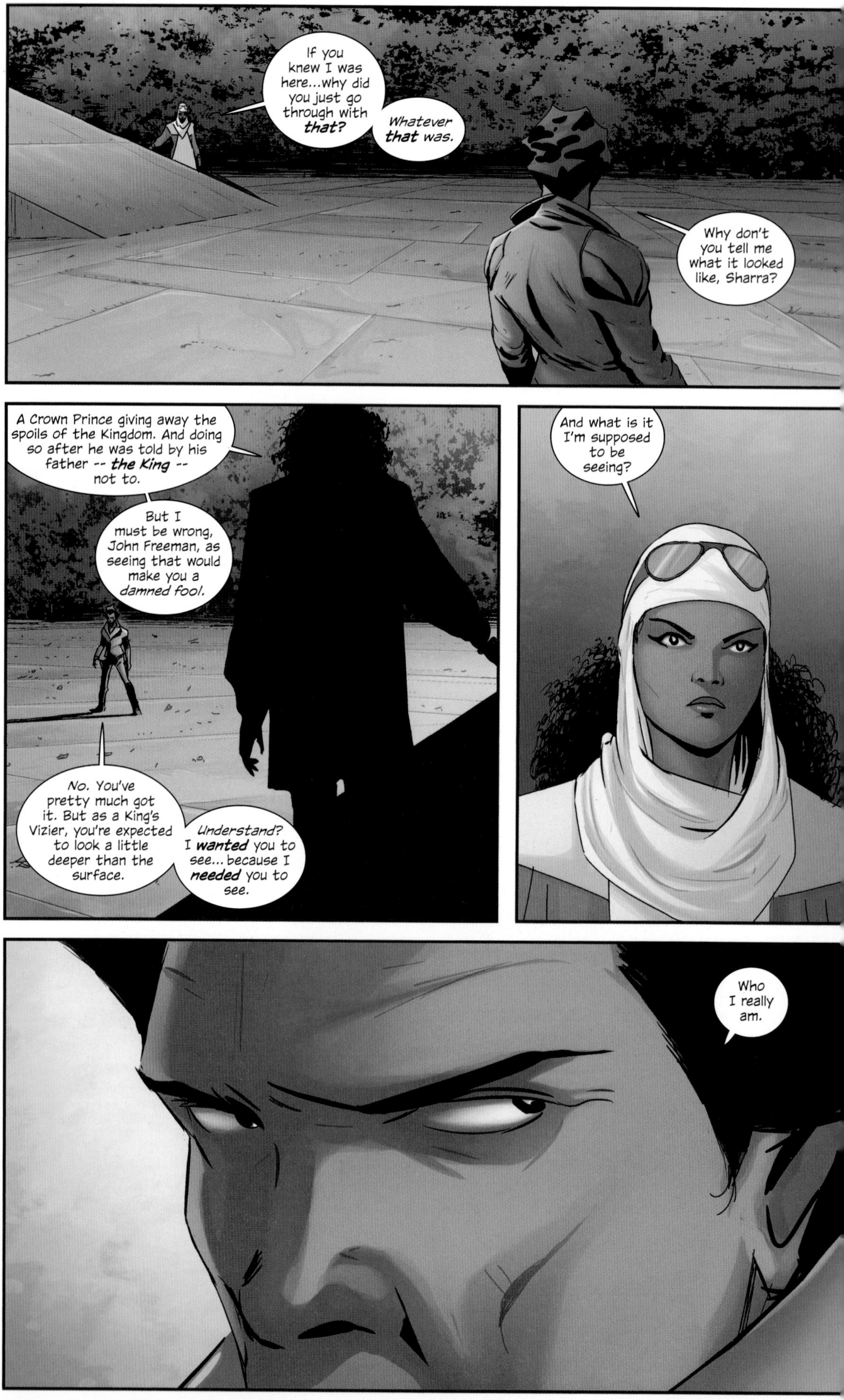
If you knew I was here...why did you just go through with **that?**
Whatever **that** *was.*
Why don't you tell me what it looked like, Sharra?
A Crown Prince giving away the spoils of the Kingdom. And doing so after he was told by his father -- **the King** -- not to.
But I must be wrong, John Freeman, as seeing that would make you a *damned fool.*
And what is it I'm supposed to be seeing?
No. You've pretty much got it. But as a King's Vizier, you're expected to look a little deeper than the surface.
Understand? I **wanted** you to see... because I **needed** you to see.
Who I really am.

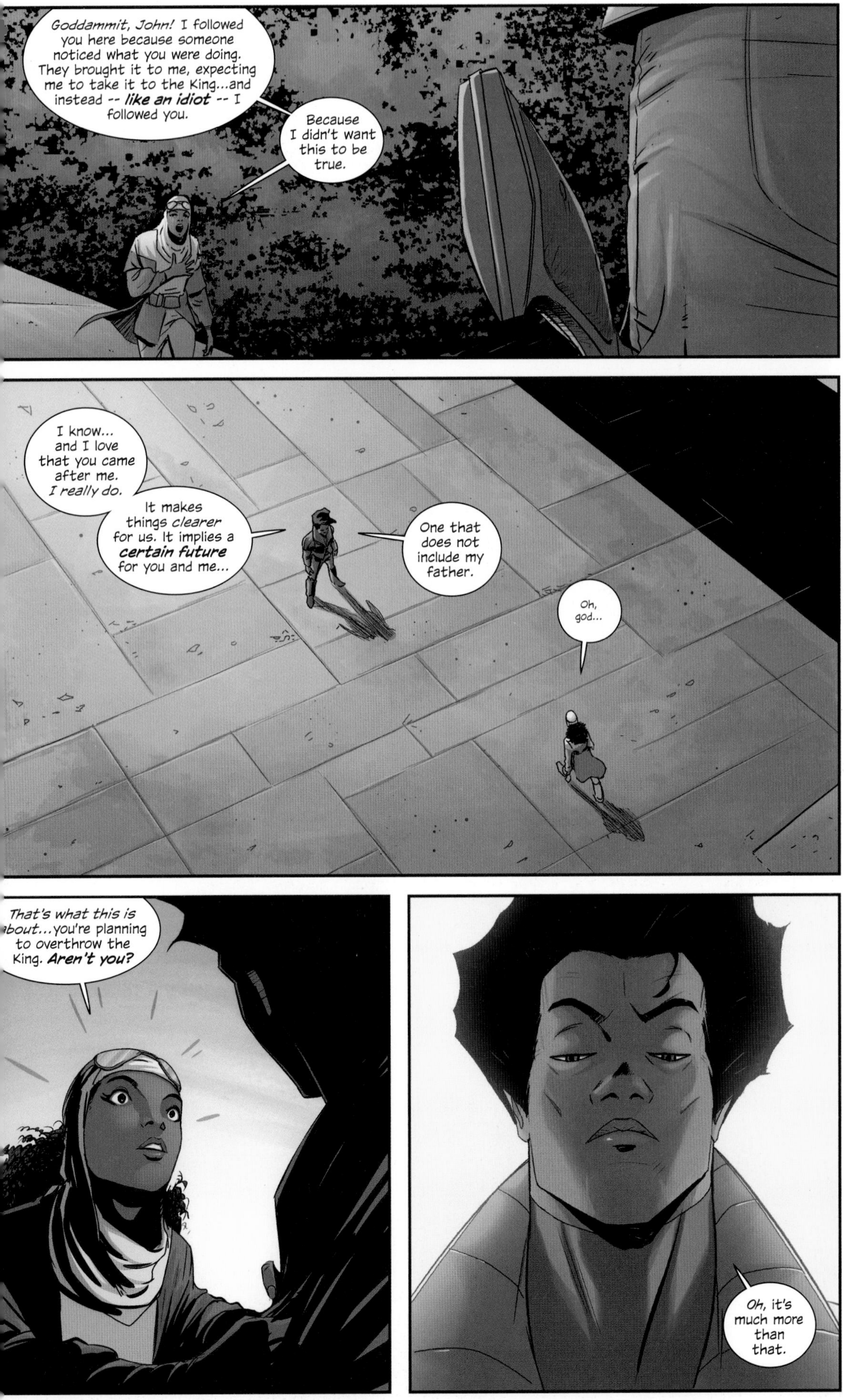

Goddammit, John! I followed you here because someone noticed what you were doing. They brought it to me, expecting me to take it to the King...and instead -- like an idiot -- I followed you.
Because I didn't want this to be true.
I know... and I love that you came after me. I really do.
It makes things clearer for us. It implies a certain future for you and me...
One that does not include my father.
Oh, god...
That's what this is about...you're planning to overthrow the King. Aren't you?
Oh, it's much more than that.

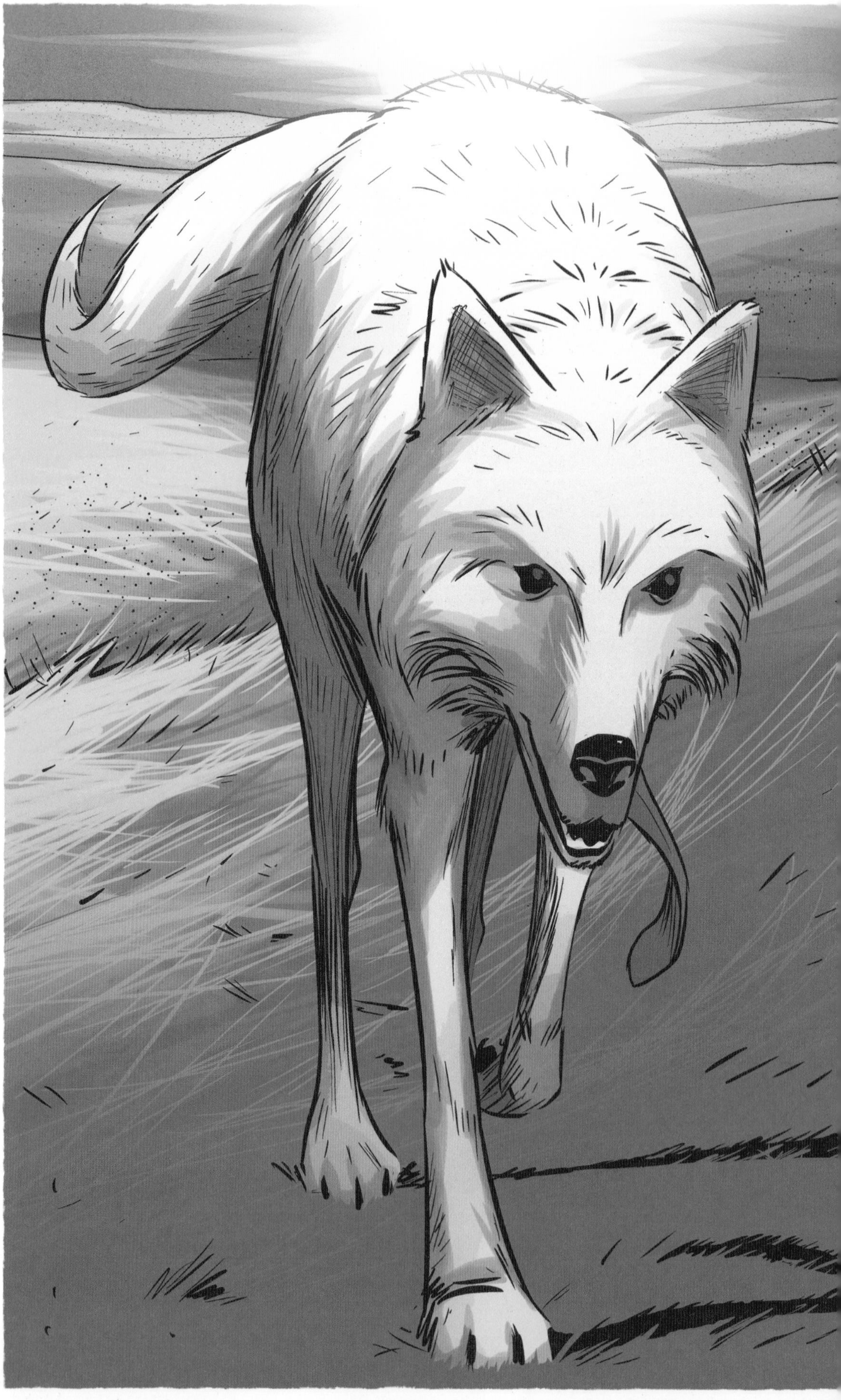

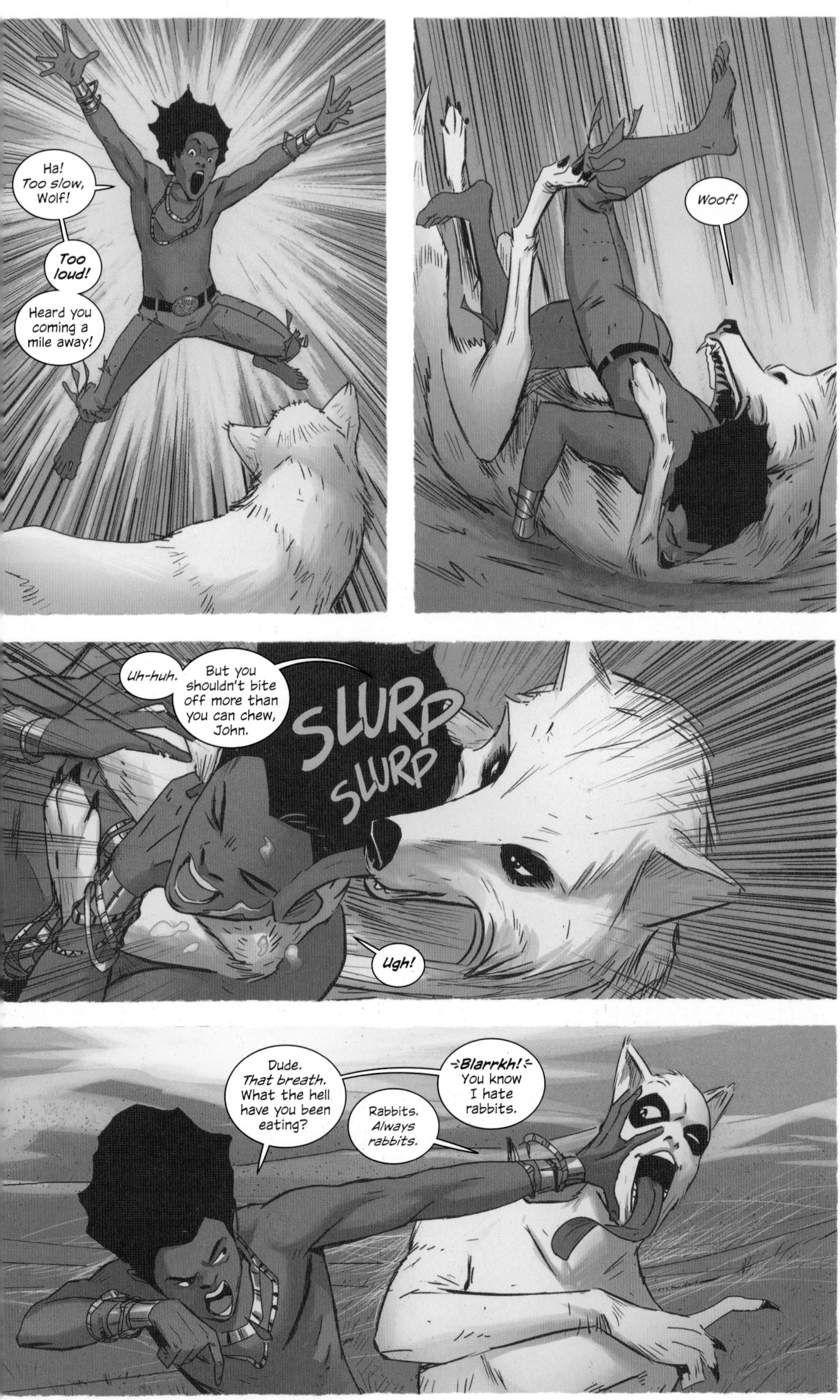
Ha! Too slow, Wolf!
Too loud!
Heard you coming a mile away!
Woof!
Uh-huh.
But you shouldn't bite off more than you can chew, John.
SLURP SLURP
Ugh!
Dude. That breath. What the hell have you been eating?
Rabbits. Always rabbits.
Blarrkh! You know I hate rabbits.

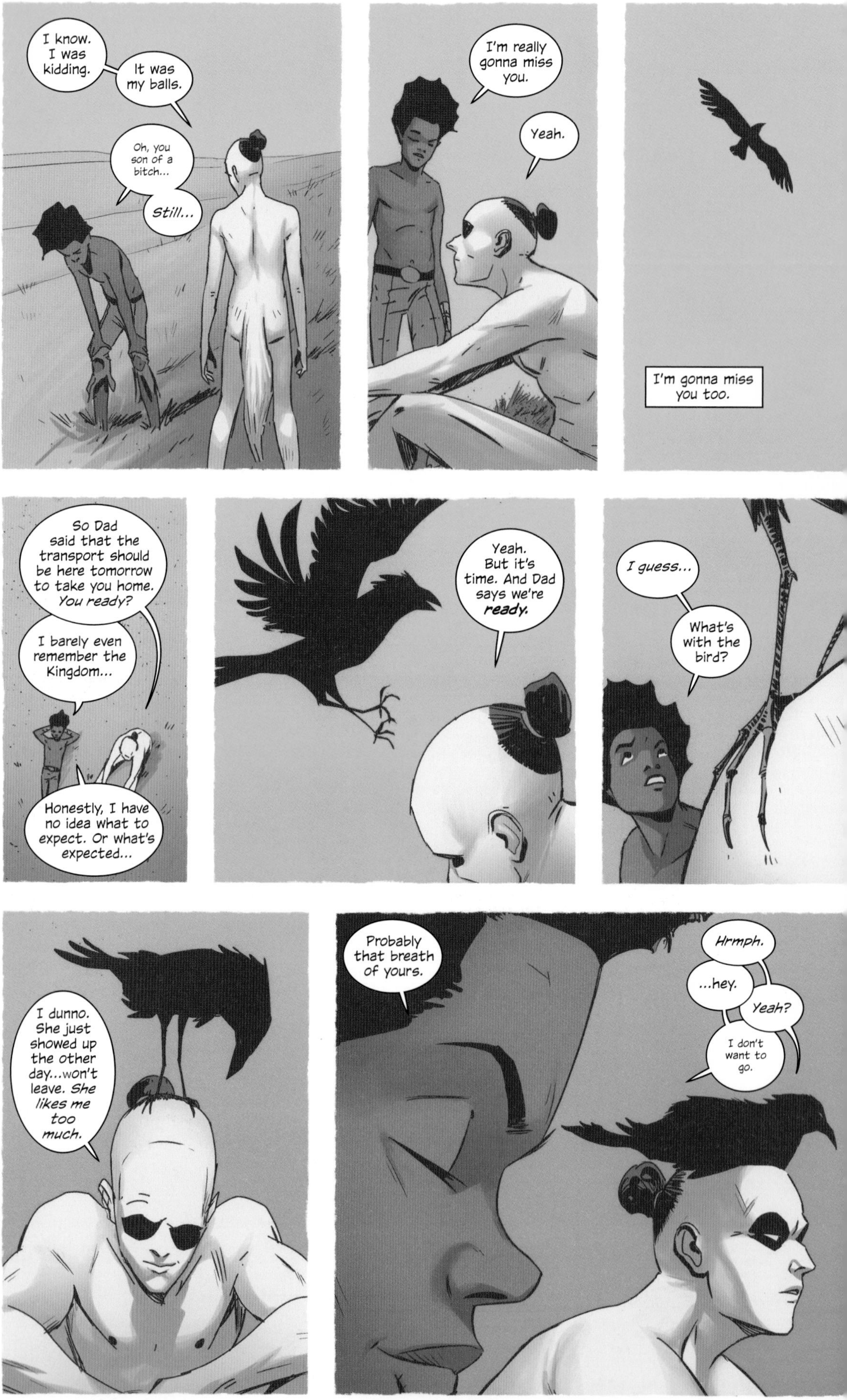
I know. I was kidding.
It was my balls.
Oh, you son of a bitch...
Still...
I'm really gonna miss you.
Yeah.
I'm gonna miss you too.
So Dad said that the transport should be here tomorrow to take you home. *You ready?*
I barely even remember the Kingdom...
Honestly, I have no idea what to expect. Or what's expected...
Yeah. But it's time. And Dad says we're ***ready.***
I guess...
What's with the bird?
I dunno. She just showed up the other day...won't leave. *She likes me too much.*
Probably that breath of yours.
Hrmph.
...hey.
Yeah?
I don't want to go.

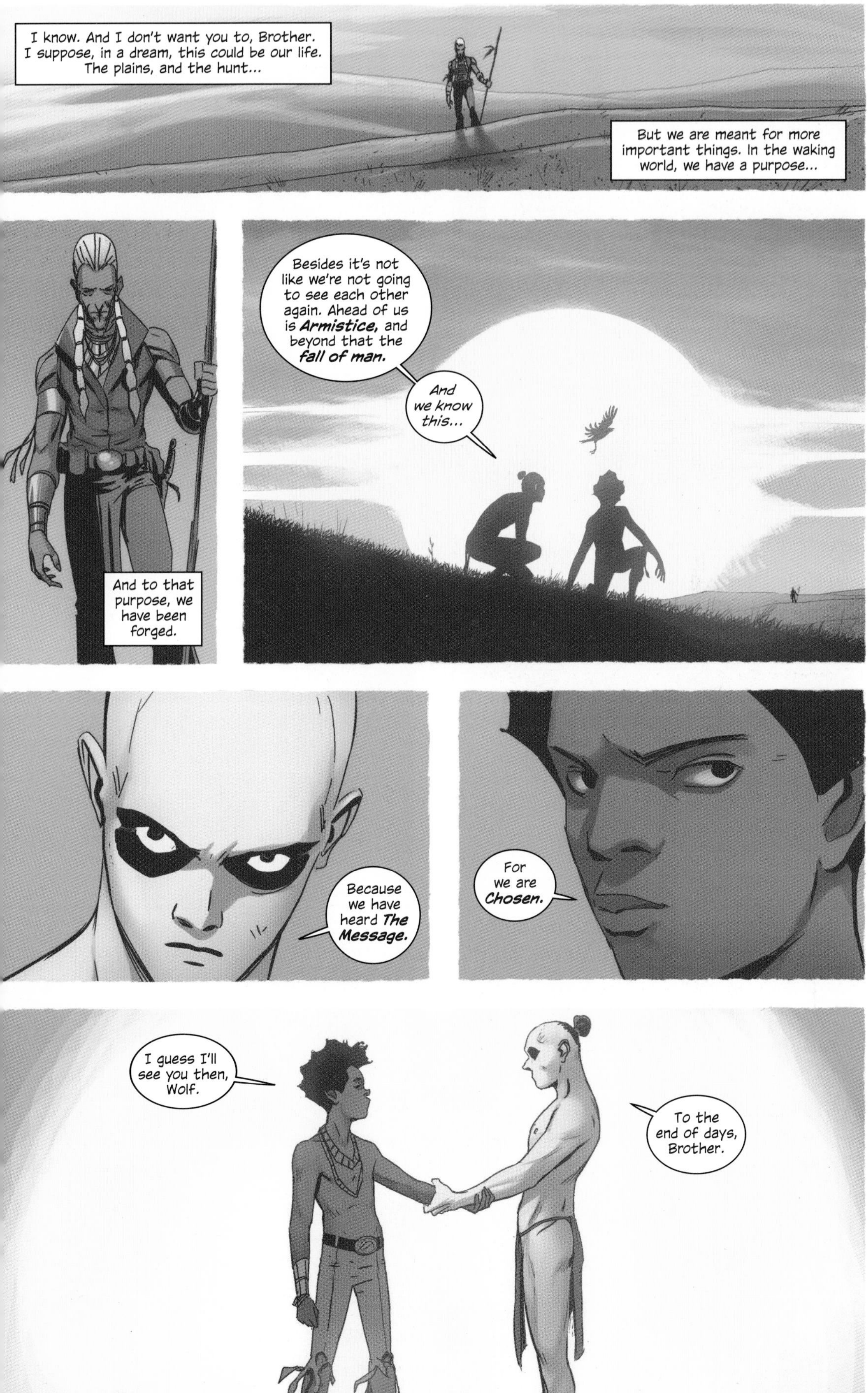
I know. And I don't want you to, Brother. I suppose, in a dream, this could be our life. The plains, and the hunt...
But we are meant for more important things. In the waking world, we have a purpose...
And to that purpose, we have been forged.
Besides it's not like we're not going to see each other again. Ahead of us is **Armistice,** and beyond that the ***fall of man.***
And we know this...
Because we have heard ***The Message.***
For we are ***Chosen.***
I guess I'll see you then, Wolf.
To the end of days, Brother.

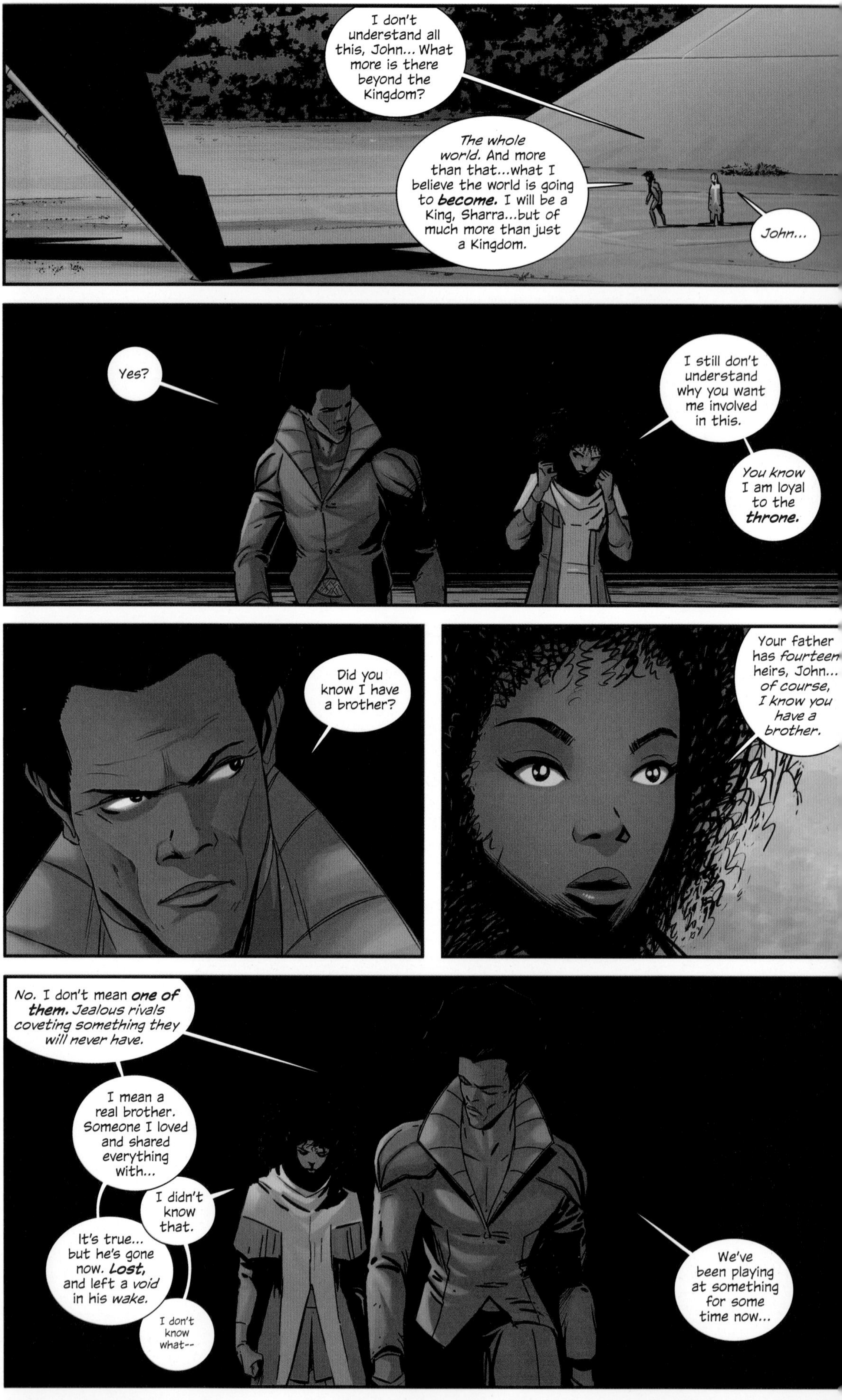
I don't understand all this, John... What more is there beyond the Kingdom?
The whole world. And more than that...what I believe the world is going to ***become.*** I will be a King, Sharra...but of much more than just a Kingdom.
John...
Yes?
I still don't understand why you want me involved in this.
*You know I am loyal to the **throne.***
Did you know I have a brother?
Your father has *fourteen* heirs, John... *of course, I know you have a brother.*
No. I don't mean ***one of them.*** *Jealous rivals coveting something they will never have.*
I mean a real brother. Someone I loved and shared everything with...
I didn't know that.
It's true... but he's gone now. ***Lost,*** and left a *void* in his *wake.*
I don't know what--
We've been playing at something for some time now...

And I'm tired of not having certain things in my life. I know that I've been hiding all this from everyone -- *from you* -- and I don't want to do that anymore.

I want to share everything with you, and, *if you'll have it,* make you a *queen.*

What?

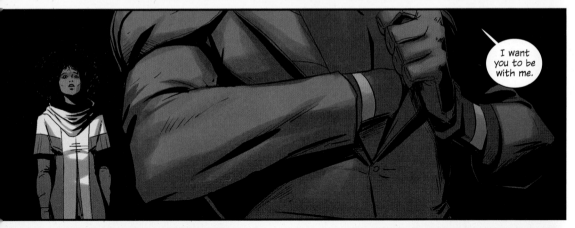

I want you to be with me.

I want you to know me.

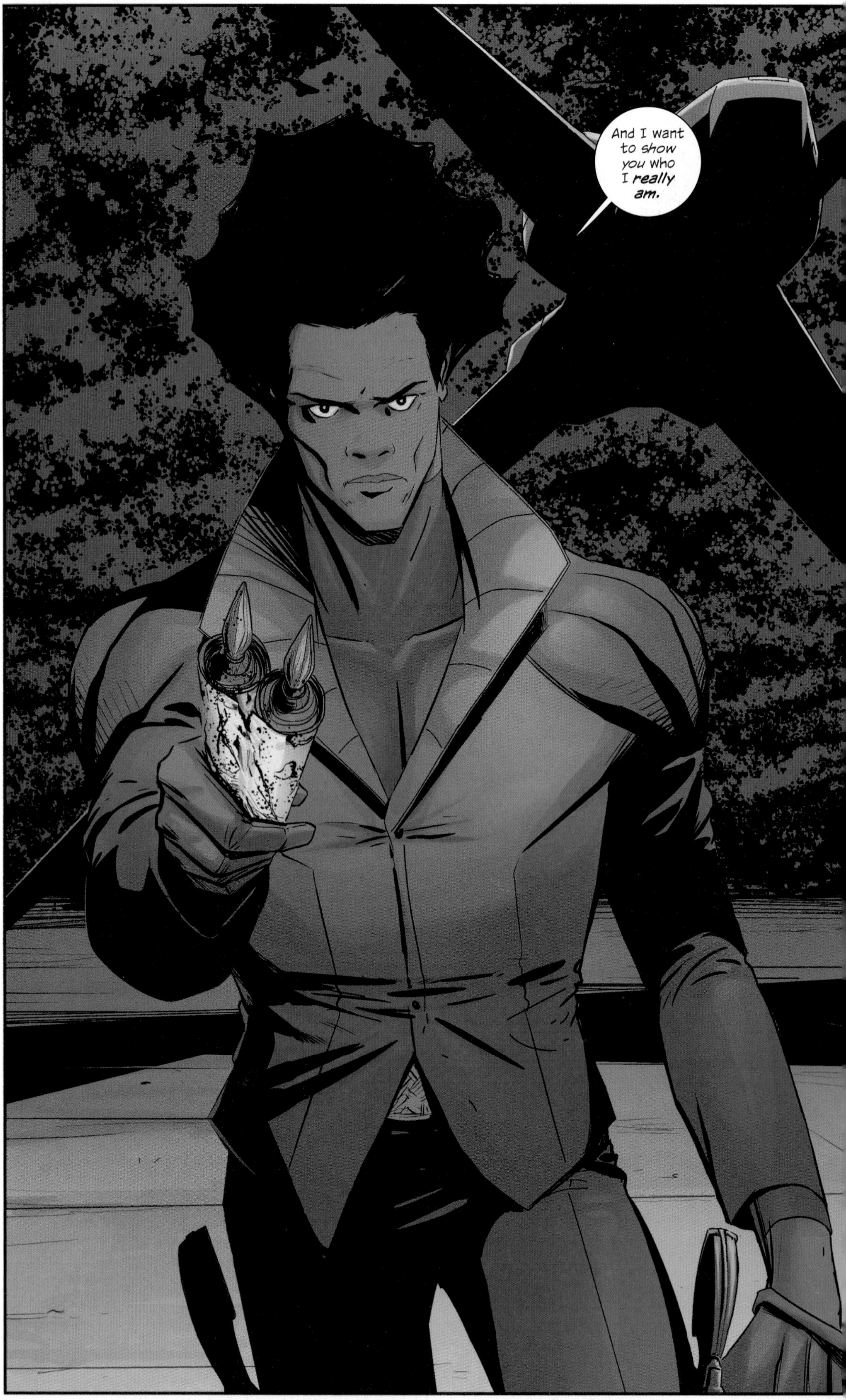
And I want to show you who I **really am.**

Urrhhhhh...

There's an **art** to persuasion.

Especially when *persuading* those who are blind to a *right* and *proper* path...

So I choose my words **carefully**.

Ahem.

"...to you, who has been summoned by the Prophet Orion, the living word, to a convocation of--"

Rrrrarrrr. Apologiesss, Orion...

But trying too hard isss never a good look. Perhapsss 'assssembly' there inssstead of 'convocation'?

Sssubtlety, I sssay. Alwaysss an ally in the doomsssaying.

That will be quite enough from you, Buer... For I am the prophet -- and won't be **rewritten**.

Urrhhhhh...

And you!..

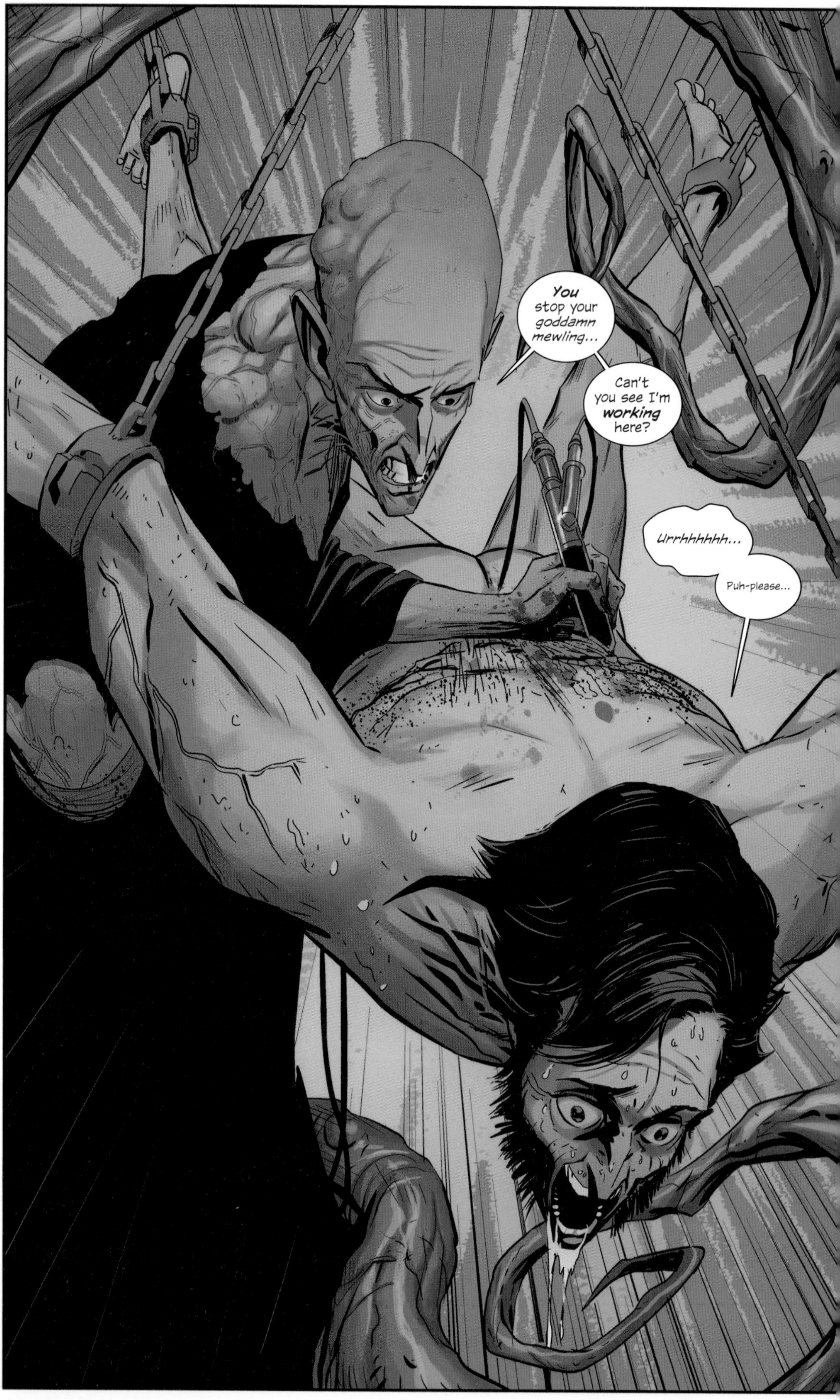

You stop your goddamn mewling...
Can't you see I'm working here?
Urrhhhhhh...
Puh-please...

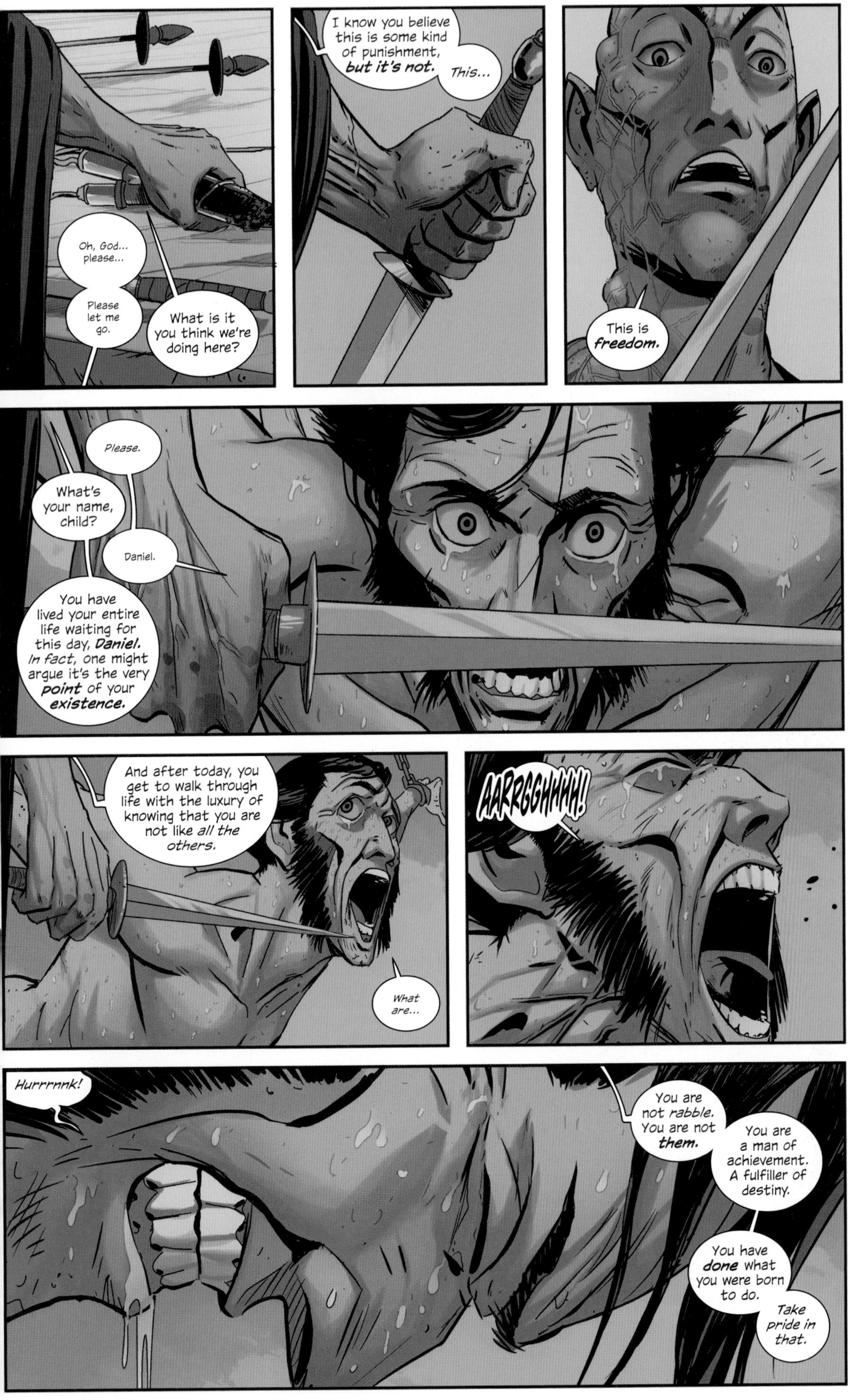
Oh, God... please...
Please let me go.
What is it you think we're doing here?
I know you believe this is some kind of punishment, **but it's not.**
This...
This is **freedom.**
Please.
What's your name, child?
Daniel.
You have lived your entire life waiting for this day, **Daniel.** *In fact,* one might argue it's the very **point** of your **existence.**
And after today, you get to walk through life with the luxury of knowing that you are not like *all the others.*
What are...
AARRGGHHHH!
Hurrrnnk!
You are not *rabble.* You are not **them.**
You are a man of achievement. A fulfiller of destiny.
You have **done** what you were born to do.
Take pride in that.

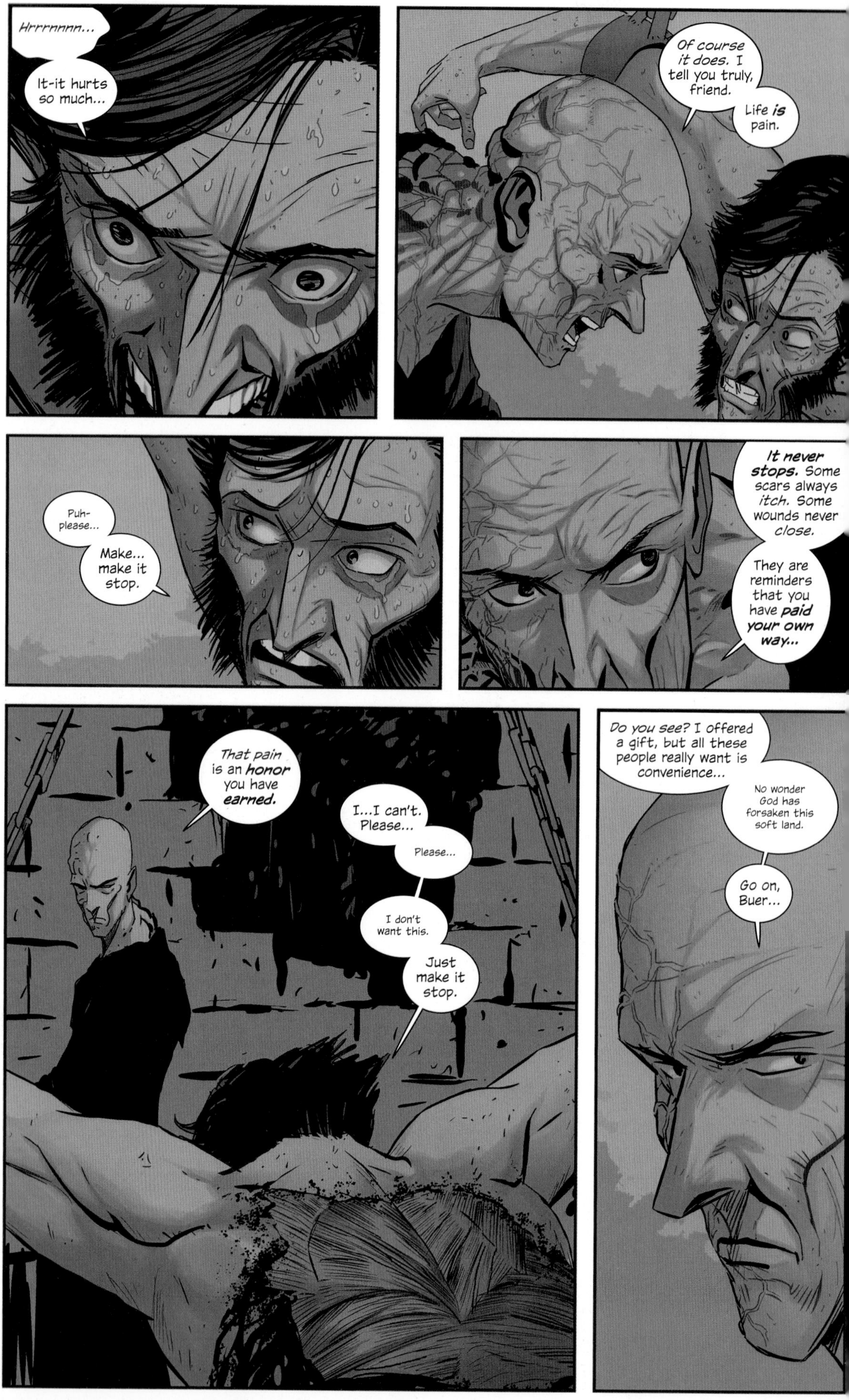

Hrrrnnnn...
It-it hurts so much...
Of course it does. I tell you truly, friend.
Life is pain.
Puh-please...
Make... make it stop.
It never stops. Some scars always itch. Some wounds never close.
They are reminders that you have paid your own way...
That pain is an honor you have earned.
I...I can't. Please...
Please...
I don't want this.
Just make it stop.
Do you see? I offered a gift, but all these people really want is convenience...
No wonder God has forsaken this soft land.
Go on, Buer...

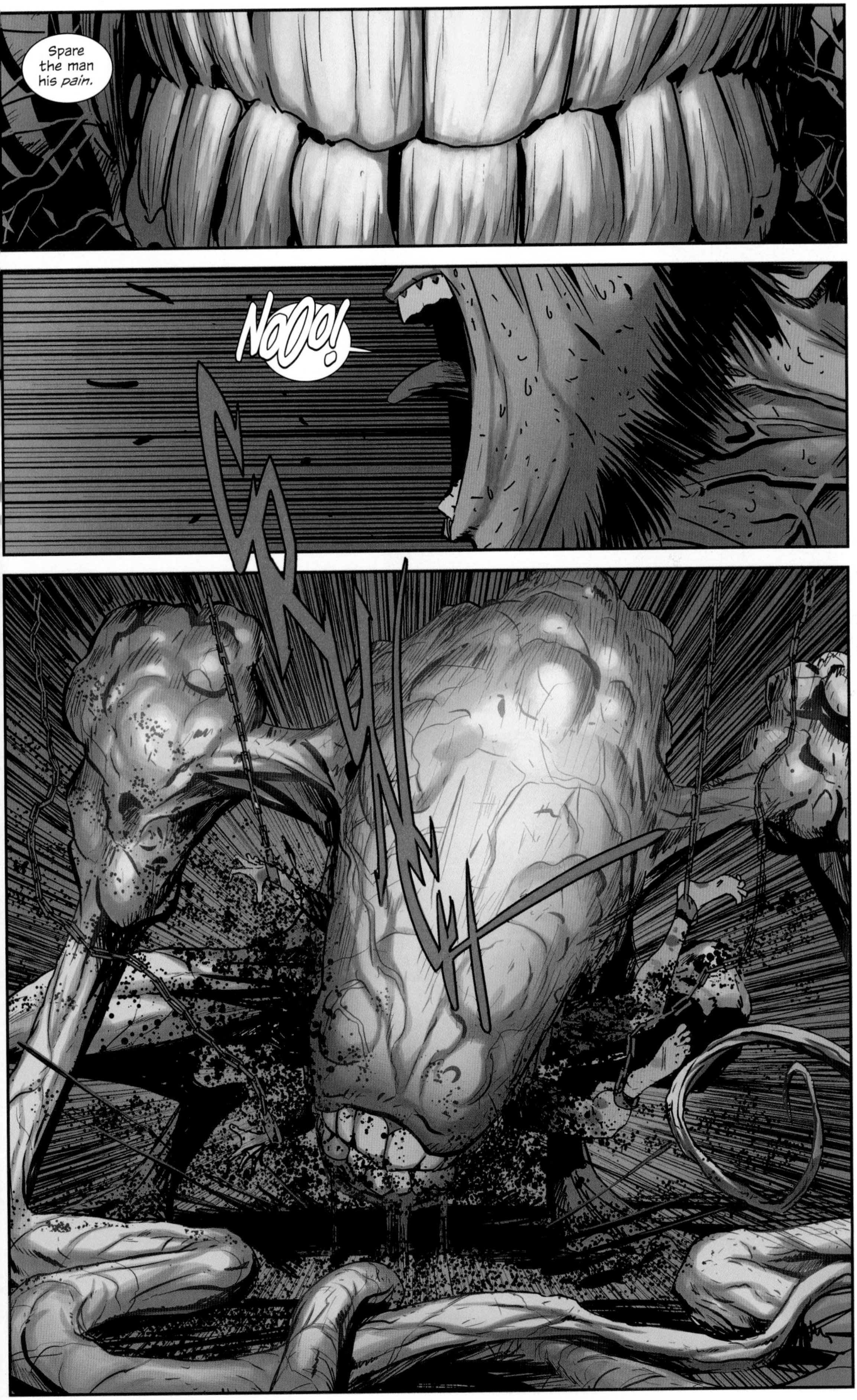
Spare the man his *pain*.
NOOO!
CRUNCH

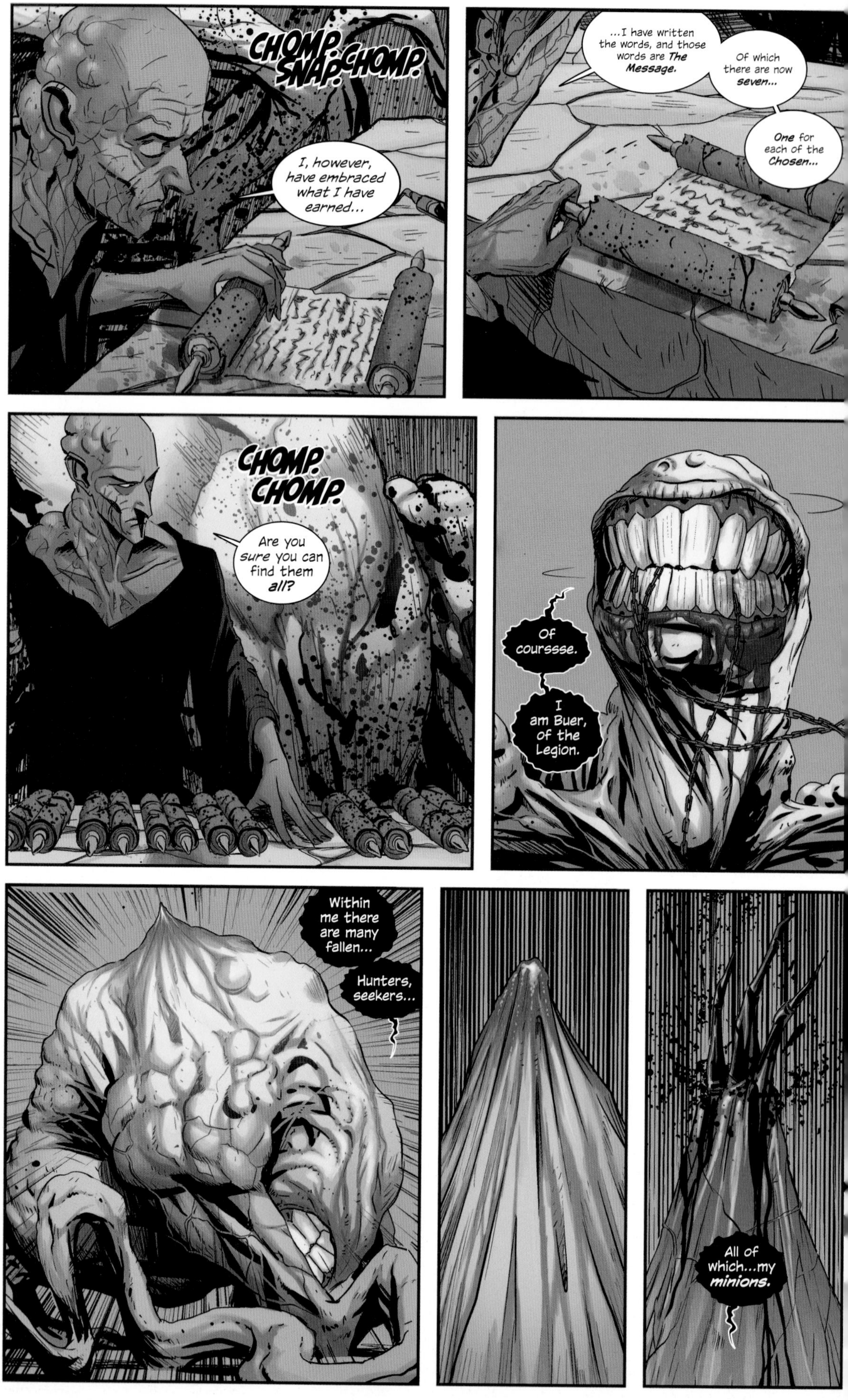
CHOMP. SNAP. CHOMP.
I, however, have embraced what I have earned...
...I have written the words, and those words are *The Message.*
Of which there are now *seven...*
One for each of the *Chosen...*
CHOMP. CHOMP.
Are you *sure* you can find them *all?*
Of coursse.
I am Buer, of the Legion.
Within me there are many fallen...
Hunters, seekers...
All of which...my *minions.*

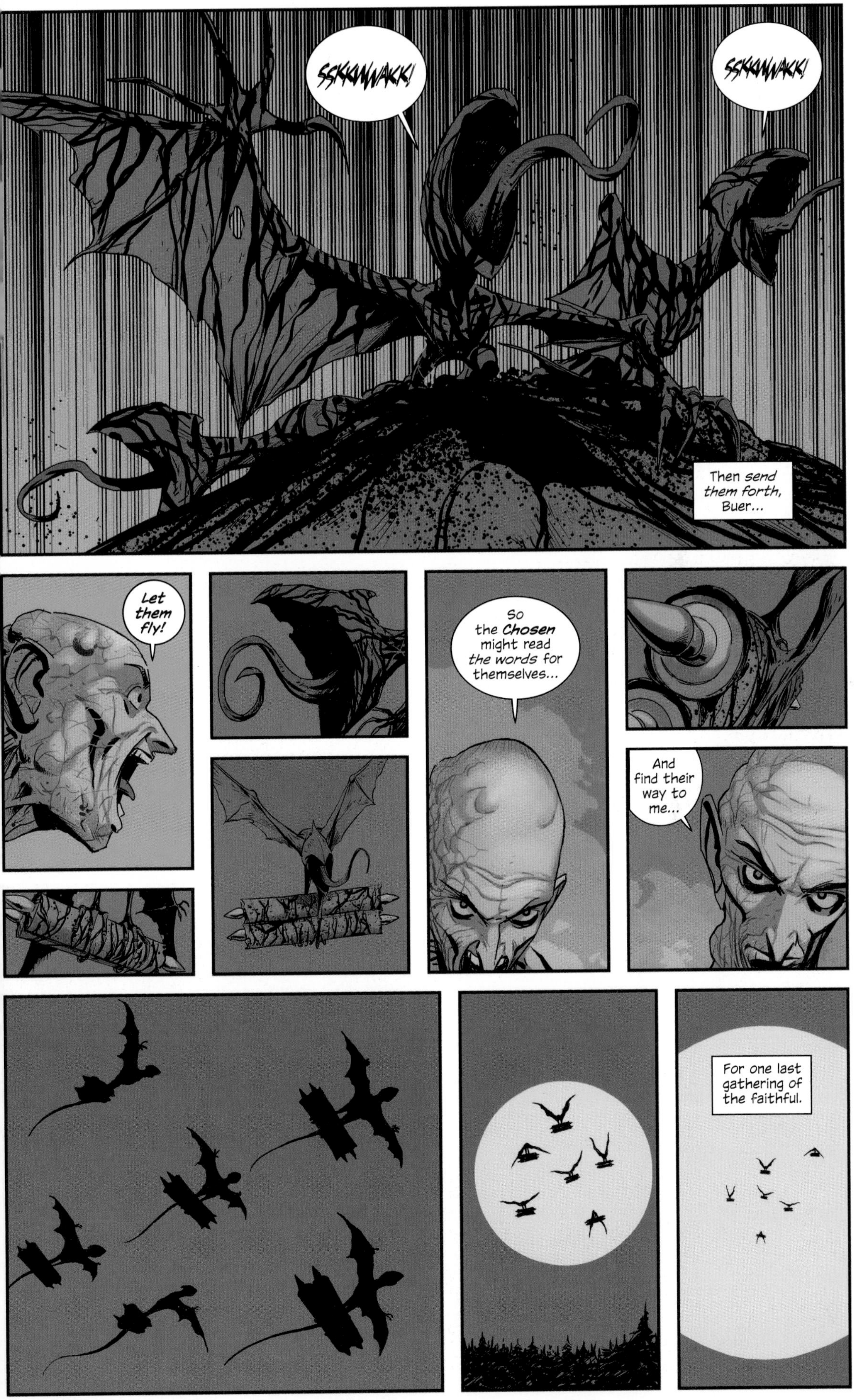
SSKKWAKK!
SSKKWAKK!
Then send them forth, Buer...
Let them fly!
So the Chosen might read the words for themselves...
And find their way to me...
For one last gathering of the faithful.

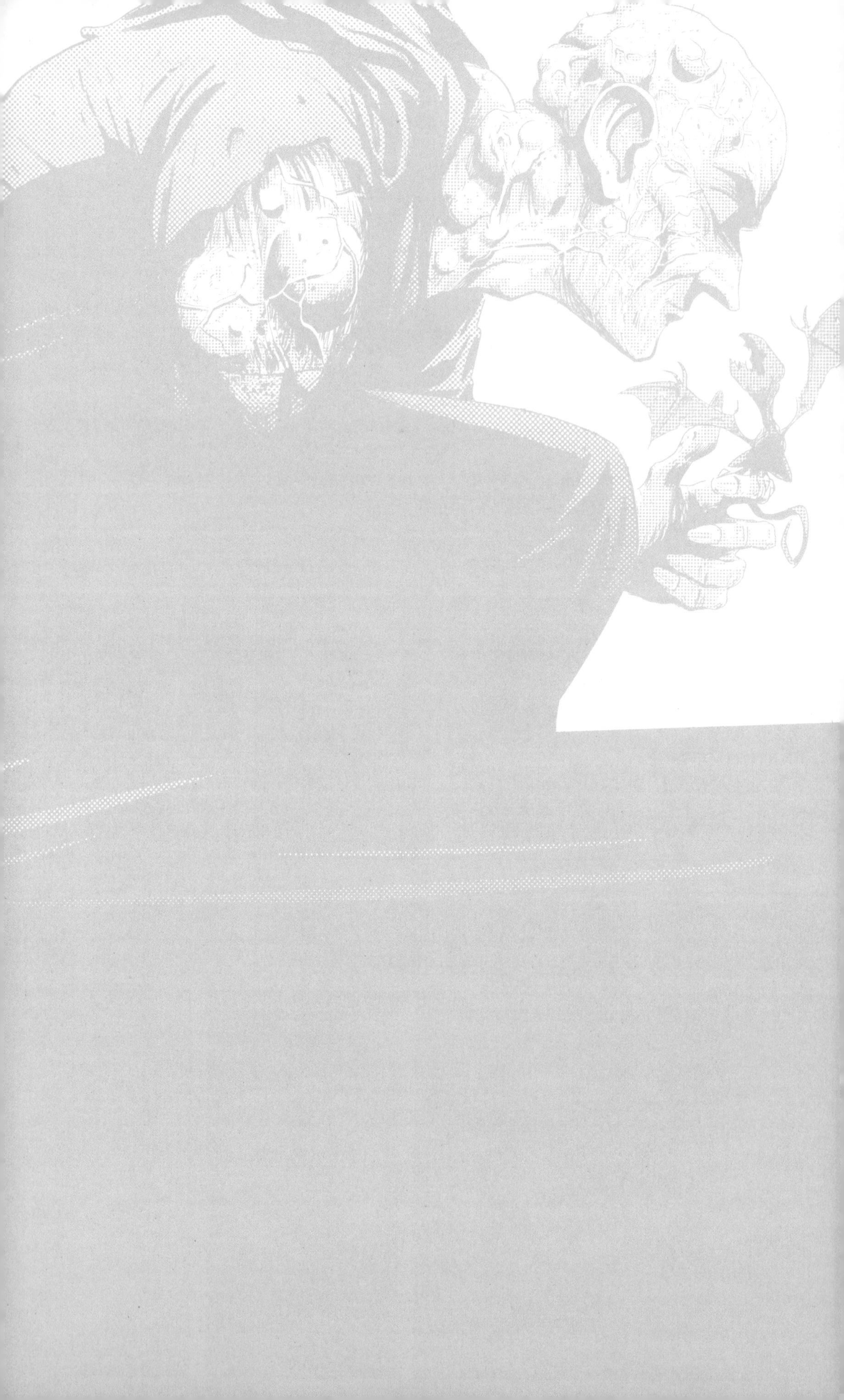

24

TWENTY-FOUR:
THE **LEGION**
BRINGS **WORD**

I devoured the three-fold **Message** at the fall of Armistice and became the **Living Word.**

Apocrypha made flesh.

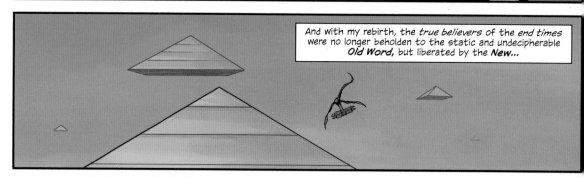

And with my rebirth, the *true believers* of the *end times* were no longer beholden to the static and undecipherable **Old Word,** but liberated by the **New...**

By *me,* for I am *true providence.*

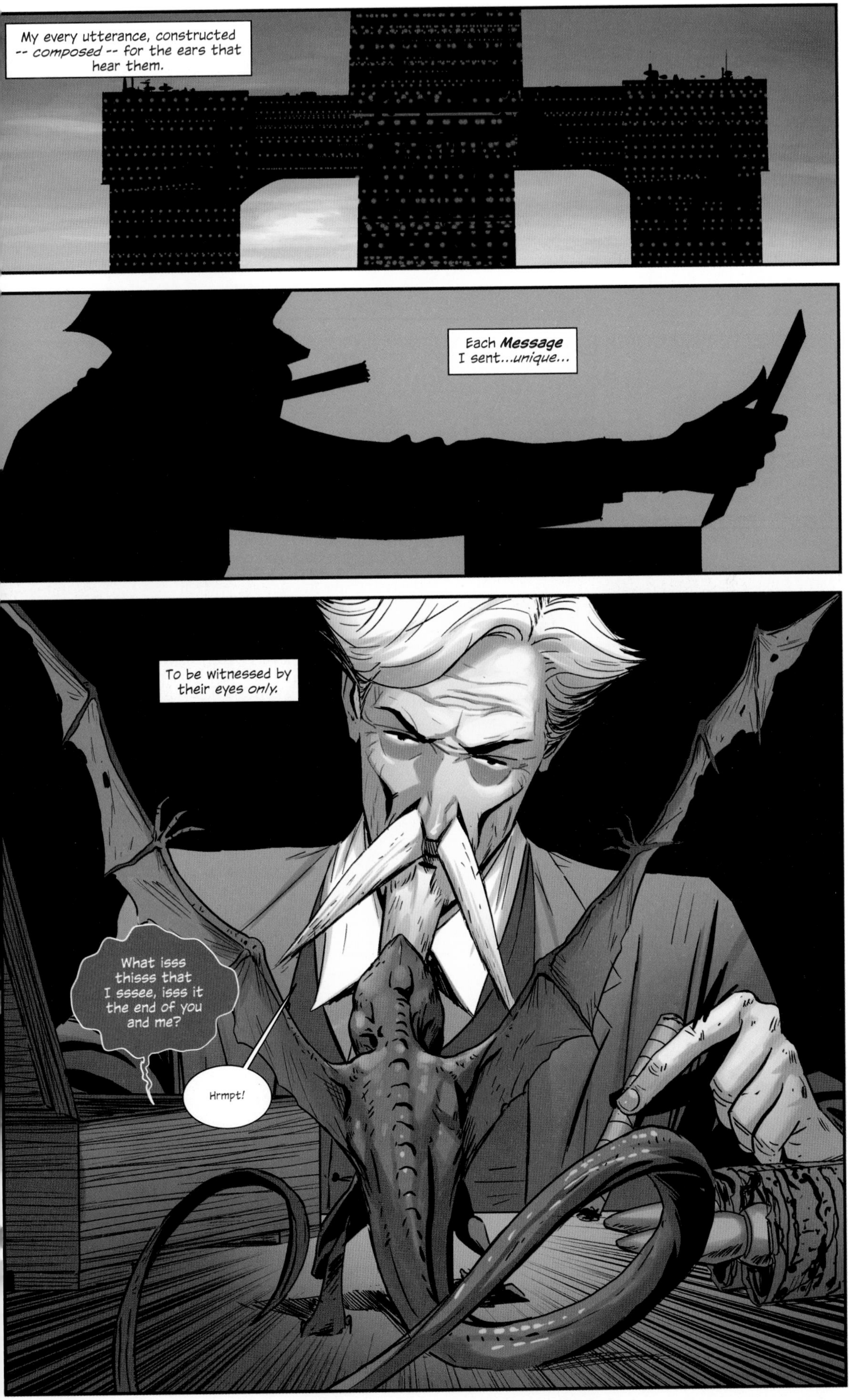
My every utterance, constructed -- composed -- for the ears that hear them.
Each Message I sent...unique...
To be witnessed by their eyes only.
What isss thisss that I sssee, isss it the end of you and me?
Hrmpt!

We have all cast off our old skins, and *put on* our new ones.

The true *Chosen* have revealed themselves...

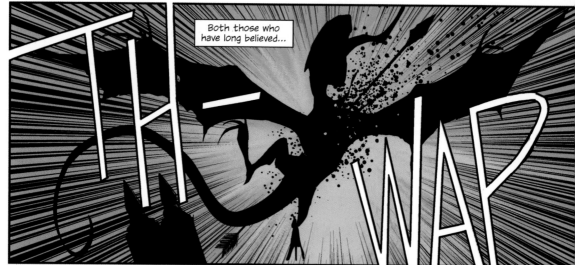

Both those who have long believed...

TH-

WAP

And those who *have not.*

Send someone to fetch that.

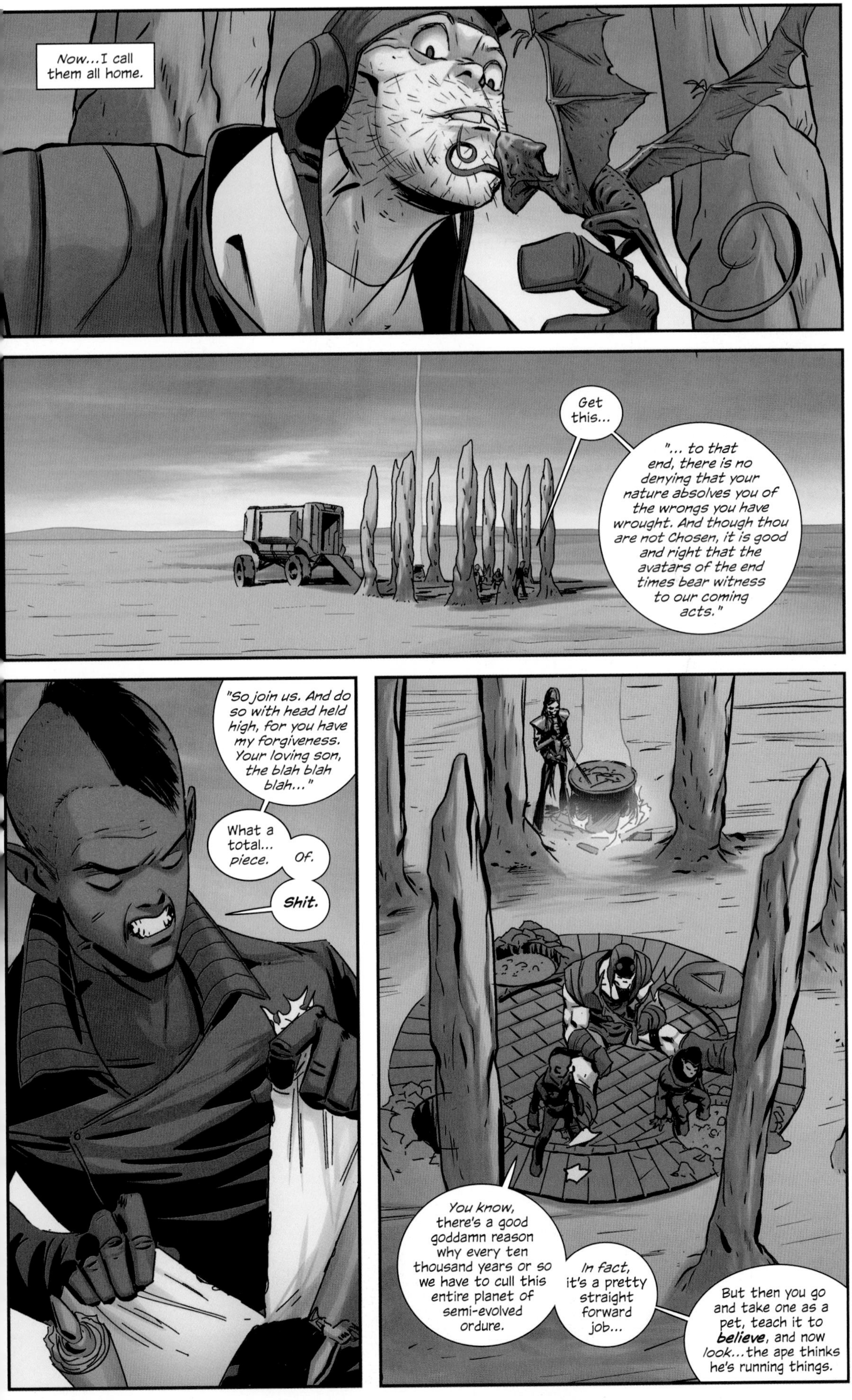
Now... I call them all home.
Get this...
"... to that end, there is no denying that your nature absolves you of the wrongs you have wrought. And though thou are not Chosen, it is good and right that the avatars of the end times bear witness to our coming acts."
"So join us. And do so with head held high, for you have my forgiveness. Your loving son, the blah blah blah..."
What a total... piece.
Of.
Shit.
You know, there's a good goddamn reason why every ten thousand years or so we have to cull this entire planet of semi-evolved ordure.
In fact, it's a pretty straight forward job...
But then you go and take one as a pet, teach it to believe, and now look... the ape thinks he's running things.

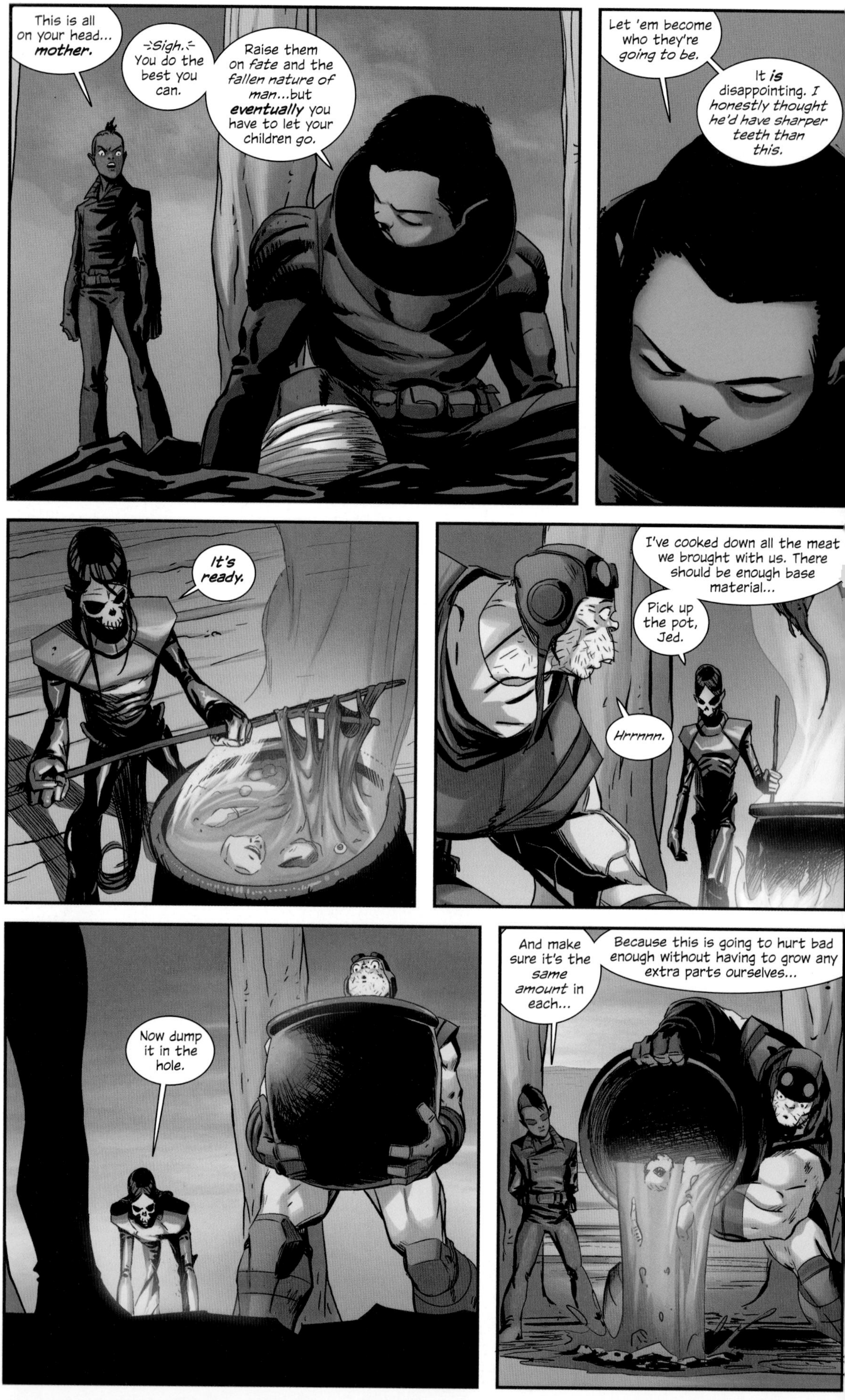
This is all on your head... **mother.**
-Sigh.- You do the best you can.
Raise them on *fate* and the *fallen nature of man*...but **eventually** you have to let your children *go.*
Let 'em become who they're *going to be.*
It **is** disappointing. *I honestly thought he'd have sharper teeth than this.*
It's ready.
I've cooked down all the meat we brought with us. There should be enough base material...
Pick up the pot, Jed.
Hrrnnn.
Now dump it in the hole.
And make sure it's the *same amount* in each...
Because this is going to hurt bad enough without having to grow any extra parts ourselves...

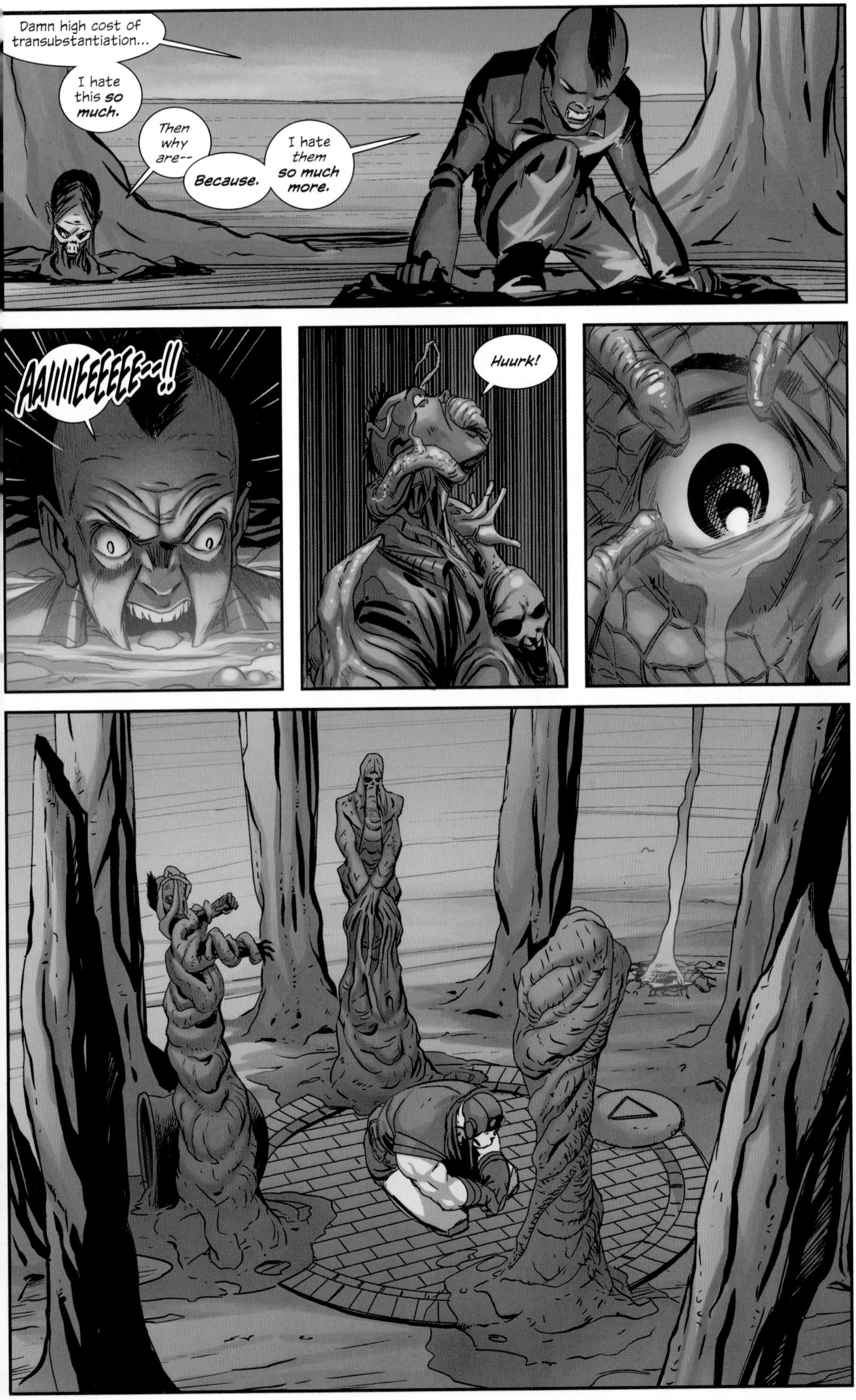
Damn high cost of transubstantiation...
I hate this so much.
Then why are--
Because.
I hate them so much more.
AAIIIIEEEEEE--!!
Huurk!

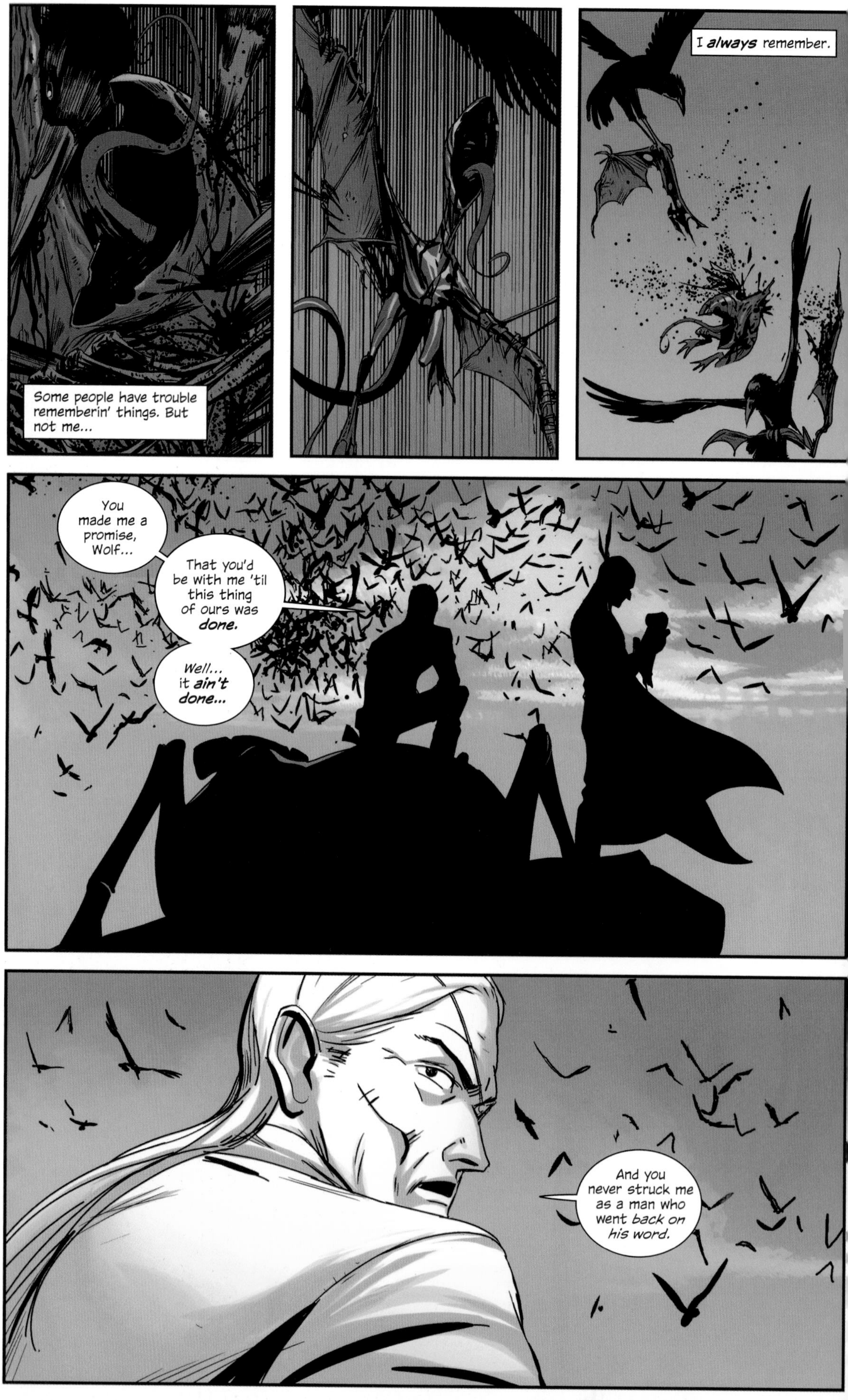
Some people have trouble rememberin' things. But not me...
I *always* remember.
You made me a promise, Wolf...
That you'd be with me 'til this thing of ours was ***done.***
*Well... it **ain't done...***
And you never struck me as a man who went *back on his word.*

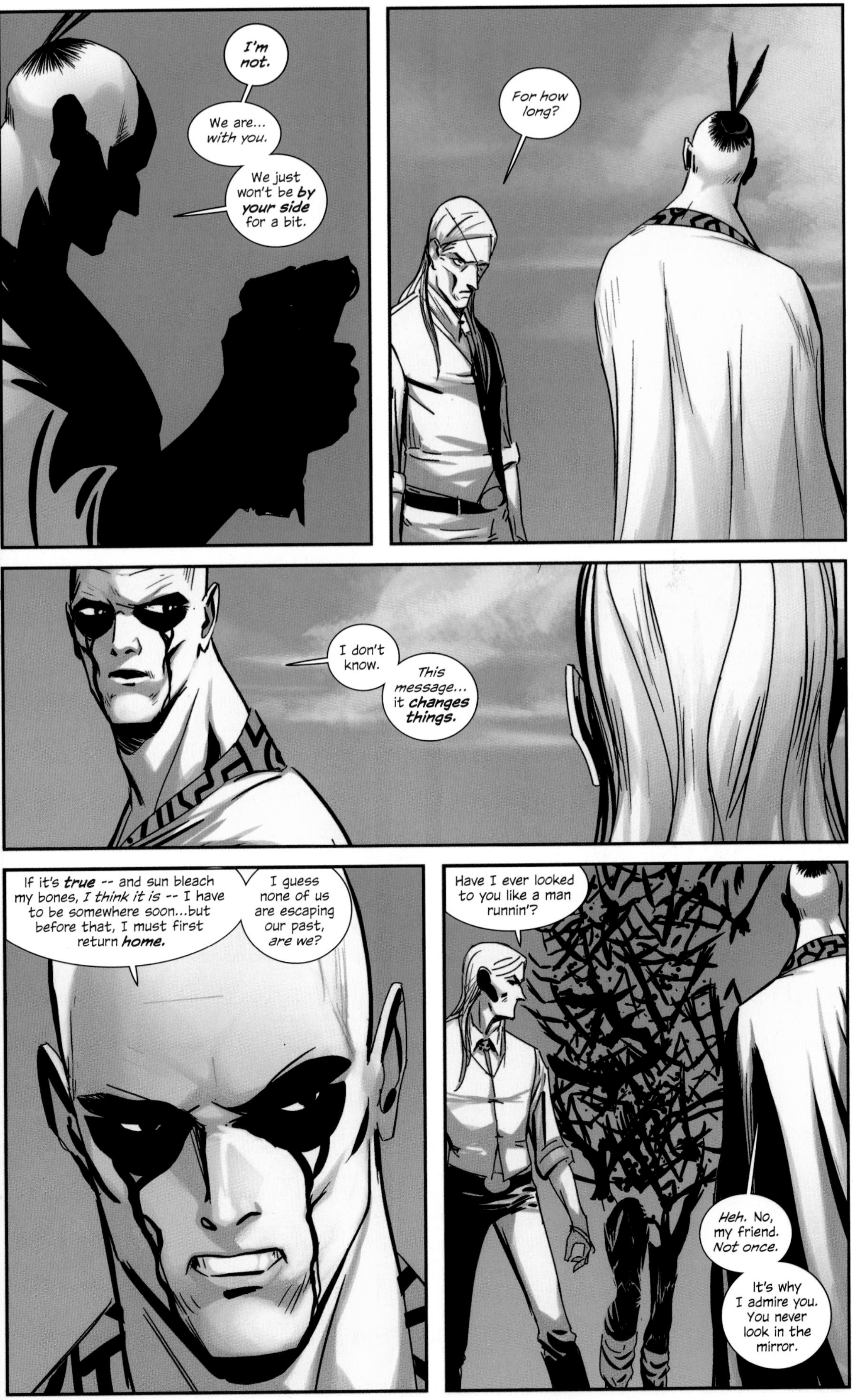
I'm not.
We are... with you.
We just won't be by your side for a bit.
For how long?
I don't know.
This message... it changes things.
If it's true -- and sun bleach my bones, I think it is -- I have to be somewhere soon...but before that, I must first return home.
I guess none of us are escaping our past, are we?
Have I ever looked to you like a man runnin'?
Heh. No, my friend. Not once.
It's why I admire you. You never look in the mirror.

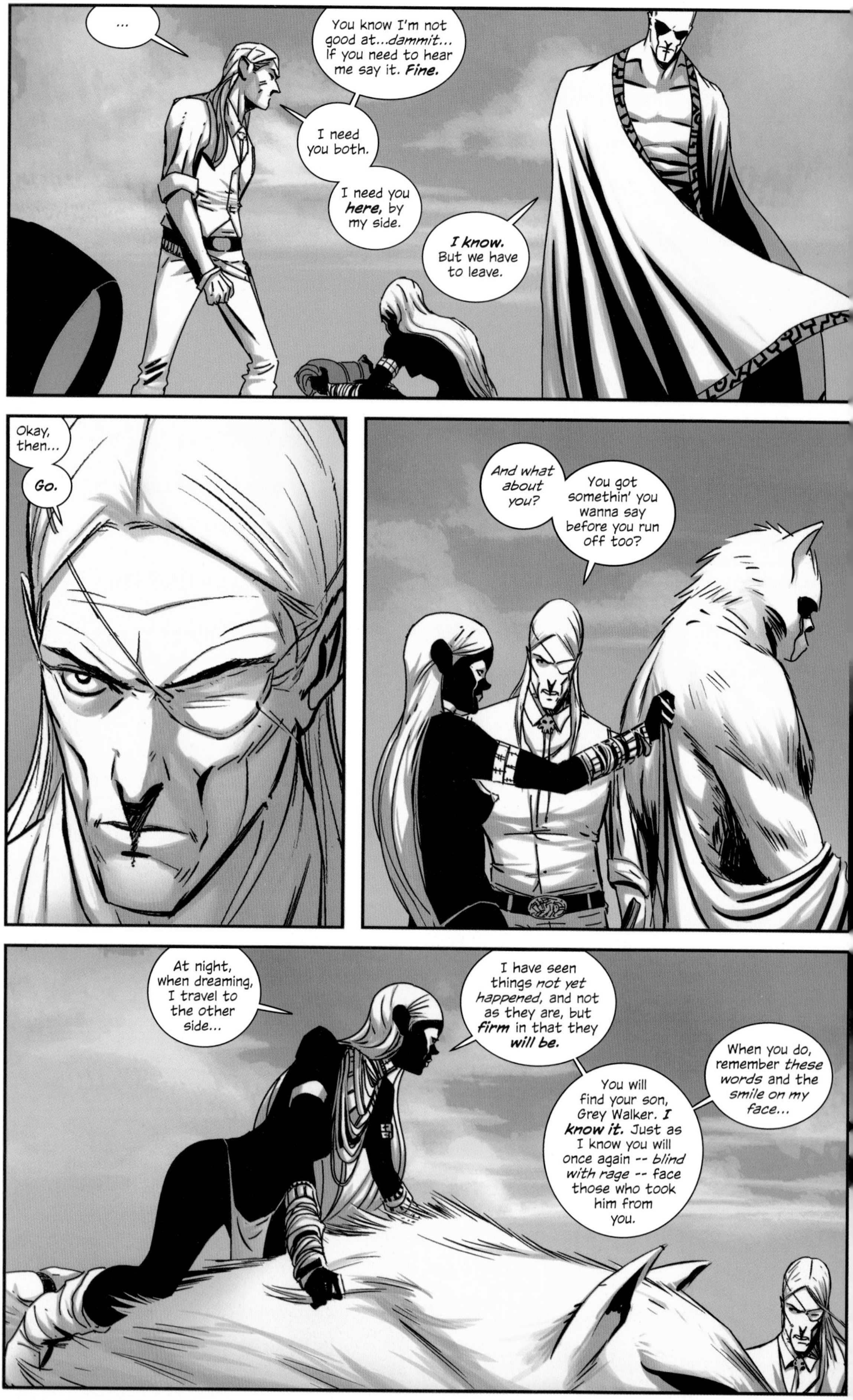
...
You know I'm not good at...*dammit*... If you need to hear me say it. ***Fine.***
I need you both.
I need you ***here,*** by my side.
I know. But we have to leave.
Okay, then...
Go.
And what about you?
You got somethin' you wanna say before you run off too?
At night, when dreaming, I travel to the other side...
I have seen things *not yet happened*, and not as they are, but ***firm*** in that they ***will be.***
You will find your son, Grey Walker. ***I know it.*** Just as I know you will once again -- *blind with rage* -- face those who took him from you.
When you do, remember *these words* and the *smile on my face...*

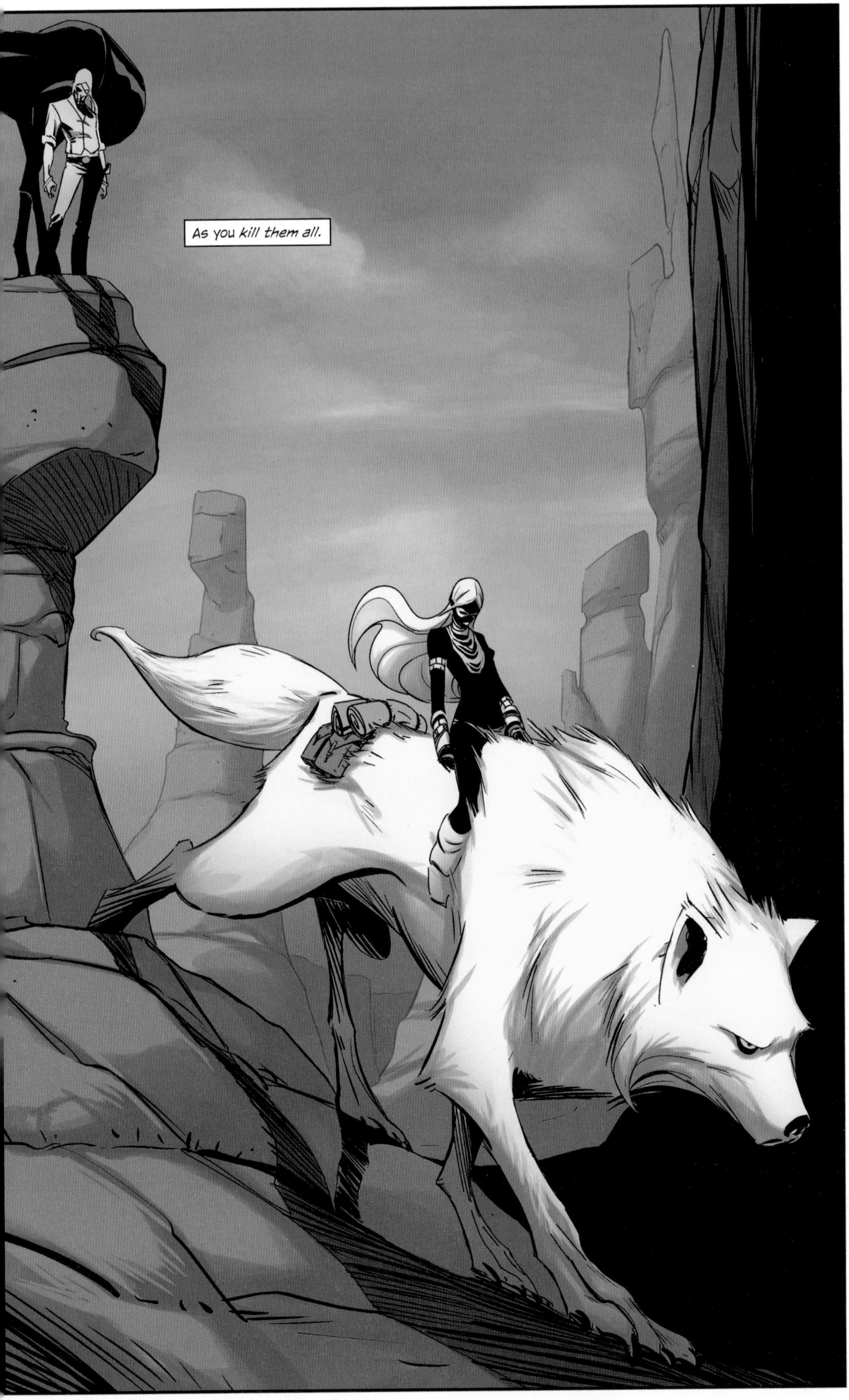
As you *kill* them all.

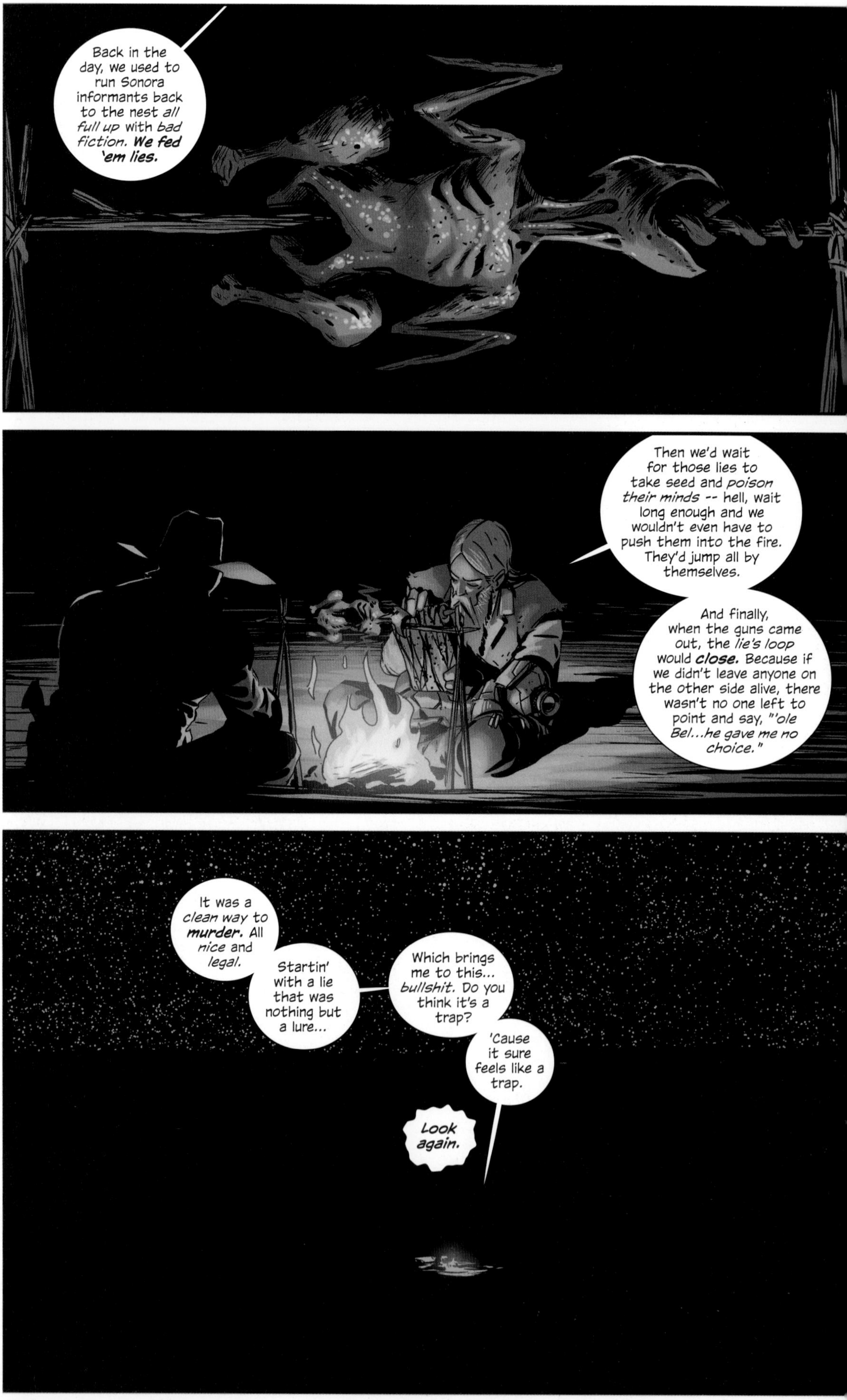
Back in the day, we used to run Sonora informants back to the nest *all full up* with *bad fiction.* ***We fed 'em lies.***
Then we'd wait for those lies to take seed and *poison their minds* -- hell, wait long enough and we wouldn't even have to push them into the fire. They'd jump all by themselves.
And finally, when the guns came out, the *lie's loop* would ***close.*** Because if we didn't leave anyone on the other side alive, there wasn't no one left to point and say, "*'ole Bel...he gave me no choice.*"
It was a *clean way* to ***murder.*** All *nice* and *legal.*
Startin' with a lie that was nothing but a lure...
Which brings me to this... *bullshit.* Do you think it's a trap?
'Cause it sure feels like a trap.
Look again.

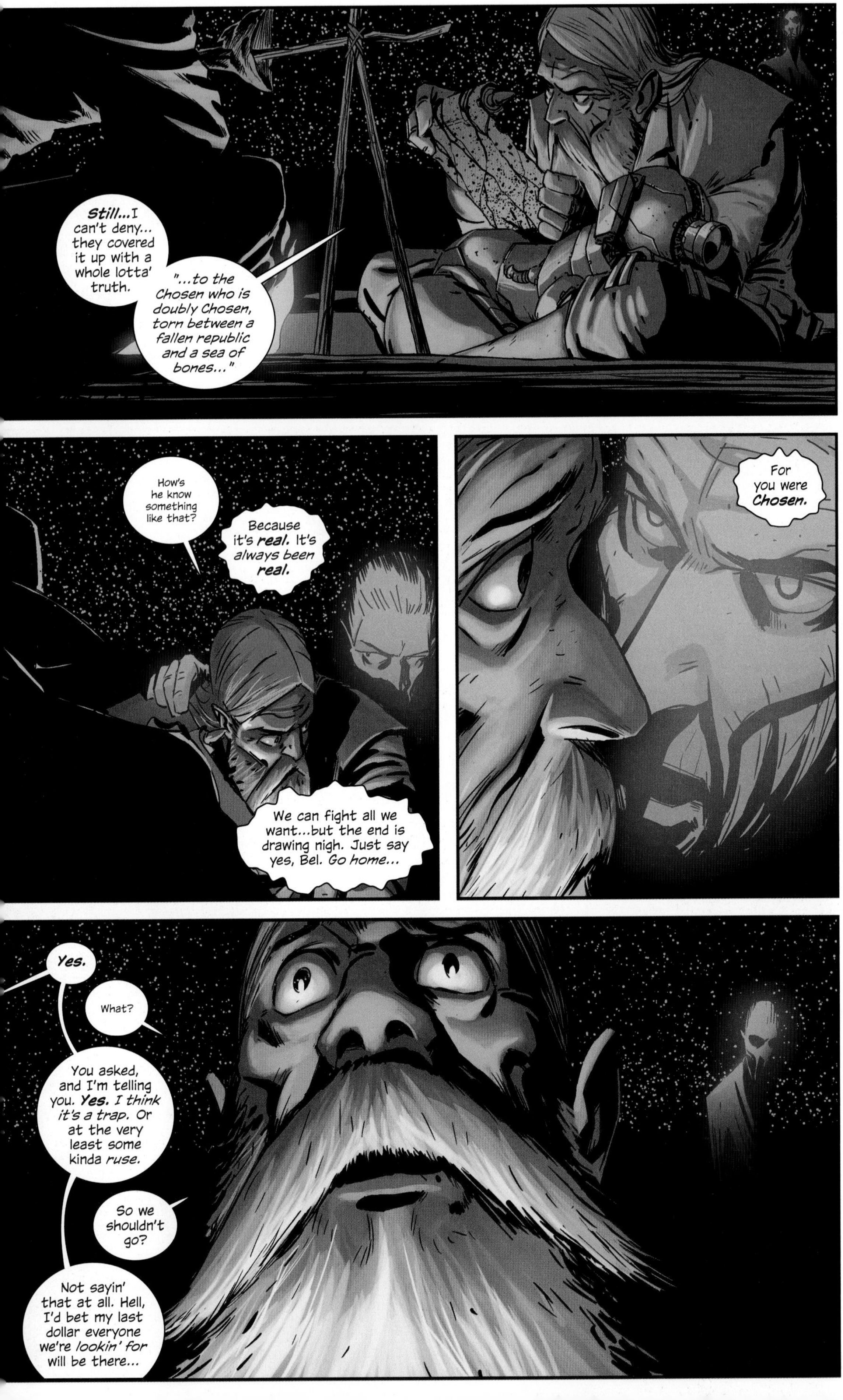
Still...I can't deny... they covered it up with a whole lotta' truth.
"...to the Chosen who is doubly Chosen, torn between a fallen republic and a sea of bones..."
How's he know something like that?
Because it's real. It's always been real.
We can fight all we want...but the end is drawing nigh. Just say yes, Bel. Go home...
For you were Chosen.
Yes.
What?
You asked, and I'm telling you. Yes. I think it's a trap. Or at the very least some kinda ruse.
So we shouldn't go?
Not sayin' that at all. Hell, I'd bet my last dollar everyone we're lookin' for will be there...

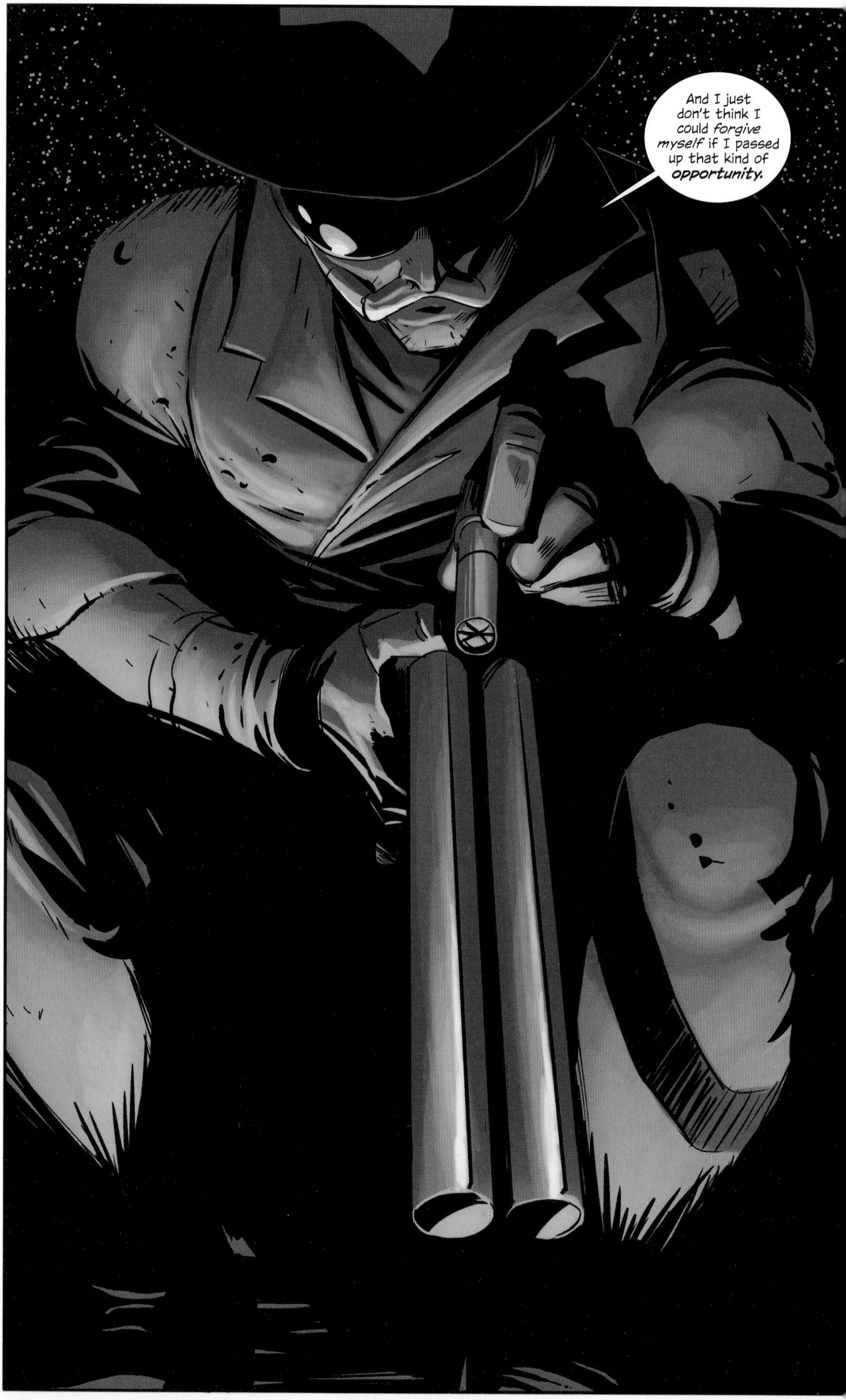
And I just don't think I could *forgive myself* if I passed up that kind of **opportunity.**

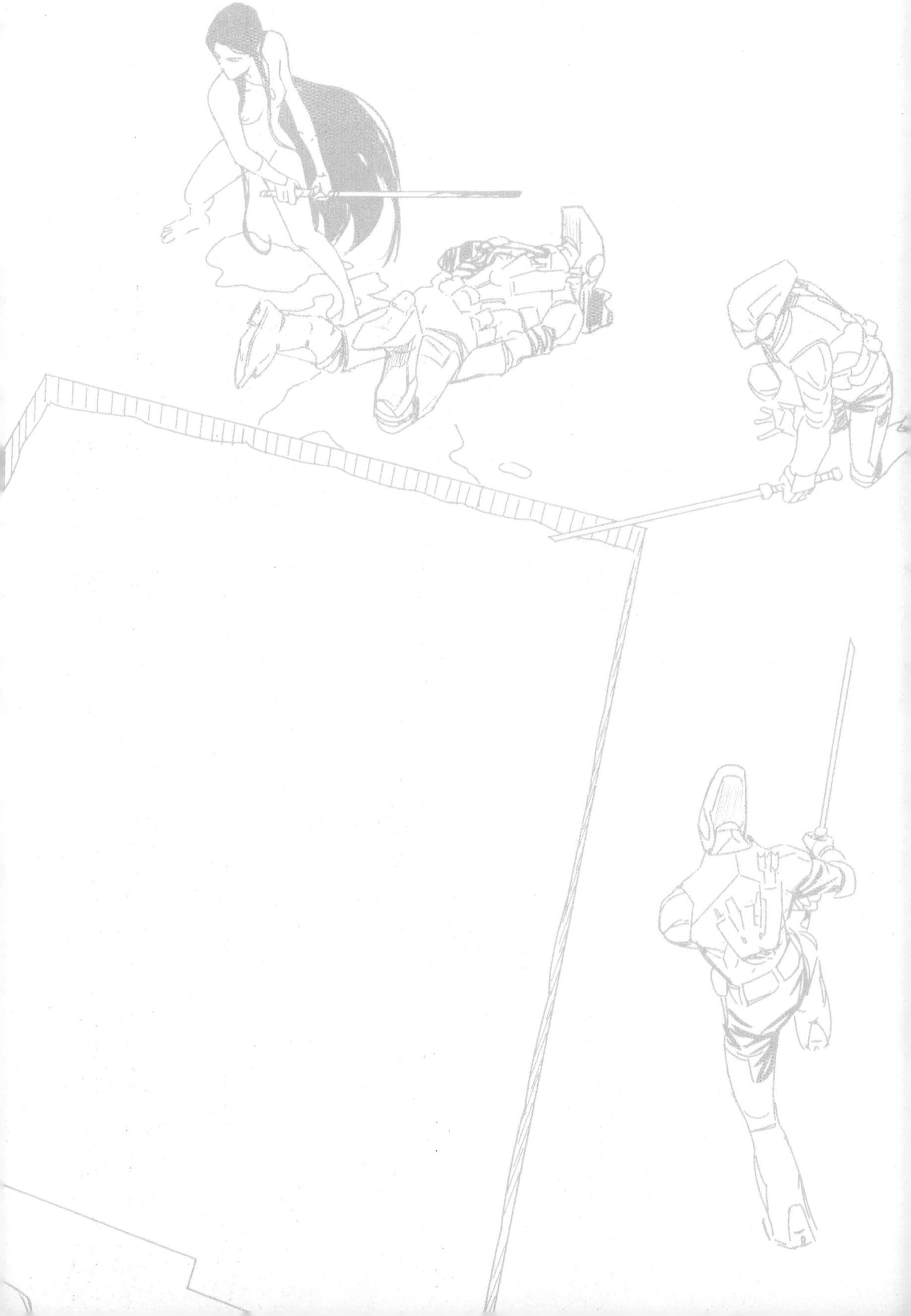

ALL MEN TELL **LIES.**
THESE ARE A **FEW** OF
THEM.

Jonathan Hickman is the visionary talent behind such works as the Eisner-nominated **NIGHTLY NEWS**, **THE MANHATTAN PROJECTS** and **PAX ROMANA**. He also plies his trade at MARVEL working on books like **FANTASTIC FOUR** and **THE AVENGERS**.

His twin brother, Marc, went missing in St. Lucia six months ago and hasn't been heard from since.

Jonathan lives in South Carolina when he isn't vacationing or searching for his brother.

You can visit his website:***www.pronea.com***, or email him at:***jonathan@pronea.com***.

·

Nick Dragotta's career began at Marvel Comics working on titles as varied as **X-STATIX**, **THE AGE OF THE SENTRY**, **X-MEN: FIRST CLASS**, **CAPTAIN AMERICA: FOREVER ALLIES,** and **VENGEANCE**.

FANTASTIC FOUR #588 was the first time he collaborated with Jonathan Hickman, which lead to their successful run on **FF.**

In addition, Nick is the co-creator of **HOWTOONS**, a comic series teaching kids how to build things and explore the world around them. **EAST OF WEST** is Nick's first creator-owned project at Image.